P9-AQK-716

Been There Prayed That:

New Day Divas Series Book Two

Been There Prayed That:
New Day Divas Series Book Two

E.N. Joy

www.urbanchristianonline.net

Urban Books, LLC
78 East Industry Court
Deer Park, NY 11729

Been There Prayed That: New Day Divas Series Book Two
©copyright 2010 E.N. Joy

All rights reserved. No part of this book may be reproduced in any form or by any means without prior consent of the Publisher, excepting brief quotes used in reviews.

ISBN 13: 978-1-60162-882-4
ISBN 10: 1-60162-882-X

First Printing June 2010
Printed in the United States of America

10 9 8 7 6 5 4 3 2 1

This is a work of fiction. Any references or similarities to actual events, real people, living, or dead, or to real locales are intended to give the novel a sense of reality. Any similarity in other names, characters, places, and incidents is entirely coincidental.

Distributed by Kensington Corp.
Submit Wholesale Orders to:
Kensington Publishing Corp.
C/O Penguin Group (USA) Inc.
Attention: Order Processing
405 Murray Hill Parkway
East Rutherford, NJ 07073-2316
Phone: 1-800-526-0275
Fax: 1-800-227-9604

Dedication

This book is dedicated to the woman who raised me as a child and up into my adulthood, my mother. To the woman who showed me what a strong, loving black mother truly is, Granny Edwards. To the woman who showed me what kind of mother a woman has to be to raise a son, Mom Marsh (Ross). To the woman who showed me (probably without even knowing) how to be a holy mother while first being a holy wife, Pastor Sherry Broomfield. And to all the women God placed in my life to raise me up in His Word; Auntie Gwen Davis, Sister Shelly Benton, Sister Alberta Thompson, and Sister Deborah Morgan.

Without Him and without Him working through each of you, I never would have made it . . .

Acknowledgments

To the Father, the Son and the Holy Spirit, whom I love, adore, praise, worship, glorify, magnify, welcome, and allow to abide in me; I first acknowledge you in all my ways and thank you for directing my path.

Next, I want to acknowledge my earthly father, Gary Edwards, whom I also love and adore. Thank you for allowing me to be daddy's little girl even still while I'm pushing forty. I love you!

To Pastor Howard Williams, I couldn't conclude without acknowledging the role of spiritual father you played as I first learned to grow in the Word. May God continue to bless your ministry at Victorious Life Christian Center.

To Apostle Maurice Broomfield, the man God chose to spiritually adopt me into Power and Glory Ministries, International. Even though I was adopted into the ministry only a couple of years ago, you've made me feel as though I was born there.

Last, but not least, to the father of my wonderful children, who I don't think I could love and adore anymore than I do at this very moment. I can't imagine my life without you anymore than I can imagine breathing without air. It's been the best thirteen years of my life! (Okay, eleven out of thirteen, at least . . . but you know what I'm saying—smile).

Chapter One

"What the Jacks Daniels was Mother Doreen thinking when she vouched for this woman to be the new leader of the New Day Single's Ministry?" Unique spoke in a loud whisper to the woman next to her who responded with a shrug, wondering the same thing herself. "Better yet, what was Pastor thinking to approve such a thing?" Rolling her eyes, she added, "Heck! For that matter, they could have named me leader, seeming just any ol' everybody can lead a ministry around here these days. Do you even have to be a member of the church to be a leader anymore?" Once again, the woman she was venting to shrugged.

The room was full of hushed whispers, teeth sucking, neck snapping, and eye rolling as Sister Lorain took the podium in front of the twenty-five members of the New Day Temple of Faith Single's Ministry. She appeared oblivious to all that was going on around her. Instead, she was delighting in the fact that she was doing God's kingdom work. She was a leader in a church; a place not too long ago she thought she'd never step foot in, let alone be operating a ministry. But here she stood, holding the torch, or as church folk would say, the mantel. It had been passed down to her from Mother Doreen, the former leader of the New Day Single's Ministry.

It was a new day all right. With this being only her second meeting since taking over as the new leader, several men had joined the ministry, which was something the past leader had been unable to achieve. Up until recently, the ministry had consisted of nothing but single women. Today, although the men remained out numbered, there were at least seven of them.

Lorain credited this now co-ed ministry to God for moving her to personally invite the single men of the congregation to join the ministry. But some of the other women—most of the other women—okay, all of the other women—credited her short skirts, three-inch pumps, and low cut blouses for the sudden increase in male attendance. And those Mary Kay cosmetics she sold on the side and tried to push on the women at every church function was partly to blame as well.

Although all the women thought these things about Lorain, only Unique was bold enough to say it out loud, with the intent of Sister Lorain overhearing her. But Sister Lorain seemed completely unaware of all the negative energy and comments being made around her and about her. So Unique figured the next time she'd have to say it even louder.

The young twenty-two-year-old, Unique, was raised in project housing in Columbus, Ohio that was now called Rosewind Terrace, but would always be known as the former Windsor Terrace. A mother of three children with three different fathers, Unique was one of the less diplomatic members of the ministry. And it had nothing to do with the fact that she was raised in the projects, but had everything to do with the way she was raised by her single mother of five children with five different fathers.

It was only two years ago when Unique moved to Malvonia, Ohio with her sister, who was also a single mother of two children with two different fathers, that she began to change her ways for the better. Prior to moving in with her sister, Unique had been evicted from her apartment for nonpayment of rent, which had only been $25 dollars a month thanks to her Section 8 Housing voucher that paid the bulk of the rent. But between her drinking, smoking weed, and paying babysitters while she went out partying, Unique never even had $25 left over from her welfare check to pay the rent.

Unique's sister took her and her kids in with opened arms the day the sheriff came with an order that allowed for all of her and her children's belongings to be placed on the sidewalk. Now, two years later, the seven of them were still making the best of the three bedroom finished basement house her sister was leasing.

Unique was still on welfare. She was no longer partying like she used to, although she'd hit the club every now and then if one of her girlfriends in Columbus called her up and talked her into doing so. These occasional nights out with the girls sometimes led to a little bit of smoking and a drink or two. But since getting saved, joining New Day, and getting baptized a year and a half ago, she'd made great strides toward giving up things of old. With her occasional backsliding she was nowhere near where she needed to be in Christ, but she was far from where she used to be. But no one judged her then, and no one judged her now. Nope, nobody at New Day judged anybody . . . with the exception of Sister Lorain that is. So it was probably safe to say that things were about to change up in New Day Temple of Faith.

As Sister Lorain opened up the meeting in prayer, invisible stones, shattering glass house after glass house, hurled through the room.

Yes indeed. Judgment day was near.

Chapter Two

"I don't know what I would have done had you not been by my side."

"Them are words for Jesus only." Mother Doreen entered her younger sister Bethany's hospital room just in time to hear her sister speak those words to the man that sat at her bedside.

With a bouquet of fresh cut flowers in hand that she'd just picked up at Floweroma on her way to the hospital, Mother Doreen continued speaking. "No man on earth is deserving to have those words spoken to him." Mother Doreen looked the man at her sister's bedside up and down. "Not even a pastor."

"Mother Doreen, it's a blessing to see you on this fine day that the Lord has made. It's even better to see you glad and rejoicing in it."

Mother Doreen's eyes narrowed. Was the good pastor being sarcastic, she wondered?

Pastor Frey stood from the chair next to Bethany's bed he'd been sitting in for the past hour. He held in a smirk. He had to admit that his comment drooled with sarcasm. He silently repented to the Lord. He then offered the seat to Mother Doreen with a gesture of his hand.

"No thanks. I'll stand." Mother Doreen rolled her eyes and proceeded to arrange the small flower bouquet she'd placed in the window sill. "I don't want to sit in that chair and get them spirits all over me," she mumbled to herself.

Clearing his throat, Pastor Frey looked to Bethany and

said, "I, uh, guess I better get going now that you have company. Besides, I have to teach Bible Study this week plus give the word on Sunday. I need to go get with God."

"Well, thank you for stopping by." Bethany extended her hand to Pastor Frey. "I know you're a busy man."

Taking Bethany's hand into his and patting it, Pastor Frey replied, "A pastor's work is never done. But checking in on the sick and shut in members is part of it, so I don't mind at all."

"Assistant pastor," Mother Doreen chimed in as both Bethany and Pastor Frey looked over at her. "An assistant pastor's work is never done. And you are just the assistant pastor of Living Word, Living Waters; correct?"

Straightening his tie that was already straight, Pastor Frey uncomfortably replied with a, "Well, uh, yes. I'm just sitting in for Pastor Davidson while he's in consecration this week. "

"But a pastor nonetheless," Bethany said in the assistant pastor of her church's defense while cutting eyes at Mother Doreen. She then turned toward Pastor Frey. "And a fine pastor you are." Pastor Frey returned the smile.

"Speaking of fine," Mother Doreen chimed in, directing her attention to Bethany, "Child, that mighty fine husband of yours called the house this morning to talk to the kids before I got them off to school."

"Did he?" Bethany asked, removing her hand from Pastor Frey's once she realized that it was still resting there.

"He did indeed. He says he hopes to finish his truck run a day early, which will put him back in town in two days instead of three." Mother Doreen walked over to Bethany and stood by her side. "That's a good man you got, Bethany. God must really love you so to bless you with someone who spends days in and days out driving that big ol' semi truck across the country in order to provide for his family. It can't be easy for a man to be away from his wife and children for so long." Mother

Doreen directed her next comment to Pastor Frey. "Just as soon as God blesses you with a wife and family of your own, Pastor Frey, you'll know what I mean; spending all that time with God and doing God's work and all will trump the time you can spend with your family."

Straightening his already straightened tie one more time, Pastor Frey excused himself without responding to Mother Doreen's comment. "Well, ladies, enjoy the rest of your day, and God bless."

"Thanks again for stopping by to check on me," Bethany called out to Pastor Frey as he exited the room nodding a *You're welcome*. Bethany immediately turned her attention to her sister once Pastor Frey was out of sight. "What is wrong with you, *woman of God?*" Bethany spat.

"I'm just fine." Mother Doreen proceeded to fluff up Bethany's pillows behind her head. "Is that comfortable enough for you? I can always ask the nurse for another pillow."

"I'm fine, Reen," Bethany said, calling Mother Doreen by her family nickname, "but I beg to differ the same about you."

A confused look covered Mother Doreen's soft facial expression. She pat down her salt and pepper ear length hair that she wore in a roller set. Some of the curls fell on her olive colored forehead. Petite, calm, and passive was how Mother Doreen had once been described. But these days she had a holy boldness about her that seemed to have turned her into a ball of fire.

"How do you do that?" Bethany seemed agitated as her olive colored skin appeared tainted with a touch of red. She was the spittin' image of her older sister, minus the salt and pepper hair. Her hair was still its natural brown.

"Do what?"

"Go from being as sweet as southern sweet tea to as sour as a box of Lemon Heads. This just isn't like you, sis. I mean, you are the kindest and most caring woman I know. You were always the peacemaker between Mama and Daddy's four daughters. Between everybody. Now all of a sudden you're a hell raiser."

"Child, I don't know what you're talking about," Mother Doreen said in the most genuine tone.

Bethany observed her sister's expression for a moment; the sincerity of it. It was at that moment that she knew her sister didn't realized how out of character she became whenever she was around Pastor Frey. "You really don't know what I'm talking about, do you?"

Mother Doreen was clueless as to what Bethany was talking about. A peacemaker she was, so her sister accusing her of raising hell baffled her. She'd always been a calm, passive person, the voice of reason, so she had no idea where Bethany was coming from.

"Every time you get around Wallace, you act like a totally different person," Bethany said.

"The devil is a liar," Mother Doreen spat and shooed her hand as if her sister was talking nonsense. "You know me. I've always been the same person. I don't put on a show for nobody. Not for the Lord, not for church folks, and certainly not for no *Pastor Frey*."

"See there," Bethany pointed at Mother Doreen in an accusatory manner, "that's what I mean. Do you hear how you even say the man's name? As if his name is laced with rat poison, and you're gonna get poisoned and die just for allowing it to rest on your tongue."

Mother Doreen just stood there, taking in Bethany's words and playing back her own words and actions toward Past Frey. She wanted to examine her ways and see if there was any truth to what her sister was accusing her of. Had she been anything but Christlike when it came to Pastor Frey?

"That man has never done anything to you or said anything outside of a godly kind word," Bethany continued. "I wish I could say the same for you. I always talk you up to him and my church family about what an awesome woman of God you are, and this is how you act. I'm embarrassed." Bethany rolled her eyes and positioned herself to a point where her back was almost to Mother Doreen. "Now I've let you get away with it for over a month now; ever since you've been here. But it's time for this nonsense to stop."

There was silence while Bethany paused in order to allow her sister to digest her words. Bethany turned her head around slightly, only to see the regretful look that filled Mother Doreen's eyes.

"Reen, I know how much you love me. You being the oldest, you always felt the need to take care of me. So I know it must make you a tad jealous to see others taking care of me. But the spirit of jealousy is not of God, so you're going to have to let it go. Visiting and praying for the sick and the shut in is part of Pastor Frey's duties as assistant pastor. That man has such a big heart, he'd do it even if it weren't in the by-laws as part of his duties." Bethany turned all the way back toward her sister. "I know you gave up your life in Ohio to come down here and take care of me, and I thank God for that. I need you, sis. No matter who else God sends to look out for me as well, I'll always need you. So don't ever think for one minute that your coming here was in vain." Bethany extended her hand and smiled.

Mother Doreen rested her hand inside her sister's and returned the smile. It was at that moment that Mother Doreen began to question her own behavior. Because Bethany was her only living sibling left, the other two having lost the battle to diabetes and high blood pressure, was she being over protective? Had she allowed her flesh to rise up so much that it overshadowed her spirit man? She could have sworn she'd heard clearly from God; that He'd sent her there to Kentucky to intercede on behalf of her sister. But had she allowed some deep rooted seed of jealousy to interfere with her assignment from the Lord?

"I'm sorry," Mother Doreen apologized. She shook her head, wondering if she ever would have known just how ugly she had been acting had Bethany not pointed out her behavior.

Even though it wasn't cause for her to be rude, she couldn't deny that there was still something about Pastor Frey that didn't sit well within her spirit. Bethany was right; the man had never been anything but kind to her, and his kindness toward her or anybody else she'd seen him interact with always appeared to be genuine. She'd seen him pray, praise, worship, exalt, teach, and preach God's Word. Nothing about Pastor Frey appeared to be staged, phony, or make believe.

Confusion began to set in with Mother Doreen because although she was convinced that Pastor Frey was a man after God's own heart, she was also convinced that he was after something else as well.

Chapter Three

"He's blessed me once. He's blessed me twice. God has blessed me every day of my life. And if God don't do nothing else, He's done enough."

Tamarra couldn't believe that after all the time she'd known Paige, that Paige could sing the way she was singing today. Just a few weeks ago, when Paige had mentioned to her that she was going to join New Day's praise and worship team, she thought about that white girl, Kim, on the reality show, *The Real Housewives of Atlanta*. Tamarra had never heard her best friend sing, hum, or even mention a desire to sing. So she didn't know what to expect when just last week Paige informed her that she'd be singing her very first solo, and on Easter Sunday no less, when the sanctuary would be full for sure. Would Tamarra pretend that Paige really could sing like Sheree did with Kim on the television show, or would she keep it real like Ne Ne did? From the way Paige was hitting them notes and allowing the Lord to use her to bless His name, she knew she'd be able to keep it real.

Tamarra just couldn't take sitting down any longer, so she rose to her feet. She'd been in awe while sitting; feet frozen to the ground. The persons on either side of her had been standing since the praise and worship team hit the first note. Not one to stand just because everybody else was standing, or even because her best friend was doing a solo, Tamarra had remained sitting. She preferred to sit, close her eyes, and allow the sweet song of the praise and worship team to summons the Spirit of the Lord into the sanctuary. Then she stood to show reverence to God.

For Tamarra, when the Holy Spirit showed up, sitting on that pew was no longer an option. Sitting on that pew was like sitting on God. It didn't take someone yelling at her from the pulpit not to sit on God either. She didn't stand for man, she stood for God. And at this very moment, the Lord had definitely showed up, and He'd used the voice of her best friend to invite Him there.

By the time Paige finished her song, the church was in a state of worship. The atmosphere had been set for New Day's pastor to bring the Word forth, and a mighty Word it was. The pastor's message was so powerful, that church went overtime by a half hour.

"I know we're running a little late," Pastor stated, "but don't worry, I'm sure the buffet line at your favorite restaurant will shorten, and God has angels watching over that roast in the oven and food in the crock pot in your homes."

The congregation let out a few chuckles and laughter at their pastor's humor.

"But I can't take it for granted that everyone in this place knows Jesus Christ as their Lord and Savior," Pastor continued, "so I can't end service without first making an altar call."

The pastor nodded to Maeyl in the sound booth, which was his signal to put on music conducive for altar call. After doing so, Maeyl exited the sound booth and stood in the aisle. Most of the ministers and leaders at New Day were women. Just in case some additional male assistance was needed during altar call, Maeyl always made sure he was close by, especially if Sister Perrin went up for prayer. She always seemed to fall out in the Spirit if Pastor just looked at her, let alone prayed for her.

Sister Perrin weighed all of three hundred pounds dry. So if she'd danced in the spirit and worked up a sweat, no telling how much she weighed. And Lord have mercy on the poor saints assigned to catch her before she hit the ground.

Tamarra had once overheard a couple of teens in the bathroom laughing and comparing Sister Perrin falling out in the Spirit to a bowling ball rolling down the aisle, hitting every last pin for a strike. After reminding the two teens that God didn't like ugly, and once the girls were out of earshot, Tamarra had to muffle a few chuckles of her own.

Tamarra, knowing Maeyl's regimen, looked over her shoulder and smiled at him, while trying not to admire his smooth bronze skin. But it was hard to ignore the features of the six feet tall, bald, goatee sporting man. Afterward, she thanked God for putting such a wonderful man in her life. They'd been through a lot in the time they'd been a couple, including a couple of break ups and make ups. They had faith that as long as they kept God first in their relationship, He would see them through a holy matrimony and a happily ever after. After all, He was in the process of doing it for Paige and her fiancé, Blake, so surely He'd do it for them.

"If there is anyone under the sound of my voice who wants to be saved today, who needs to be saved today, please make your way down to the altar," the pastor requested as a handholding couple made their way down to the altar. "Praise God. Do we have anyone else? Don't be embarrassed. This is not the time nor the season to be embarrassed. Planes are falling out of the sky. Boats are sinking. Animals are attacking. Fires are burning. Lightning is striking folks down. Tomorrow is not promised. Will you be ready? Come now. Come get ready."

The pastor looked around to see if anyone else was making their way down to the altar. When no one stood, Pastor looked among the congregation and said, "Pray, saints. This is a matter of life and death. Intercessors, intercede. Pray, for the Spirit tells me that there is someone else who needs to be down at this altar giving their life to the Lord. Pray, saints, pray."

Prayers, chants, mumbling, and foreign tongues could be heard about the sanctuary as Pastor made one final call. "Make today the day you know Jesus Christ as your Lord and Savior. Don't put it off until you *get right*. You can't get right without Him. So won't you come?" Once again, Pastor looked amongst the sanctuary, then suddenly a smile spread across Pastor's face. "Praise God. We have another."

Clapping filled the sanctuary as prayers were answered and one last woman, tears streaming down her face, stood and began to walk forward. Tamarra smiled with joy and looked to Maeyl. His eyes were still closed from praying that the Spirit would touch someone's heart and lead them down to the altar. Once again, Tamarra couldn't help but thank God for giving her such a wonderful man, a praying man, a God fearing man.

Tamarra's own eyes began to get moist as she looked at Maeyl. As if he could feel her eyes watching him, he opened his to see her smiling face. He smiled at her, then turned his head to see the soul that his prayers would help save.

Tamarra noticed that just as quickly as the smile had spread across Maeyl's face, it had disappeared. His jaws tightened and beads of sweat began to two-step on his forehead. Any minute now it looked as though he would puke right there in the middle of the aisle. He was frozen stiff. His eyes were frozen stiff; set on something. Set on someone.

Tamarra followed Maeyl's frozen stare down to the altar. Her eyes landed on the woman who'd just gone down to the altar to turn her life over to Christ. She then allowed her eyes to settle back onto Maeyl. She blinked, then decided to once again follow his eyes, praying that they landed on something different. Someone different. Anything other than that woman. God was definitely into answering prayers today, as indeed, Maeyl's eyes were no longer set on the woman. Instead, they were set on the owner of the little hand that was cupped inside the woman's hand. When Tamarra's eyes fell upon the child, her legs felt limp, and she let out a loud gasp that drew the attention of the two women next to her.

"Are you all right, Sister Tamarra?" one of the women asked, holding onto Tamarra's arm to balance her.

"Do you need some water or something?" The other woman fanned Tamarra vigorously as both women gently aided her in sitting back down on the pew.

"No, I'm fine," Tamarra told them, still trying to look at the little girl in between the persons sitting and standing in front of her.

Why, today of all days, had she been running late for church and had to sit farther back than normal? Had she made it to church on time, she'd have been much closer and able to get a better look at the child. But she didn't need a better look. She knew what she'd seen. She'd seen that child's eyes, dark brown, almond shaped eyes that she'd, without a doubt, seen before. She'd seen that complexion before as well, and that nose and those lips. She'd seen them before, only not on the little girl. She'd seen them on Maeyl.

Chapter Four

"Excuse me, Sister Unique, do you have a moment so that I can talk to you?"

After giving Lorain the once over, Unique reluctantly agreed. "Sure, but only a second because I have to get my kids from Children's Church."

Sister Lorain turned toward her mother, whom she'd invited to church with her that Easter Sunday. "Mama, they've got coffee and donuts in the Welcome Center." Sister Lorain pointed. "Why don't you go help yourself while I talk to Sister Unique for a minute, then I'll be right in?"

The sixty-year-old woman, who didn't look a day over forty-five, happily obliged. "Okay." She peeked into the room referred to as the Welcome Center. "Sounds fine with me. And take your time," she said to Lorain as she admired a couple of gentlemen entering the room, "'cause I see some sugar that will go mighty fine in my coffee, if you know what I mean." She playfully elbowed her daughter and walked off.

Lorain shook her head and turned her attention back to Unique. She ran her hand down the back of her hair that was tapered down her neck. The short, edgy, spiky looking style was very becoming on Lorain's long, thin face. The golden, honey tint complemented her mocha brown skin. "You'll have to excuse my mother. She just lost one hundred and fifty pounds on that Bariatric surgery and can't nobody tell her she ain't fine. She's been trying to get a man ever since."

"Like mother, like daughter," Unique tried to say as if it were a compliment, even though her obvious tone said otherwise.

"Pardon me?" Lorain was taken back by Unique's blatant rudeness, which was all the more reason she knew she needed to talk to the girl.

"No disrespect intended. I just meant with you being the new leader of the Single's Ministry; you must be trying to get a man too." Unique looked Lorain up and down. She turned her nose up at the snug fitting button up white blouse Lorain was wearing. Her 38 D's were barely contained. Unique thought if Lorain sneezed, one of those buttons would fly off and take her eye out.

"Actually, my purpose for joining the ministry wasn't to get a man." Lorain decided to play fair game. "After all, look at me." She ran her hands down her voluptuous size twelve figure. "Does it look like I have a problem with getting a man?" Not waiting for Unique to respond, she stated, "But you wouldn't know anything about that." Giving Unique a taste of her own medicine, Lorain looked the young, petite girl, thirteen years her junior, up and down.

"So what are you trying to say?" Unique was in full sister-girl mode by now. Her hands were on her hips and her head was bobbing.

Lorain noticed that Unique's stance was drawing attention. The last thing she wanted was to make a scene. All she'd wanted to do was to confront the girl. She'd heard about some of the little comments Unique had been making about her during the Single's Ministry meetings. She'd even heard some of them herself, but chose to ignore them. But after learning from one of the sisters at New Day that Unique had gone as far as calling her a Jezebel, Lorain felt it was time to call her on her actions.

She had no intentions of having any type of altercation with Unique. In fact, she thought herself the bigger person by coming to Unique. She simply wanted to clear the air between them. Lorain felt that maybe if Unique got to know her better, then she'd realize that all those things she thought about her weren't true. Perhaps the two might even have been able to become friends. Lorain had few of those nowadays, so she thought that being friends might benefit both of them. But from the looks of it, there would be an ice storm warning in hell before the two of them would ever be friends.

"Never mind," Lorain said with a sway of her hand as if she were dismissing Unique. "No need in me wasting my breath or your time. I know you have to go get *all* of those kids of yours."

"Look, if you got something to say, then I suggest you come on with it," Unique said.

"And I can say the same to you with all the whispering you've been doing about me," Lorain shot back.

"Whispering? Who's whispering around this piece? Everything I've said I've said loud enough for you to hear, or at least I thought I was."

Lorain shook her head. "I don't even know why I bothered. I should have known I couldn't come at someone as ghetto as you and expect any other results but something ghetto."

"Ghetto?" Unique said as she began unsnapping her large, hoop earrings from her ear.

"Yes, ghetto, and you're proving my point now by removing your earrings like you want to fight me right here in God's house." She looked down at the large knock-off designer bag that rested on Unique's arm. "And let me guess, I bet next you're going to pull out a jar of Vaseline, huh? And you're shocked that I called you ghetto. What else would you call a girl with four kids by four different daddies living in a house with ten people?"

"See, that's why you don't know what you're talking about. I don't live with no ten people, and I only have three kids," Unique corrected her.

By now, both women were speaking loud enough for anyone walking by to hear. Even those who couldn't hear could tell a heated and indignant conversation was going on between the two by the way they were both bobbing heads, snapping necks, hand hipping, and pointing.

"Oh, I stand corrected; three kids with three different daddies. Either way it goes, I'm sure that on Father's Day you have to install a revolving door in your front room."

Rage rushed through Unique like a flowing river as she balled her fist.

"There you are, Unique. Your kids were looking for you."

Thank goodness the Children's Church teacher's assistant in training came around the corner when she did. She had Unique's three children in tow. Had her timing not been perfect, Unique probably would have caught a case for assault as her fist was balled and ready to swing on Lorain. As wrong as she would have been for doing it, Unique wanted to knock Lorain's block off, but, she didn't want her kids to witness such a thing. Although things got rough sometimes, she always tried to be the best mother she could be by setting an example in front of her kids, which was why they were none the wiser about her drinking, smoking, and partying. She certainly didn't want them to know she was a fighter and would beat a chick down in a heartbeat like she used to do back in the projects.

"Mommy!" Unique's children, ages three, four, and five, said as they ran toward her with open arms.

"We thought you left us, Mommy. Gave us away. Where were you?" her oldest of three boys said to her.

"Oh, sweetie, I would never give you away. Never." Unique kneeled down and basked in the hugs and kisses her children covered her in.

Witnessing such genuine affection, Lorain suddenly felt awful. She wished she could take back all the things she'd just said to those beautiful children's mother. How had she allowed herself to stoop to such a level? And here she was calling herself the bigger person. She was the bigger fool. She knew better. She was older than this girl, so if anything, she should be setting an example. Instead, she was about to take her earrings off too and pull out her lip gloss, since she didn't have any Vaseline.

"We still going to McDonald's after church today?" Unique's middle child asked her.

"Didn't I promise you we would?" Unique asked, standing.

All her children replied in unison. "Yes!"

"Then let's go. We'll walk to the bus stop that's closest to the McDonald's restaurant." Unique looked to the Children's Church assistant. "Thank you, Sister Helen."

"Not a problem," Helen replied, staring at Unique's interaction with her children in admiration. She couldn't help think about what it would have been like had she had children. But ever since she started facing the demon of an abortion she had years ago, she didn't feel worthy of ever becoming a mother and having children of her own. Being an assistant in the Children's Church was part of her healing process that the pastor had suggested. Maybe caring for other people's children would eventually prove to her that she was not only capable, but worthy.

"We'll see you next Sunday, Sister Helen." Unique walked away with her children, but not before cutting a look at Lorain that read, "My children saved you from a butt whooping, but this ain't over yet by far."

Letting out a deep sigh, Lorain headed toward the Welcome Center, preparing in her head an excuse for her actions once confronted by the pastor about it. "You ready to go already?" Lorain asked her mother who came waltzing out of the Welcome Center.

"Child, yes! My work in this place is done," her mother said excitedly. "I got me a phone number!"

Chapter Five

"It feels so good to be out of that hospital," Bethany said as she sat at the kitchen table with Mother Doreen, her four-teen-and-a-half-year-old daughter, Sadie, and her son, Hudson, who was going on seventeen.

"Child, I know it does. Seems like you been in and out of the hospital for the past two years now," Mother Doreen said before eating a forkful of meatloaf.

"Yes it has, and Lord knows I missed a good home cooked meal." Bethany closed her eyes and let a mouthful of buttered mashed potatoes slither down her throat. "I know y'all's Auntie Doreen got y'all spoiled rotten with all of her cooking," Bethany said to her two children, who confirmed such with head nods. "Well, don't think for one minute I'm gonna be throwing down like this. It's back to the basics. Won't be none of this meatloaf, fresh cut greens with onion and tomatoes, and mashed potatoes." Bethany shook her head as she took in a bite of greens. "Frozen dinners, beanie weenies, here we come!"

Everyone chuckled.

"Now don't you think for a minute I'm going to let you back in the kitchen as long as I'm here," Mother Doreen stated, pointing her fork at her sister. "Besides, you ain't alltogether well; just too well to be laid up in somebody's hospital. And our goal is for you to get even better, and that's not going to happen eating stuff like frozen dinners with all that sodium. No sir; we gon' keep your diabetes under control, and part of doing that is changing your eating habits and diet."

"Blah, blah, blah." Bethany teased Mother Doreen the same way she used to when they were young girls.

"Watch it now," Mother Doreen warned. "I can still mop the floor with you the same way I did when we were girls."

The two women giggled.

"Old lady," Bethany teased, "you ain't gon' do nothing."

"Old? Don't go calling me old. It ain't my fault Mama and Daddy waited until I was twenty-three years old to have you," Mother Doreen replied. "The oops baby."

"They wanted to save the best for last," Bethany gloated.

"Oooh, Mom; and you talk about Hudson and me bickering," Sadie said, playfully shaking her head.

"I'm sayin'," Hudson agreed, finishing up his food, chomping on the last bite of meatloaf.

Both Mother Doreen and Bethany looked at Hudson like he was speaking a foreign language. "I'm sayin'?" the two sisters said in unison.

He looked back and forth from one sister to the other. "I mean, uh, I mean, uh..." his words trailed off after not being able to find the right words to express his sentiment. His mother had told him a million times about not speaking proper English in full sentences. "May I be excused?"

"Um, hmmm." Bethany rolled her eyes at him.

"Me too," Sadie said as she stood up.

"Don't forget we got that apple cheesecake for dessert," Mother Doreen reminded the teens as they put their dishes in the dishwasher.

"We won't," they said.

"Especially me." Hudson kissed his aunt on the cheek. He then turned and kissed his mother as well. "Welcome home, Ma."

"Thanks, son." Bethany smiled as her kids exited the kitchen.

Mother Doreen finished her last few bites, and then began to clear the kitchen table.

"Oh, let me help you." Bethany stood up.

"You'll do no such a thing. Remember, I'm here to help, and that's exactly what I'm going to do. Now sit down, and talk to me while I finish up."

"Talk about what?" Bethany asked as she sat back down.

"I don't know." Mother Doreen shrugged. "How about we talk about that husband of yours? How are things between you two?"

Now Bethany shrugged. "I don't know. Same ol' same ol' I guess. I mean, we've been married for ten years, so there's nothing new to speak on." Bethany and her husband had lived together for seven years and had already had both of their children by the time they decided to get married. "You know the drill; Uriah's been on the road. I've been in the hospital. When ever we both are at home, seems like we're still never home. I'm doing church business; he's catching up with his mama and sister, who as you know, live seventy-five miles east of us. We're like passing ships in the night."

"That doesn't surprise me none," Mother Doreen stated. "I mean, what man wants to come home and stay home when all he's got waiting on him is frozen dinners and beanie weenies?" Mother Doreen couldn't hold back her laughter.

"You so bad." Bethany balled up her napkin and threw it at her sister.

"But I'm telling the truth. Child, you got to do better than that. He's probably running over to his mama's house to get some real food."

"We do have real food here...on occasion. The sisters at church will sometimes take turns fixing meals for us, and Pastor Frey will bring it over on his visits."

Before Mother Doreen could reply, the doorbell rang.

"I got it," Bethany said, stopping Mother Doreen in her tracks as she started toward the door. "I ain't altogether helpless you know."

Mother Doreen picked up the napkin that had been thrown at her and threw it at Bethany's back. The two shared a giggle before Bethany made her way to the door, looked out the peephole, and opened it.

"Speak of the devil," Bethany said as she opened the door.

Mother Doreen looked over her shoulder to see Pastor Frey entering the house, and mumbled to herself, "And the devil appears."

Bethany was right; Mother Doreen's entire demeanor did seem to change whenever that man came around. Mother Doreen tried to convince herself that it was something about Pastor Frey that just outright vexed her spirit. But that wasn't the case. Now, with him showing up on her sister's doorstep at seven o'clock in the evening, it wasn't him Mother Doreen had issues with. It was his intentions. And so help her God, she was going to find out exactly what they were.

Chapter Six

"Is everything okay?" Tamarra asked Maeyl as the two ate lunch at Family Café.

It was the usual busy Wednesday evening crowd. Maeyl appeared to be distracted, barely touching his meal that had been sitting in front of him for at least twenty minutes. Certainly it was cold by now.

"Hello . . . Earth to Maeyl," she said when Maeyl didn't respond to her query.

"Oh, pardon me. Did you say something?" Maeyl asked, snapping out of his daze.

"Yes, I did." Tamarra dropped her fork in frustration.

She was fed up with Maeyl's lack of attention toward her these past few days, ever since Easter Sunday to be precise. Once the most attentive man she'd ever known, Maeyl's daily phone calls to check up on her had been shortened. It was as if he really didn't have time to talk to her, if he bothered even calling her at all. Today was the first time they'd seen each other since Sunday, which was unusual. Normally the two would have met up a couple of times by now, even if it were just for a cup of coffee or a stroll in the park.

Even on Sunday after church, the two of them were supposed to meet Paige and Blake at the Golden Coral Buffet. Once upon a time, that was Tamarra and Paige's meeting spot after church, but that was before men came into their lives. Paige normally would have had Easter dinner with her parents, but they were going out of town to have dinner with her father's brother's family. Running her own catering business, Tamarra cooked for a living, so the last thing she wanted to do was whip up a feast. The Golden Coral had a special menu just for Easter, and Tamarra had planned on partaking in it with Maeyl. Instead, it was just her, Paige, and Blake, as well as a few other New Day members who'd decided against cooking as well.

Before leaving church, Maeyl had informed Tamarra that he'd suddenly come down with stomach discomfort and didn't want to go out to eat. He voiced his concerns about being afraid that he was coming down with a stomach virus or something.

He'd been just fine the earlier part of Sunday; that was until that mystery woman and child turned up. Tamarra didn't want to jump to conclusions, but she sensed something other than a stomach virus kept Maeyl from keeping their date. If her senses were on point, she guessed it had something to do with that woman and little girl.

For a moment, Tamarra thought that maybe the woman was Maeyl's long, lost sister that he hadn't told her about. It could happen. After all, she had a brother that she'd never bothered telling him about, for reasons of which she felt justified. Her own blood brother had raped her. After doing something so despicable to her, he was dead as far as she was concerned. In her mind, she didn't have a brother, and as far as everyone else in Malvonia was concerned, she didn't have a brother. That was one of the reasons why she'd moved from Cleveland, Ohio to the small town of Malvonia; to have a better chance at living a lie without anyone knowing. And it helped to have a new last name. She'd kept Davis as her last name even after her divorce.

Maeyl's reaction in church on Sunday had been nagging at Tamarra all week long. By now she thought she would have been able to pick Maeyl's brain in order to find out what was going on, fishing for some type of clue. Unfortunately, he hadn't given her any opportunity, being short in conversation or not even having a conversation at all. Even now, at their pre-Bible Study dinner, she thought it would have been her golden opportunity to get to the bottom of things. But he was too distracted to even hold a conversation, let alone give her straight answers. But she thought she'd give it a try anyway.

"As a matter of fact, I've been saying something for the last few days, but you probably haven't heard a word I've said," Tamarra continued, losing her appetite and pushing her plate away with half her meal remaining on it.

Maeyl sighed and dropped his fork. He, too, then pushed his plate away. "I'm sorry, Tamarra, you're right. I have been a little out of it these past few days. It's just that I have a lot on my mind."

"Like what?" Now Tamarra was getting anxious as she shifted in her seat and leaned forward as if Maeyl was about to share top secret government information with her.

Maeyl was silent as he looked into the eyes of the woman he'd fallen in love with, the woman he'd been through so much with in so little time. The woman who had to ask him to forgive her over and over again for the many mistakes she'd made in the process of their forming a relationship. Now that they'd made it through the fire, there was a chance that, once again, their relationship would be threatened. But this time, it would be Tamarra on the forgiving end, hopefully, otherwise, there was a chance that somebody might get burned.

Maeyl hesitated before replying to Tamarra. He was debating whether or not to move forward with the conversation he knew he needed to have before it was too late. Deciding that there was no time like the present to share exactly what had been bothering him for these past few days, he began to speak.

"Tamarra, honey, there's something—"

"Was the food all right? This is a first for the Family Café; for folks not to finish their meals."

Tamarra and Maeyl looked up to see their waitress, Zelda, standing over them. Tamarra shot her a look of irritation. She felt that Maeyl was just about to spill the beans without her even having to pick his brain, and now Zelda's bad timing could have possibly ruined it.

Maeyl, on the other hand, let out a deep sigh of relief and gave Zelda a look of thanks for coming to his rescue. *Guess it wasn't God's perfect timing,* he thought.

"Oh, no, Sister Zelda, the food is just fine, as always." Maeyl smiled. Even though Zelda no longer attended New Day, or any other church for that matter, Maeyl was still in the habit of calling her Sister Zelda. As far as he was concerned, she didn't have to be a church member to be his sister in Christ. *"We're all God's children,"* is what he'd been taught since his childhood Sunday School days.

"All right, then," Zelda said, not sounding too convinced. "But I've seen birds outside the window eat more food than the two of you put together." She placed their bill on the table, and then lifted their plates. "I'll put them in some to-go boxes for y'all." She then walked off.

"Thanks, Zelda," Maeyl called out to her as she headed in the kitchen. He then turned to Tamarra who had a sour look on her face. "What?" he shrugged.

"What?" she repeated. "Getting you to talk has been like pulling hen's teeth, but now all of a sudden you can't stop talking to Zelda, that's what."

Maeyl chuckled while reaching across the table to pat Tamarra's hand. "Now, Tammy, don't tell me you're jealous." He knew darn well Tamarra wasn't jealous. He knew exactly what she was getting at. He just didn't want to get caught up in her trying to get him to go there.

"I asked you not to call me that!" Tamarra snapped, raising

her voice, causing a couple of customers to turn their heads to look. Brushing off her embarrassment, she said to Maeyl. "I'm sorry. It's just that my name is Tamarra."

Maeyl put up his hands in defense. "My apologies. I'm sorry. I know you've told me before not to call you that. I slipped."

Calming down, Tamarra replied, "That's okay." She looked up at the clock that was hanging on the restaurant wall. "We better get going. Bible Study will be starting soon, and you know Pastor makes the last person who walks into the classroom give the opening prayer," Tamarra reminded Maeyl as she gathered her purse and wrap. The April weather didn't require a jacket or heavy coat.

Maeyl pulled out his wallet and paid the bill, adding a few extra dollars for the tip. He then stood up and assisted Tamarra with putting her wrap on.

"You all set?" Maeyl asked Tamarra, who replied with a nod. "Good, then let's go."

They each headed for the exit door so that they could make their way to their own individual cars. They'd met up at the restaurant like they did almost every Wednesday before Bible Study. Driving separate cars was suggested in one of the Single's Ministry meetings that both Maeyl and Tamarra now attended. Two single people who were simply dating should drive separately and meet out whenever possible; that was the suggestion. Avoiding the cliché "too close for comfort" was a means of avoiding the lust demon, which could ultimately keep the couple out of a compromising position, literally.

"Don't forget your food," Zelda called out right before the couple exited the restaurant.

"Oh, thank you." Maeyl took both boxes and handed Tamarra hers. "I almost forgot all about this."

"I'm sure you did," Tamarra said before all but snatching her box of food from Maeyl's hands, wondering how long she'd have to wait before she could finally get Maeyl to talk to her one on one. But little did she know, it wouldn't be soon enough.

Chapter Seven

"And just what are you doing here?" Unique snapped as she stood in the waiting area outside of Pastor's office. "Let me guess; waiting to tattle on me to Pastor."

Lorain stood up from the chair she had been sitting in. Although Unique was trying her patience and Christianity with the first few words out of her mouth, she'd promised herself she'd never let that woman take her out of character again. So she flattened out her skirt and said with a cool, calm, and collected voice, "Actually, I'm not here to tattle on you. I'm here to tell on myself."

"Yeah, right." Unique smacked her lips and rolled her eyes as if she didn't believe Lorain's claim. "You here to give Pastor your side of the story first, but it looks like I got here just in time to intercept."

"There's nothing to intercept," Lorain insisted. "Like I told you, I'm not here to try and rake you through the coals with Pastor." An inquisitive look crossed Lorain's face. "But if you don't mind me asking, why are you here?"

Before Unique could respond, the Pastor's office door opened. "Sister Unique, Sister Lorain, I see you both have arrived as scheduled," Pastor greeted.

Both women looked at each other in confusion, and then turned their attention to their pastor.

"Since you both called and wanted to talk about the same matter, I figured we'd kill two birds with one stone," Pastor said, extending a hand to invite both women into the office.

"Thank you for showing up a few minutes early so that we can discuss whatever it is that is on you ladies' minds before Bible Study." Pastor closed the office door and remained standing along with Unique and Lorain.

"Shall we pray first?" Pastor held each of the women's hands. Noticing that the women hadn't joined hands to lock in the prayer circle, Pastor gave each of them a glance, then nodded toward their hands. Once the women somewhat reluctantly joined hands, Pastor proceeded to pray.

Upon completing the prayer, Lorain and Unique came into agreement with an Amen, and then upon Pastor's request, took a seat in front of the desk. "So Sister Lorain, I know when you phoned you said that you wanted to speak with me about the Single's Ministry." Pastor took a seat behind the large desk and looked to Unique. "Sister Unique, you made the same exact request. I found it to be a coincidence at first, until I heard something about what appeared to be a heated discussion between the two of you this past Sunday."

Both Lorain and Unique were quiet. They knew the chances were slim to none, but Monday morning when they'd each phoned Pastor, they both did it with the intentions of speaking about what had taken place between the two of them. Their goal was to do it before other members could get to Pastor. Both women had decided that they wouldn't mention to the pastor directly that they wanted to talk regarding the other. Instead, they used the subject matter of the Single's Ministry to open up the door to discuss an issue they were having with one of the members. But like Pastor had just informed them, it wasn't hard to put two and two together after hearing about their verbal altercation. And Unique was willing to bet the entire bank that the church secretary was the one who'd ratted them out.

That busy body needs to get her some business, Unique thought to herself before Pastor interrupted her deliberations.

"Sister Unique," Pastor said, "would you care to share with

me what it was you wanted to discuss pertaining to the Single's Ministry?"

Never one to be a coward, Unique cleared her throat, sat straight up in her chair, and began to speak. "Yes, Pastor, I would. I wanted to discuss the leadership of the ministry."

Lorain leaned in toward Unique to let her know that she was all ears; ready to see just what she had to say about the leadership. Pastor was at full attention as well, only with less attitude than Lorain.

"What about the leadership?" Pastor asked.

"I just question what Mother Doreen might have been thinking when she passed the mantel to Sister Lorain here." Unique nodded toward Lorain. "Lorain just joined the ministry. It's almost like a slap in the face to women who have been members since it started and who know a lot more about it and how to lead it."

"I see how you and other members might feel that way," Pastor started, "but I assure you that if God hadn't told Mother Doreen that Sister Lorain was the one to take over, then Mother Doreen would have never presented her to me as a candidate."

Lorain's lips parted into an I-told-you-so smile. This hit a nerve with Unique.

"Well, perhaps Mother Doreen didn't hear as clearly from the Lord as she thought she had," Unique reasoned. "After all, she had a lot on her mind with her sick sister and relocating to Kentucky and all."

"I could see where you might think that as well, Sister Unique," Pastor said, "so I prayed on it as well, and when I picked up the telephone to call Sister Lorain to tell her about what God had showed both Mother Doreen and me pertaining to her work here at New Day, she just happened to be on my telephone line. She'd been in the process of calling me to tell me that God had told her it was time; it was time for her to become one of His servants in His kingdom. That it was time for her to be more than a pew viewer and become a pew doer. This was just further confirmation."

Once again, Lorain's lips parted into an I-told-you-so smile. Once again, this hit a nerve with Unique.

"Pastor, you know I'd never question your authority or the fact that you hear clearly from God—" Unique shifted in her seat. For the first time ever, she appeared to be struggling with her words. "But are you sure God specifically said that it was the Single's Ministry and not the Usher's Ministry?" Unique looked Lorain up and down before saying to the pastor, "Or even the Janitorial Ministry? I'm sure Sister Nita could use the help in taking out the trash."

Lorain looked appalled at what Unique might have been insinuating with her last comment.

"I'm quite sure, Unique," Pastor told her. "Trust me; I don't appoint kings and queens without hearing from God about it. You know me, someone coming up to me telling me what they used to do at their old church or what they feel they are called to do has never prompted me to just appoint them to positions. I take everything to God because it is He who validates a person, not man. Do you understand what I'm saying, Sister Unique?"

Defeated, Unique sunk down into her chair and replied, "Yes, Pastor. I understand."

Just when she was about to give up, a sudden thought came to Unique's mind. "Pastor, and again, I'm not trying to question your authority, but perhaps God did call Sister Lorain to be the Single's Ministry leader, just not right now, but later." As far as Unique was concerned, later meant after she was married off and didn't belong to the ministry anymore. That way she wouldn't have to deal with the likes of Lorain. "I mean, even though Mother Doreen was the official leader, Sister Deborah pretty much ran the ministry. She was like the co-leader. So it only seems fit that Sister Deborah would be the next in line."

Not losing an ounce of patience with Unique's relentlessness, Pastor replied, "Once again, Sister Unique, I can see where you would think that, but as you know, Sister Deborah is on a sabbatical for I don't know how long, until whenever the Lord releases her. But even if she weren't, before going onto the sabbatical, she made it clear that God had called her to focus on other things."

Unique sighed. For the first time since she could remember, she was out of words.

"Sister Lorain." Pastor turned toward Lorain. "I don't want to monopolize all the time up with just Sister Unique's concerns regarding the ministry. You had some concerns as well?"

"Actually, I just wanted to inform you of my behavior on Sunday, apologize, and assure you that it will never happen again. As a leader in this church, I'm truly going to step up. I've already prayed and asked God to help to become the best leader that He called me to be."

"Sounds good, Sister Lorain." Pastor smiled then looked at the clock on the wall. "Well, it looks like it's time for Bible Study to begin, ladies, so we're going to have to end our discussion here." Pastor wasn't feeling one-hundred percent certain that the issue had been completely resolved. "Shall we close out in prayer?"

Pastor closed out the discussion with a prayer that God would speak to the situation speedily and that everything would turn out for His good and glory in the end. Pastor then opened the door and dismissed the women to Bible Study. "Ladies, wait," Pastor called out before Unique and Lorain were out of the door. "I have an idea," Pastor said as if suddenly experiencing a revelation regarding the situation at hand. "The Holy Spirit just deposited something into my spirit. Come in and sit back down."

Both Unique and Lorain returned to their chairs, with Pastor once again closing the door behind them. Pastor began to share with the two women what God had just deposited, knowing that more than likely, neither woman would be pleased with God's solution to that matter. Nope, they wouldn't be pleased at all.

Chapter Eight

"Well, Pastor, looks like you have to open in prayer to-night," Maeyl said when he saw Pastor tailing into the Bible Study classroom behind Unique and Lorain.

"My apologies for running a little late," Pastor said, heading toward the podium, then looking at the clock and noting that it was four minutes after seven o'clock.

After allowing Unique and Lorain time to find a seat, Pastor asked the class to stand for prayer. Everyone in the class obliged.

"Hold up, Pastor," someone called out, "looks like you're not the last one to enter the room after all."

Everyone looked toward the doorway. There stood one last visitor, well, two if the toddler was to be included.

"Sorry, I'm late." The woman looked mortified as every eye in the room appeared to be glued on her.

The pastor, noticing the expression on the woman's face, let out a chuckle. "Oh, it's okay, my sister. We just have a little thing we do here at New Day where the last person who enters Bible Study has to open up with prayer."

"Oh." The woman seemed much more relaxed now.

"But we'll give you a pass since it's your first time attending one of our Bible Study sessions. We don't want to put you on the spot," Pastor stated. As a matter of fact, this past Sunday had been her first Sunday attending New Day. Pastor had noticed the woman when visitors were greeted and asked to stand during Sunday morning service. The woman had chosen not to stand, in spite of the urging eyes of those around her who knew that she was a first time attendee. Pastor understood her choice not to do so. Lots of first time visitors opted not to stand for fear they would be asked to speak.

"Well, I don't want to break any rules," the woman said, "so if you don't mind, Pastor, I'd be honored to pray."

"Well, all right, woman of God," a couple of people said.

"Y'all heard the sister," Pastor said happily. "Let's bow our heads and grab hands while Sister . . ."

"Sasha," the woman stated.

"While Sister Sasha leads us in prayer."

Maeyl had found himself staring at the woman the entire time, the same way he'd stared at her this past Sunday. She just looked uncannily like someone he'd met once upon a time. He thought it was her. He hoped it wasn't her, but it sure looked like her. Those were the thoughts that had been in his head all week and had returned to the tenth power once he saw her standing in the doorway. After hearing the woman state her name, he was now most certain it was her. Sasha McCoy.

He'd thought that was just her stage name, the name she gave out to the guys who tried to pick her up. She'd assured him over a cup of coffee that Saturday night he'd met her, about four years ago, that Sasha McCoy was her given name. She'd assured him again at her doorstep in the wee hours in the morning after he'd insisted on following her home from the coffee shop to make sure she'd made it safely. She'd assured him again after inviting him inside her apartment . . . *just to talk.*

"You're such a gentleman," she'd told him as they sat on her couch. "I know where I work is called a gentlemen's club, but trust me when I say it ain't often I find too many gentlemen up in there."

Within minutes, it seemed, after Sasha had given Maeyl

such a compliment, he had thrown caution to the wind, along with that title. And hours after that, he found himself tiptoeing out her front door with his shirt untucked, carrying his shoes, and arriving home with barely enough time to make it to Sunday morning service. He'd repented and cried uncontrollably at the altar that Sunday, wishing he'd never let the guys from his job talk him into going to that stupid strip club in the first place, the place where he'd met her.

Sasha McCoy. That was her name all right. She'd trusted him with her full given name because she thought he was a gentleman. She'd trusted him with her body because she thought he was a gentleman. All he had trusted her with was his first name and an empty spot next to her bed.

"Maeyl," Tamarra whispered in his ear after attempting several times to hold his hand for prayer.

"Oh, huh, what?" Maeyl stammered from his daze.

"Your hand. Give me your hand," Tamarra stated.

Maeyl slowly lifted his hand and took hold of Tamarra's.

"Yuck!" Tamarra said louder than she meant to as the woman started to pray. "Oh, sorry," she apologized when several people lifted their bowed heads and opened their eyes just long enough to shoot her a snappy look. She stood, all five feet and nine inches of her, in embarrassment.

Tamarra quickly slid her hand from Maeyl's and wiped it down her slacks, leaving a moist smear. She was disgusted by the transferring of the sticky sweat from his palm to hers. Tamarra looked at Maeyl only to find that it wasn't just his palms that were sweaty. Sweat drizzled down his forehead that wrinkled due to the scrunching of his face. To Tamarra, he looked as though he'd just filled his mouth with a handful of sour grapes.

For Maeyl, the prayer couldn't have ended soon enough. "I'll be back. I have to go to the men's room." He placed his hand on his mid section. "My stomach is acting up again," he whispered to Tamarra as he headed toward the door.

Tamarra watched as Maeyl stumbled over feet, purses, and Bibles trying to get out of the door. He acted as if he couldn't get out of that door fast enough, and he couldn't. But as far as he was concerned, he'd gotten out of there just in the nick of time, as he could hear Pastor asking the woman to introduce herself and her child.

"Sasha," Tamarra repeated the woman's name after she reintroduced herself. The word fell off of Tamarra's lips in a hushed whisper. The name sounded so exotic; so mysterious, just like the woman herself who stood there with honey caramel colored skin and shoulder-length, black, wavy hair. And those gray-blue eyes were just piercing. But if Tamarra had anything to do with it, the woman, nor that child of hers would remain a mystery for long. At least now Tamarra had a name. She'd have to get the story behind the name from Maeyl; she'd try to anyway.

"And this is my three-year-old daughter, Sakaya," the woman stated in conclusion of her formalities.

"Well, welcome to New Day Temple of Faith," Pastor said before instructing the woman to find a seat for her and her child.

Now Tamarra was the one staring at the woman, then at the child. The more she looked at the child, the tighter the knot in her stomach got. She didn't have any concrete evidence, but something was telling Tamarra that about three years ago, Miss Sasha had a knot in her stomach too, a big one. And from the looks of things, that little girl was the cause of it. And if Tamarra's instincts were correct, the child was now the cause of her daddy's stomach issues too.

Chapter Nine

"It's so good to have you back in fellowship with us, Sister Bethany." Pastor Davidson gave Bethany a hug as he stood at the altar shortly after giving the benediction.

He always hung around the sanctuary for a few minutes after service to meet and greet the congregation. His sole purpose for doing so was so that he could get a chance to speak with any visitors or potential members. Pastor Davidson was big on numbers as far as membership. He knew the more members that belonged to his church, the more tithes and offerings he could collect, which meant the more kingdom work he and the church could do. But it always seemed as though the same old members rushed up to speak with him, taking up so much of his time that he could rarely catch up with all the visitors before they left. Some of the folks that always made sure they were the first to get to Pastor Davidson were even ministers and leaders, people who talked to or saw him on a regular basis. Then there were those who acted like church wasn't church unless the pastor laid hands on them. The devil is a liar.

"And it's so good to be back, Pastor Davidson," Bethany replied. "I can't thank Living Word enough for all the prayers and acts of kindness toward me. My family and I so much appreciate it." Bethany looked next to her at Mother Doreen. "And I don't know what I would have done without my dear sister here as well." Bethany rubbed Mother Doreen's back, who bowed her head in modesty.

"Yes, Mother Doreen," Pastor Davidson greeted her with a handshake. "You know it's always a pleasure to have you here at Living Word, Living Waters too." He gave her hand a pat before releasing it. "You know, we'd like it even more if you became a member and blessed us with those wonderful gifts and talents God has blessed you with." Pastor Davidson winked.

"Oh no, Pastor." Mother Doreen smiled while shaking her head. Pastor Davidson was an excellent minister of the Word in Mother Doreen's opinion. With all of the wonderful ministries and evangelistic works he oversaw at Living Word, Mother Doreen didn't doubt that he was about God's business. His only flaw, as far as she could see, was his aggressiveness in seeking membership. "That's flattering, but I'm praying that once I finish my business here with my sister, God will send me back to Ohio and allow me to resume my works at New Day."

"Been there prayed that one." Pastor Davidson chuckled. "God initially sent me here as just an interim pastor." He raised his hands in the air and let them fall to his side. "But look at me now."

"And we are so blessed that God let us keep you," Bethany told him.

"Thank you, Sister Bethany." Pastor Davidson smiled before turning his attention back to Mother Doreen. "Perhaps God will let us keep you too, Sister Doreen. I mean, after all, Bethany's out of the hospital now and looking like she has the strength of Christ. I mean, look at her. She appears to be stronger than ever before. So with her seeming to be doing so well, seems like you could mosey on back to Ohio. So something must be keeping you here. Perhaps the Lord?" He winked again.

Mother Doreen didn't doubt that the Lord was indeed the one keeping her there. After all, He was the one who sent her there in the first place. Even so, she wasn't about to turn around and move back to Ohio any time soon after packing up everything she owned to move into her sister's guest room. She had a home to go back to if she wanted because she hadn't sold her house, choosing instead to rent it out to a Section 8 tenant. The home had long been paid for by her late husband, Willie, so besides any maintenance involved in preserving the property, Mother Doreen simply banked the rest of the rent.

"Oh, the Lord is definitely keeping me here indeed," Mother Doreen told Pastor Davidson with conviction. Just then Pastor Frey walked up. Mother Doreen shot him one of her looks. "But the Lord ain't the only somebody that's keeping me here." She stared at Pastor Frey.

Pastor Davidson, Bethany, and Pastor Frey proceeded to chat a bit while Mother Doreen subconsciously continued to stare at Pastor Frey. In the midst of the conversation, Pastor Davidson noticed how attentive Mother Doreen was to Pastor Frey. He couldn't help but smile internally while Mother Doreen's last comment played in his head. *But the Lord ain't the only somebody that's keeping me here.* And she had made the comment just as his assistant pastor had walked up.

Putting two and two together, an external smile appeared on Pastor Davidson's lips. He'd had a sudden thought as to how he might at least be able to keep Mother Doreen busy during her stay in Kentucky.

Chapter Ten

"I know I prayed to God for help, but that was not the type of help I had in mind," Lorain complained to her mother over the telephone. "I mean, I don't know if Pastor was trying to be funny or what."

"Maybe that was Pastor's way of shutting the both of yous up," Lorain's mother laughed.

"Eleanor Simpson, you always could make a joke out of serious things," Lorain stated, calling her mother by her name.

"Oh, chile please. It ain't that serious."

"And will you stop talking like you're from down South knowing you were raised in Youngstown, Ohio?" Lorain's voice was full of attitude, as if she didn't appreciate the way her mother was trying to lighten up a situation that she had already deemed as dark and gloomy.

"Don't go getting snippy with me, girl. I ain't but a hop, skip, and electric slide away from your tail. Grown or not, I'll come over there and remind you who the momma is in this relationship." Now Eleanor was serious.

"I'm sorry, Mama. I don't want you coming over here whooping on me. It's just that—"

"It's just that it ain't that serious is what it is, Lorain. I mean, come on, you should be used to this type of thing by now. Girls have never liked you, so what's the big deal? And apology accepted. Besides, I ain't got time to come over there and take a switch to your behind anyway. I's gots me a date. Ha-haaaa," Eleanor said in a sing-song voice.

Lorain was still stuck on the comment her mother had made about her being disliked by girls. "Girls have never liked me? Is that your way of making me feel better about all of this?"

"Get over yourself. It's not about you, Lorain. Ain't that what you always telling me your pastor says? That it ain't about you, but it's always about God? Well then, let it be about God. Obviously there's a reason why God chose for you to be connected with this Unique person."

"But wasn't going to church with her and being a part of the Single's Ministry with her enough? But for Pastor to assign her as my co-leader of the Single's Ministry is just outright evil!"

"Speaking of singles, let me get up off this phone so I can get ready for my date so that, hopefully, I won't have to be single too much longer. That fine man I gave my number to on Sunday is picking me up for a movie."

"On a weekday?"

"Yeah. I guess there's some girl who goes to y'all's church—Paige or something—who works at a theatre somewhere and gets free passes that she shares with the congregation. She gave him two."

"What's this fella's name anyway?" Lorain asked before her other line beeped. She looked at the caller ID. It was a blocked number. Sometimes she didn't answer blocked calls, but since she was caught up on all of her bills, she decided to go ahead and answer it this time. "Ma, let me take this other call. You have fun on your date."

"I will, sweetie. Bye-bye."

Lorain clicked over to the other line. "Hello."

"Yeah, this is Unique. I was just calling you like Pastor said so that we could set up a time to hook up." Unique's voice wasn't the least bit enthusiastic. It was as if someone had woken her up at three o'clock in the morning, put a gun to her head, and forced her to dial Lorain's number. Then on top of that, forced her to actually talk.

Lorain wasn't excited about having to meet with Unique to discuss matters of the Single's Ministry either. She was even less excited that Pastor had even asked Unique to assist her with the Single's Ministry by appointing Unique co-leader. Both Lorain and Unique had been absolutely floored when Pastor called them back into the office and shared with them the instructions God had ordered. Certainly God had jokes by choosing those two to work together. Or maybe it was Pastor who had jokes. Neither woman had figured it out. All they knew is that they weren't willing participants.

"God bless you, woman of God," Lorain forced herself to say. She was bound and determined to approach this situation with the understanding that she was doing God's work. And if doing God's work meant having to battle with the devil, then so be it. She'd just put on her full armor.

"Yeah, um, hmm," Unique said.

Lorain could just visualize Unique rolling her eyes up in her head. And she figured she probably had a scarf tied, Aunt Jemima style, on her head over all of that long black weave she wore. She was probably picking at her long, neon polished acrylic nails too. And batting those fake eyelashes with an entire tube of mascara on them. Lorain felt that Unique wore so much make-up that no one had any idea what her natural complexion was underneath it. She looked orange to Lorain.

"So Pastor said we should meet to go over what our vision is for the New Day Single's Ministry. Are you free this Saturday?" Lorain asked.

"Oh no, girl. My Saturday is on lock. *BET* picked up the sitcom series called *The Game,* and they showing re-runs all day starting at nine o'clock in the morning. I been waiting on this for a month. How about next Saturday?"

Lorain could already foresee there was going to be issues

with who put in more work regarding the ministry. "We could do it one day during the week," she suggested.

"I've got way too much going on during the week," Unique was quick to say.

Lorain sighed and rolled her eyes up in her head. "I guess you would with three children and all." Lorain sucked her teeth. "Next Saturday is fine. We can meet—"

"Sounds good. You can pick us up at around one o'clock if that's cool with you."

Lorain cleared her throat. "I was thinking we could meet somewhere. My place isn't that big, and with all your kids—"

"Oh, we're used to being crowded. You should see how we work it out with all of us living here at my sister's place. Grab a pen and write down the address," Unique ordered.

Lorain removed the phone receiver from her ear and stared at it as if to say, "Is this chick bossing me, telling me what to do?" She then heard the words her mother had just reminded her. *"It's not about you, Lorain."* She located a pen and slip of paper, returned to the phone, and wrote down the address Unique rattled off. "Okay, well I'll—"

All of a sudden there was a loud crash in the background.

"Awww, I'm tellin'. You gon' get it," Lorain heard a child say in the background.

"Nique!" Lorain now heard an adult yell. "Come and get your child before I—"

"I've got to go," Unique said. "My kids done broke up something else in my sister's house."

Before Lorain could say good-bye, Unique had hung up the phone. She looked around at her modest townhouse that was decorated with nice things. She made a mental note to stop by U-Haul and purchase boxes to pack some of her nicer things away before Unique and her brood paid her a visit next Saturday. Just thinking about having that woman and all her children in her house made Lorain tense up.

Lorain wanted to kick herself now for even praying to God about help with being a leader. Next time she was going to be a little bit more careful about what she prayed for just in case God decided to give it to her.

"Now Lord, I said I needed help, but I thought my help cometh from the hills." Lorain paced in anger. "Not from that ghetto—" She stopped herself before any explicits rolled off of her tongue. She'd been two years free of the cussing demon, and she wasn't about to let it creep back into her life.

Flopping down on the couch, Lorain took a deep breath. "It's not about you, Lorain," she reminded herself over and over again while taking several more deep breaths to calm her nerves. *But Lord, what is this about? Please show me what this is about?*

Chapter Eleven

"But can you believe he had the nerve to not even come back into Bible Study and tell me good-bye?" Tamarra fussed to Paige through the phone receiver as she pulled the large, aluminum pan of macaroni and cheese out of the oven. That was her signature dish, which just happened to be Maeyl's favorite and the dish that snagged him as her man in the first place. She was so glad she'd decided to make the dish for the very first Single's Ministry dinner. She was even gladder that Maeyl had shown up to the event and fell in love with the dish, and her.

Macaroni and cheese was also the final dish she needed for the catering affair she was about to go to. Her client had specifically requested the dish for Tamarra to prepare, stating that she'd come highly recommended by a friend who'd used Tamarra's catering services and that the mac and cheese had been a hit.

Tamarra could vouch that word of mouth was the best advertisement. It seemed like every new client she'd received lately had been a referral. If God continued to show favor on her business, allowing it to continue to prosper, she'd have to hire a couple more employees, making her current staff of four people grow to at least a half dozen.

"He just gon' creep on by the door and leave." Tamarra continued her rant.

Paige couldn't hold in her laughter.

"Oh, and my best friend thinks it's funny. I must be missing something." Tamarra sat the pan on the cooling rack that lay across her counter. The phone that had previously been locked between her shoulder and cheek was now cupped in her hand.

"Girl, my bad," Paige said as her laughter trailed off. "I can just picture Brother Maeyl tippy-pausing down the foyer, trying to get by that door without you seeing him."

"Yeah, well, I don't think I'm the only one that he didn't want to see him." Tamarra sighed.

"So you really think he knows this Sasha chick from somewhere?" Paige asked.

Tamarra had filled Paige in on all that had occurred since Sasha and the little girl had gone down to the altar on Easter Sunday. She'd also filled her in on her suspicions that Sasha was someone from Maeyl's past. She was too embarrassed to even mention that she thought there was a chance that the little girl could even be Maeyl's child.

She'd lost her ex-husband of fifteen years to a woman and a child he'd had as a result of his affair with the woman. She couldn't imagine finding herself in a similar circumstance, and especially not with just a *boyfriend*. Maeyl hadn't even reached fiancé status by proposing to her. Maybe she would have entertained the thought of involving herself in such drama if he'd at least proposed to her by now. Even though she and Maeyl hadn't even been dating a year, marriage was something she'd consider. In fact, she would welcome it with open arms. This was something she never thought possible after the heartbreak of her divorce from a man whom she'd still been deeply in love with on the day she signed the divorce papers. But eventually, love was replaced with hate, then bitterness, then no feelings for the man at all.

She'd known Maeyl much longer than Paige had known Blake, yet Paige had accepted Blake's proposal and was already in the planning stages of their wedding. But Tamarra didn't want to compare her relationship with that of her best friend's. That was just the devil's way of trying to rear his ugly head and spit venom poisoned with jealously. Tamarra had to admit, though, that she'd much prefer that trick over the one the devil was trying to play on her now with this Sasha woman.

"I'm almost positive he knows this Sasha person . . . from where, I don't know." Tamarra sounded so sure of herself.

"Well, I'm not understanding why you don't just flat out ask him about the woman. I can hint around about it at choir rehearsal if you want me to. You know he comes sometimes to do the music."

"Nahh," Tamarra replied.

"Then just ask him yourself. I mean, what have you got to lose?"

"My Christianity if that fool comes at me with some bull."

Once again, Paige was overcome with laughter. "Slow your roll now, Sister Tamarra, and remember who you are and whose you are. You are a child of the King, and God is not going to allow one of His children to run around here and be made a fool of. If something ain't kosher with Maeyl and Miss Sasha, be sure that God will reveal it to you, if you ask." Paige could tell by Tamarra's silence that she hadn't yet prayed on the matter and asked God to reveal the situation to her. "But even more so, God won't put more on you than you can bear."

Tamarra knew God's Word to be true. And no load He'd given her thus far had been too heavy for her to carry. But for once, she just wanted happiness without having to go through hell and high waters to get it. She wanted to bypass the wilderness and go straight to the Promised Land. Was that too much to ask of a God who could do anything? Couldn't He do that one small, tiny favor for her just this once?

"I know He won't dish out more than I can handle, Paige." Tamarra sighed. "It's just that I'm so tired. I just want to be happy."

"Well, Mary J. Blige used to say that same thing, and look at her now. She's happy. You can tell by her music. She used to sing stuff that made you want to cut your own wrist, or your man's wrist. But now she sings all those happy songs that have women all over the country posing in the mirror."

This time Tamarra laughed. "You are a mess, in a good way. But a mess no less."

"Speaking of mess," Paige said, "I need to get off this phone and do something with my house. Blake is on his way over. We're going over some wedding stuff."

"Well, don't get too engulfed in wedding stuff before the wedding, if you know what I mean."

"Don't you worry. My mom and dad are meeting us here too. After all, they are paying for the majority of the wedding, so I thought it was only fair that we allow them as much input as possible in the planning of it."

"Have you guys come up with a color scheme yet?"

"I was thinking of a chestnut brown and—"

Tamarra's line clicked. "Hold on real quick," she told Paige before clicking over and greeting the other caller. "Hello."

"Well, hello to you too, stranger."

"Mom," Tamarra said with enthusiasm. Once an estranged relationship, Tamarra now looked forward to talking with her mother on a weekly basis. She'd missed talking with her mother last week. Well, actually, she'd only spoken with her briefly. When her mother had called last week, Tamarra was on her way out the door to a catering affair, so she'd told her she'd call her back. She had noticed her mother's phone number on her caller ID a couple of times since then, making a mental note to return the call. She'd never gotten around to it though, and now here she was practically on her way out the door again. "I have Paige on the other line. Hold on for a second, Mom." Tamarra clicked over and ended her call with Paige, then clicked back over to her mother. "Okay, Mom, I'm back."

"I missed talking to you last week."

"Same here, Mom." Tamarra switched and swayed in her gourmet size kitchen, boxing up things she needed to load into her Jeep Cherokee for the catering affair. She'd recently been contemplating getting a van for her business. With extra employees and an extra vehicle, she might land herself in a position to be able to do two catering events at one time.

"Did I catch you at a bad time again?" her mother asked, hearing all the hustle and bustle in the background.

"Uh, well, no, Mom." She looked down at her watch. "I've got a minute," Tamarra lied. She only had half a minute. She'd wasted more time than she'd thought venting to Paige on the phone. She figured if she could dedicate that much time to fussing about her relationship issues to her best friend, she could surely take a moment to chat with her mother.

"Good, because there's someone else who wants to talk to you."

Tamarra's heart began to race. She couldn't think of anyone else there with her mother who'd want to speak with her. Her father was the only other person who now shared a home with her mother, and for as long as she'd been estranged from her mother, she'd been estranged from her father even longer. It had taken her years to finally begin to work on forgiving the two for the role they played in her being raped repeatedly as a child by her own brother, their son. She blamed her father for having porn in the house, which helped to arouse her brother in the first place. She blamed her mother for not knowing sooner that something was going on. She blamed them both for the cover up.

During all this time, her father had avoided her like the plague. Never even speaking with her on the phone. Tamarra felt as though he acted as if he were mad at her for everything that had happened. She'd been seeking God in the matter and had come to realize that everyone had a part in it, including herself. She should have told her parents the first time it happened. She should have told.

"You still there, baby?" Tamarra's mother asked.

"Yes, Mom, I'm still here."

"Did you hear what I said? Someone wants to speak with you."

"Yeah, Mom. Fine. Sure," Tamarra said as she rested the phone receiver between her ear and shoulder, then picked up the pan of macaroni and cheese to load it into the jeep. As she walked toward the garage door to her vehicle, she nervously waited to hear her father's voice come through the other line. What in the world would she say to the man? Before she could come up with anything, she heard the voice on the other end of the phone.

"Hey, Tammy. It's me."

The voice Tamarra had expected to hear was anything but her father's. The voice she did hear, though, sent an electric wave through her body that caused the phone to hit the ground simultaneously with the large pan of macaroni and cheese.

It can't be, Tamarra thought to herself as she stood in a daze. *It can't be him. He's dead. I know he's dead because I killed him.*

Chapter Twelve

"I thought I heard voices," Mother Doreen said as she came down the steps and entered the living room. "Am I dreaming, or is that the best brother-in-law in the whole wide world standing right there, smack in the middle of the living room?" A huge grin spread across Mother Doreen's face as she noticed her sister's husband, Uriah, standing in the living room with two duffle bags at his feet.

"Doreen, my favorite sister-in-law." Uriah smiled and stretched his arms open wide, welcoming her. He gave Mother Doreen a hug and a kiss on the cheek.

"Isn't this a blessing?" Mother Doreen turned and asked Bethany, who was sitting on the couch with her feet tucked under her bottom doing crossword puzzles.

"A blessing indeed it is," Bethany replied. "God is good." She scribbled down a word, but then erased it when it didn't fit into the boxes.

"Well, I hope you're staying longer than one night, unlike the last time you were here," Mother Doreen told her brother-in-law, poking him in his chest. "Heck, you were here one minute, I went to the bathroom, came out, and you were gone," she joked.

"I know. I know, but until we get out of this adjustable rate mortgage mess I got us into, I have to take every truck run that comes my way. And with the price of diesel fuel—need I say more?"

"Oh, that's right." Mother Doreen shook her head. "Bethany told me y'all got caught up in that balloon mortgage mess. Hopefully President Obama's stimulus plan can help y'all out."

"I hope so too, even though some people feel like it shouldn't. But I wish I could let America know that I didn't get myself into a house I couldn't afford on purpose. In the beginning, every time the payments increased, I paid them just fine. But then the cost of gas went up, and with me owning my own truck and trying to take every load I could, I wasn't making as much money. Then with Beth in and out of the hospital and those bills accumulating, I just couldn't seem to make ends meet anymore." Uriah sighed. "I tried my best. I'm still trying. That's why I'm always on that road driving across the country. I don't want America's tax dollars to bail me out like they've been doing all those corporations and banks. I'd rather they bail out the schools. A loan modification or refinance at a lower interest rate will do me just fine. In the meantime, I gotta keep hustling for the sake of my family. You know."

"I understand you're trying to do everything you can to look out for your loved ones, but a man's still got to take care of his family in the physical." Mother Doreen looked to Bethany, who she felt should have been the one giving the pep talk to her husband. "Isn't that right, Bethany?"

Without even looking up from her task at hand she said, "Oh, yeah right, sis," then continued scribbling down words.

Mother Doreen looked her brother-in-law in the eyes. "God will provide all that other stuff."

Feeling encouraged, Uriah smiled. "Yes, Doreen, I know that God is a provider."

"And don't you forget it," she playfully scolded. Flattening out her blouse, she then changed the subject. "I sure do wish I'd known you were coming. I would have made up some-thing real special in the kitchen." Mother Doreen looked to

Bethany. "Did you know he was coming home? Why didn't you tell me?"

"Sis, I'm just as surprised as you," Bethany told her, still not looking up from the crossword puzzle.

"Oh, don't worry about it," Uriah told Mother Doreen. "I wanted to take my family out to dinner anyway. It's not often I can do that. So dinner is on me tonight." Uriah looked down at his watch. "It's three o'clock now. Bethany, what time do the kids usually get home?"

"They have band practice today, so the activity bus won't get them home until about five-thirty," Bethany answered, finally looking up, but not at her husband. Straight forward, as if she had to think about her answer.

"Well, that gives me time to get cleaned up and take a little cat nap," Uriah said to Bethany before turning toward Mother Doreen. "Sis, you'll be joining us too, right?"

"I wish I could, but I'm having a dinner meeting with Pastor Davidson this evening."

"Dinner? With Pastor?" Bethany jumped in. Finally, something had pulled her attention away from that crossword puzzle.

"He says there is something he wants to talk to me about," Mother Doreen replied. "But maybe I can cancel. It's not every day we all get to have dinner together."

"Oh no, I wouldn't want you to do that," Uriah said.

"Please, that man is just trying to wine me and dine me into becoming a member of his church." Mother Doreen shooed her hand.

"Reen!" Bethany said in a shocked tone. She was now looking at Mother Doreen.

"Oh child, please. Don't even try to act shocked. If they had a word for pastors chasing folks to become a member of their church like they do attorney's who chase ambulances—"

Uriah chuckled. Bethany shot him a look. It was the first

time Mother Doreen noticed her looking at her husband at all.

"Come on, honey, you know she's right," Uriah agreed. "I love Pastor Davidson to death, but he's bar none when it comes to filling that sanctuary with members."

Bethany shook her head and fought to hide her smile. She knew both her husband and sister were speaking the truth. Pastor Davidson took evangelism and discipleship to a whole new level.

"Anyway, sis, you go ahead with your meeting with Pastor," Uriah told her. "Maybe the next time I blow through town I'll give you a heads up so you can make something real special. How about that?"

"I'm gonna hold you to that," Mother Doreen told him. "And it better be real soon. I had planned on whipping Bethany and the kids something up to eat before I headed out, but since you're taking them out to dinner, I don't have to worry about that now. Guess God wanted to free me up some time to go get prayed up before my meeting with Pastor Davidson."

Bethany smacked her lips and dropped her pen. "Reen, you act like you got a meeting with the devil. It's Pastor Davidson for goodness sakes." Bethany was almost offended at this point.

"Child, I don't care if I was meeting with Jesus Himself. I always want to be prayed up and ready. So I'm just gonna pray that God be in the midst of our conversation and that I hear and follow no other voice but His, that's all I'm saying. Because I know Pastor Davidson is a man of God, but even a man of God's flesh can get in the way of his spirit man if there's something he wants badly enough." She shot her sister a peculiar look. "You know what I mean?" Bethany fidgeted with her pen and went back to her crossword puzzle. Mother Doreen took that as a 'yes,' then made her way up the stairs to get her prayer on.

***

"Reen . . . Wallace?" Bethany's tone was laced with a bit of anger. "What are you two doing here? Together?" Bethany did everything but fold her arms and tap her foot while she waited for a response. Her lips were pouted. Yep, the folded arms and tapping foot were the only things missing from her visible temper tantrum.

"Why, uh, Sister Bethany, it's mighty fine to see you up and out of the house enjoying your evening." Pastor Frey looked over Bethany's shoulder at Uriah, who was standing behind her with his hands on her shoulders. "And uh, you too, Brother Uriah." Behind Uriah stood the couple's children. Pastor Frey nodded them his hello.

"It's good to see you too, Pastor Frey." Uriah walked around his wife and shook Pastor Frey's hand. "It's funny we ran into you. I was just telling my wife on the drive here how I had to call the church and thank them for looking out for my family. And I want to thank you especially, Pastor Frey. Beth tells me how you have been taking real good care of her."

Pastor Frey swallowed hard.

"Checking on her regularly while she was at the hospital and praying for her and all." Uriah was specific.

Pastor Frey appeared to exhale. "Oh, yeah. Well, uh, it was no problem at all. It's always an honor to be doing God's work. I'm just blessed that He chose me."

"Well, my wife and I are blessed that God chose you too," Uriah told him. He then looked to Mother Doreen. "Looks like I'm gonna get to have dinner with my sister-in-law after all. Why don't we all have dinner together?"

"Oh, no," Mother Doreen was quick to say, holding up her hand in refusal. "You and your wife spend this priceless time together with your children."

"Are you sure?" Uriah asked. "Beth, the kids, and I would love for you two to join us. Right, honey?" He looked to his wife, who was still standing there waiting on a response to the question she'd posed moments ago.

"Doreen, you said you were having dinner with Pastor Davidson," Bethany said in an almost scolding manner. "This don't look like no Pastor Davidson."

Mother Doreen felt like a child being caught after curfew by her parents. Being caught by her parents after curfew with a boy. Being caught by her parents after curfew with a boy on her front porch smooching. The flesh inside of her wanted to stand up, point her finger in her little sister's face, and tell her that she wasn't the boss of her and that she could have dinner with anybody she wanted. But thank goodness she'd prayed herself up and that the spirit man prevailed.

In a nice, kind, and gentle voice, and with a smile plastered on her face, Mother Doreen looked to Pastor Frey and said, "Will you excuse me for a moment, Pastor Frey? I need to go to the ladies room."

"Oh, by all means." Pastor Frey stood while Mother Doreen stood to her feet.

"Bethany, can you come with me?" Mother Doreen, with the smile still resting on her face, looked back and forth between the two gentlemen. "I guess it never seems to matter what age a woman gets; we always have to go to the bathroom in pairs." After letting out a chuckle, and the men returning a chuckle of understanding, Mother Doreen took Bethany by the arm and led her into the women's bathroom.

"Have you lost your God given sense?" Mother Doreen said to her sister once they were behind the closed bathroom door. "If I didn't think there was some funny business going on between you and that Pastor Frey before, well your actions sure did confirm it just now."

"Puhleeze! I don't know what you're talking about." Bethany's arms were now folded, and she was tapping her foot. She was in full temper tantrum mode.

"The heck if you don't, and I'm not gonna stand here and let you force me to even spill the words out of my mouth. For starters, since when do congregation members call their pastors by their first names? That's a sign of disrespect." Bethany didn't respond. "Huh?" Mother Doreen questioned, adding enough bass in her tone to make Bethany jump. "Out there was my second time hearing you call that man Wallace. Sounds a bit too personal for me."

Bethany thought for a minute. "It must have just slipped, I mean, after all, that was the man who came to see about me dang near every day and prayed for me every day. I can't help it if I feel a sense of closeness toward the man, enough to call him by his first name . . . outside of church."

"Keep on lying to yourself, you hear? But child, you the only one you're lying to. Heck, if I noticed how foolish you were acting out there, like a jealous girlfriend catching her beau with another gal, then you best believe your husband did too."

With her arms still folded, Bethany turned up her nose. "I still don't know what you're talking about. And if you are trying to insinuate what I think you are, that's nonsense. Wall–I mean, Pastor Frey is fifteen years my senior."

"Oh, yeah? Well, they make little blue pills to fix that problem."

Bethany turned her nose up in the air. "You should be ashamed of yourself, allowing such filthy talk to come out of your mouth."

Realizing that she wasn't going to get her sister to confess anything, not now anyway, Mother Doreen decided to end their conversation before things got real ugly. That prayer and holy oil she'd anointed herself with before leaving the house could only get her so far, and she could feel her flesh battling on the inside. "Like I said, I'm not going to stand here and let the truth, as I'm starting to see it, spill from my lips. It's your sin to confess, not mine." On that note, Mother Doreen went into a bathroom stall, then heard Bethany exit the bathroom in a huff.

"Everything happens for a reason and in divine order," Mother Doreen mumbled to herself. "None of this that transpired tonight was a coincidence. God, you wanted to show me something, which is why you made it so that Pastor Davidson had to cancel his dinner with me and have Pastor Frey meet with me instead. My sister's actions are just confirmation to what you are trying to show me."

Mother Doreen had been just as shocked as Bethany had been to see Pastor Frey at the restaurant when she showed up. For a moment she was going to cancel altogether, telling Pastor Frey she preferred to meet with Pastor Davidson when he could fit her into his schedule. But then Pastor Frey mentioned that the reason why he'd asked him to fill in was because his schedule was quite full, and he didn't know when he'd be able to meet with her again. It was almost as if Pastor Davidson had covered every reason as to why Mother Doreen should go ahead and meet with Pastor Frey.

If she were being honest, Mother Doreen had to admit that the last person she wanted to be keeping company with was Pastor Frey. But figuring she could turn a bad situation into good, she decided to relent, hoping to find herself in a position to have a little talk with Pastor Frey regarding her sister. So she looked at the entire situation as a divine set up.

It was a set up all right. It was all confirmation to Mother Doreen as to why God had her in Kentucky. The look on her sister's face when she spotted her and Pastor Frey having dinner together. Her attitude, her tone, and disposition. She now knew exactly what she needed to pray for. Mother Doreen only hoped, though, that while she was praying for her sister, someone would be praying for her.

Chapter Thirteen

"Didn't your mama ever teach you that it was rude to sit outside of somebody's house and blow your horn?" Unique spat as she made her way to Lorain's car, her three children tagging close behind her. The month of May was approaching, so each child wore a nice spring, hooded jacket.

Lorain was not looking forward to their little Saturday afternoon meeting at all. Unique hadn't even made it in the car yet and already she was running her mouth.

"My bad," Lorain said sarcastically, figuring she'd speak Unique's language.

Unique paused at Lorain's mocking tone, rolled her eyes, then proceeded to put her children in the backseat and buckle them up. "I'm sure when your mama talked to you about boys picking you up, she mentioned to you how it was a sign of disrespect for them to sit in the car and blow their horn instead of walking up to the door," Unique continued her rant. She took a moment to give Lorain the once over from the backseat. "Or didn't you have any boys coming to your house?"

Everything in Lorain told her to simply brush off Unique's insult, but she couldn't let it go. "Whether boys came to my house to pick me up or not doesn't matter." Lorain gave Unique's children the once over. "But I guess it's safe to say that at least three came to yours." Lorain let out a Morris Day laugh that irked Unique, but she didn't have a quick enough comeback, so she let it go.

"Can you roll these windows up?" Unique asked as she got in the passenger's seat and put her seatbelt on. "I'm not trying to have that wind blow my hair." She pat at the clump of weave she'd worked in an up-do with a few strands hanging down.

Lorain shook her head, wondering how in the world the wind was going to mess up that capped on bird's nest. Still she obliged Unique by rolling up the windows, leaving hers cracked to Unique's dismay.

"Can we stop at McDonald's or something?" Unique asked as they backed out of the driveway. "I didn't get a chance to feed my babies yet."

Lorain knew this was going to be a long day as she made her way to the nearest McDonald's and pulled up at the drive-thru. Once the voice boomed through the outside intercom asking for their order, Unique rattled off the order of three chicken nugget Happy Meals. Lorain proceeded to the first window as instructed after the order was taken.

"That will be ten dollars and fifty-three cents, please," the cashier said.

Lorain looked over to Unique and held her hand out. Unique was fidgeting through her purse.

"Dang it—" Unique fussed. "Where's my—" Fidget. "I know I didn't —" Fidget. "I changed purses—" Fidget. "Left my dang on—" Fidget. "Wallet."

Lorain knew exactly what Unique was getting at, but she continued to hold her hand out, waiting for Unique to miraculously come up with the cash to put in it so that she could pay for the food order.

"I cannot believe this," Unique said, visibly giving up her search as she closed her purse and threw it down. "I left my wallet in my other purse. I changed purses last night when I—" Unique caught herself. She'd been out last night at a house party for one of her girlfriends, but she didn't want Lorain to know. She didn't trust her. The next thing she knew, Lorain would be sitting outside Pastor's office just waiting to leak that bit of information in order to make Pastor reconsider her being co-leader of the Single's Ministry. Although she detested the fact that her first leadership role at New Day was underneath the likes of Lorain, she wasn't going to let Pastor down. She wasn't going to let herself down. Most importantly, she wasn't going to let God down. She was determined not to let the devil drive her out of doing work for God, even if the devil was disguised in a tight blouse, mini skirt and pumps.

"Do you want to drive back to your house and get you wallet?" Lorain asked Unique.

"Naw, just forget it," Unique sighed. "Don't nobody feel like going through all that drama."

"Aw, man," the four-year-old middle son stated. "Does that mean we ain't getting no McDonald's?"

"Getting any McDonald's," his older brother corrected. "Does that mean we are not getting any McDonald's."

"Yeah, boys. I'm sorry," Unique apologized. "Mommy left her money at home."

Unmoved by the little charade Unique had tried to put on, Lorain asked Unique, "Are you sure you don't want me to take you back to your house to get your money?"

"No, I'm good." Unique waved her off.

Lorain twisted her lips and pulled out of the drive-thru line in disbelief that Unique had tried to pull the oldest trick in the book on her. Not even the weeping three-, four- and five-year-old behind her made her go into her own pockets. For all Lorain knew, Unique had trained her kids to put on that act. Real tears probably weren't even falling from their eyes.

Lorain looked into the rear view mirror to peek at the children. Okay, so real tears were falling. Little actors, were they? Still Lorain wasn't falling for it. They'd probably pulled this trick on many people prior to her. They could probably drop a tear at the drop of a dime, but Lorain wasn't falling for it. No siree!

A few minutes later, Lorain pulled up in front of her town-house and led her guests up the sidewalk to her doorstep. She usually parked in her attached garage, but she'd hoped, no, she'd prayed to be in and out of there in under an hour. The night before, she'd put together an agenda of things for her and Unique to cover in order to speed things right along. Although she was given the name Unique, to Lorain, she didn't look like someone who could come up with original thoughts and ideas to save her life.

"If you don't mind, can you take your shoes off at the door?" Lorain asked as she unlocked her front door. On second thought, she'd wished she had used the garage entrance that would have led them straight into the kitchen where she planned on having the meeting. That way she wouldn't have to trot the troop through her house since she hadn't gotten around to packing and putting away some of her breakable, valuable items.

I don't know what I should be more afraid of, Lorain thought to herself as they all entered the house and removed their shoes, *whether they are gonna break my stuff or steal it.*

"What are you, Japanese or something?" Unique asked as she stepped out of her shoes. "Or you just don't want our kind dirtying up your nice little carpet?" Unique rolled her eyes, not expecting an answer. Lorain didn't give her one.

"I figured we can work in the kitchen," Lorain said after ignoring Unique's sarcastic comment. "I made out an agenda." She led Unique and the children into the kitchen.

On the bar that separated the cooking area from the eating area, Lorain had two notebooks and pens set out for her and Unique. On the table she had three Bible story coloring books and some crayons she'd picked up from the dollar store laid out for the children. She hoped that if she kept them busy enough, they wouldn't ransack her house.

"Color, Mommy, color," Unique's three-year-old said with excitement after noticing the lay out on the kitchen table.

"I see, sweetie." Unique leaned down and kissed him on the forehead. "You gon' color Mommy a nice picture to hang up on the Shine Board?"

"Yep," he replied, then took off and claimed a seat and coloring book.

"Me too, Mommy," her middle child proclaimed. "I'm gonna shine too."

"Going to," her eldest son corrected. "It's *I'm going to shine too.*"

Once again, Lorain found herself immersed in the way Unique interacted with her children.

"It's really just the refrigerator," Unique said to Lorain when catching her staring. She assumed she was looking crazy in wonderment about what the children were referring to as Shine Board.

"Huh?" Lorain said, snapping out of her daze.

"The Shine Board; it's what we call the refrigerator that's covered with pictures the children draw, good reports, and awards from their teachers—stuff like that."

"Oh," Lorain said. She was impressed, but she didn't show it. "Shall the two of us get down to work so you and your kids can get out of here?" She paused, realizing that her words hadn't come out right. Well, they'd come out right, she just wished they'd stayed in her head where she'd meant for them to. "It's Saturday. I'm sure you all would much rather be somewhere else than cooped up in my little old place." She cleaned it up.

"Can I whip my kids up something to eat first? They'll play better and not bother us on full stomachs."

"Well, I'm not sure what I might have that the children would like," Lorain thought, kicking herself for not buying snacks to keep the children settled. "I don't do much grocery shopping with it just being me here and all."

"Child, don't even worry," Unique said as she began scrambling through the refrigerator. "I'm a single mom, which means

I'm sure I've made miracles out of less. Food stamps don't stretch as far as a person might think."

Lorain couldn't believe how open Unique had just been in her admittance of being on food stamps. Although Lorain had never been on them herself, she was certain public assistance was a thing of embarrassment, not something to be proud about, or even to tell people about for that matter.

Lorain had been fortunate as a child. Even though her mother and father divorced when she was only ten, leaving her mother to raise her as a single parent, her father paid child support and alimony, which prevented them from having to seek any type of public assistance. Lorain's father even had her on his insurance plan, so they never even had to seek as much as a health card.

A few minutes after Unique had gone through Lorain's fridge, freezer, and cupboards, she'd created her children a concoction that even wet Lorain's taste buds. Lorain watched as Unique served her children plates that had two layers of toast. In between the slices of toast, Unique had spread some spaghetti sauce. She'd somehow managed to split the little bit of mozzarella cheese Lorain had left in her fridge amongst the three children so that it melted between the toast. On top, she'd spread another layer of sauce, sprinkled parmesan cheese on it, and topped that with mushrooms she'd taken from a can that Lorain had in her cupboard.

"Thank you, Mommy. This looks delicious," the oldest child said after Unique sat the plates in front of the children.

"Thank you, honey. Now join hands and bless the food," Unique ordered.

Lorain thought that Unique would stand there and lead the children in prayer, but that wasn't the case. She made her way over to the bar, sitting down in front of her notebook and pen, while her eldest child led his younger siblings in prayer.

Lorain was absolutely beside herself. Unique, of all people, was actually training up her children in the way that they should go. Who would have thought it?

"So you ready to do this?" Unique asked Lorain.

"Oh, uh, yes. Let's get down to business, but first, we should open in prayer too."

The women closed their eyes and joined hands. Unique was about to open her mouth to begin praying, but Lorain jumped right in and led them in prayer. For the next hour or so, Lorain led everything else too, while Unique listened.

"Well, I've covered everything on the agenda." Lorain yawned after about an hour or so. "So I guess we can call it a day."

Lorain was beat. It seemed like she had been going non-stop covering different issues regarding the Single's Ministry. She'd covered a couple of things she wanted to change with the by-laws. She'd covered fundraising ideas. She'd covered Single's events and activities. Now that she thought about it, she'd done everything. But what could she say? In all honesty, she hadn't expected much out of Unique anyway.

Unique tidied the kitchen back up, washing anything she had soiled in preparing her children a snack. After the children had finished eating, Unique had given each of them a cup of water. She washed the cups too. She had the children put all the crayons back in the box and stack their coloring books up nice and neat.

"You guys can take the coloring books with you if you'd like," Lorain told the boys.

"No, we want to keep them here for when we come back the next time," the five-year-old told Lorain. Lorain was hoping that there wouldn't have to be a next time. "It's fun here. And the food is good." He smiled.

Lorain returned the smile, kicking herself for her most recent thought. Lorain led her guests back to their shoes and jackets. Once everyone was situated, she locked up behind them and drove them home.

"Hold on for a minute while I go in the house and get something," Unique said when Lorain parked her car in the driveway of their home. Unique unbuckled her children's seatbelts, got them out of the car, and then went into the house.

Lorain tapped her fingers on the steering wheel as she waited for Unique to return. She couldn't imagine what she had to go in and retrieve. A few seconds later her curiosity was answered.

Unique walked up to the driver's side of Lorain's car. Lorain had already traded the crack for an all out rolled down window.

"Here you go," Unique said as she held out her hand.

Lorain could tell something was in it, she just couldn't tell what it was. Reluctantly, she held out her hand to accept whatever Unique was offering.

"There's some gas money for you. Thanks for the ride. See you at church tomorrow—*sista*." On that note, Unique walked away, leaving the ten dollar bill, the last bit of money she had to her name, in Lorain's hand. She'd sensed back at the McDonald's drive-thru that Lorain felt she was running game on her about leaving her wallet and money. She wanted to show her just how wrong she was.

Lorain was dumbfounded. *So Unique really had left her money at home after all.* Unique hadn't been trying to play her for a fool; she just wanted to feed her children. Dread fell over Lorain. She felt as though God had turned His face from her in grief, disappointed at the actions of His daughter. Thinking God would be even more disappointed in her if she took the money, Lorain opened her door and stepped outside the car. "That's okay," Lorain called to Unique. "You keep it. I'm sure you need it more than me."

Unique paused just as she'd made it to the door. She turned around and shot Lorain a look of death. "And just what's that supposed to mean? You think 'cause you got a little transportation and a little piece of house that you better than me? That you got it going on?" Unique shook her head. "Please. I bet you grew up right around the corner from me." Unique looked Lorain up and down. "Keep the ten spot. 'Spite popular opinion, you need it more than me. Go buy yourself some character."

Lorain didn't even try to come up with a comeback as Unique entered her house and slammed the door behind her. Once again, she'd prayed to be the bigger person when it came to her and Unique, but once again, she'd failed miserably.

"I'm sorry, God," she said as she got back into her car and proceeded to drive home. She put the ten dollar bill in her glove compartment, vowing to give it back to Unique. "It's obvious I can't do this without you, God. I can't just see Unique how you see her and love her with the love of Christ." Lorain continued to pray as she drove, asking God to touch Unique so that she didn't come off so strong and raw toward Lorain and people in general. She asked God to season Unique's tongue so that she wasn't so vocal, saying whatever she wanted, however she wanted, and whenever she pleased—all the things that just got under Lorain's skin and took her out of character. She prayed to God to make Unique more settled and easier to deal with.

Just as Lorain ended her prayer, she noticed her car acting like it wanted to cut off. "What the—?" Lorain asked herself as she pumped the gas pedal, trying to keep the car moving. She looked down at her dashboard only to see her gas light on. She thumped herself on the forehead, remembering that the gas light had come on during her drive home from work last evening. She'd meant to go get gas before picking up Unique, but it had obviously slipped her mind. There was no way she was going to be able to make it back home without stopping to get gas first.

Spotting a Speedway, Lorain pulled up at the pump. Her car seemed to take its last breath just as she parked. "Thank you, Lord!" she shouted, and then went to get her credit card so that she could pay at the pump.

"Dang it—" Lorain fussed. "Where's my—" Fidget. "I know I didn't—" Fidget. "Left my dang on—" Fidget. "Purse." Lorain sighed in defeat after an endless search for her purse. Figuring she was simply going to drop Unique off, she hadn't even carried it with her. "I cannot believe this. And I don't have my cell phone either to even call anybody." She looked up. "Lord, help me."

Lorain let out a deep breath. "Fooling around with that dang on Unique, now I'm . . ." Lorain's words trailed off as she remembered the ten dollar bill Unique had just given her. She opened her glove box and the money seemed to be staring at her like the money on the Geico commercials.

Letting out a sigh of relief, Lorain picked up the ten dollar bill and headed inside the gas station. "I guess you were right, Unique," she mumbled under her breath, "I did need this more than you."

Chapter Fourteen

For the past week, Tamarra had been walking around in a zombie like state. She felt a sickness in the pit of her stomach that she couldn't seem to get rid of. Perhaps she'd caught whatever it was that Maeyl had caught. There was no perhaps about it; she knew she had that sickening virus called *The Past*.

How could this have happened? She'd buried her past so deep and for so many years. How was it that her mother was able to dig it up just like that, in a matter of minutes, and throw it at her feet? And just when the two of them were finally starting to form a better relationship? Why in the world would she go and do something like that? She had to have known how Tamarra would have felt about it.

Tamarra couldn't help but think this had all been set up, that her mother never really wanted to have a true mother-daughter relationship with her in the first place. She was sure her mother had only been setting the stage for that very moment, the moment she'd resurrect a part of Tamarra that had been dead and buried. How could she possibly trust her mother now, after the stunt she'd pulled?

On several occasions, Tamarra had had to catch herself from saying how she hated her mother for what she'd done. She'd already forgiven her once. How many more times would she have to forgive her? Even though Tamarra knew the biblical answer to that question, she just wished God would stop testing her with the forgiveness issue already. Hadn't she at least scored a C on the test when she forgave her mother and father for covering up her rape? So what if the rapist was their son? They should have protected her is how she felt.

Her rapist, her brother, was dead as far as she was concerned. She'd killed him a long time ago. She'd killed him in her mind, in her thoughts. Every fiber of her being accepted the fact that he was dead and that she was now Mr. and Mrs. Evans's only daughter. Their only child. Her brother being locked away in jail for the past several years for the rape of another child made it that much easier for Tamarra to believe that he was dead. But no. Like Lazarus being raised from the dead, her mother had performed some miracle, or should she say some voodoo witchcraft, and raised her brother back from the dead.

When she'd heard her brother, Raymond's, voice blare through the phone, Tamarra thought she'd faint. "Tammy," he'd said. He was the only person in the world who ever called her Tammy. "Come on, Tammy, it won't hurt. Don't tell Mom and Dad, Tammy. You promise, Tammy?"

Tamarra hadn't allowed anyone else to call her by that name. That was his nickname for her. His sick nickname whenever he was on top of her. His sick nickname whenever he was threatening her not to tell Mom or Dad. His sick nickname when he was adding sugar on top by offering her candy treats not to tell.

She'd buried the name Tammy when she'd buried her brother. And even though it had been over twenty something years since she'd heard Raymond's voice, now at thirty-seven years of age, she'd still never forget it.

When her phone had fallen from her ear upon hearing the sound of her brother's voice through the phone receiver, it had shattered into pieces. Ironically, the pan of macaroni and cheese had landed flat, without a spill. Tamarra took that as God's sign that Raymond was one demon she didn't have to face, or at least talk to. Even more so, she took it as a sign that Raymond was one person that God didn't expect her to forgive.

Even upon the phone shattering into pieces, she'd heard the ringing of the other phones in her house. She knew it was her mother calling back, but she had a catering affair to get to. She couldn't waste precious time running through the house trying to locate a phone. God wouldn't want her to be late due to her chatting it up on the phone with her mother and her—

Ring! Ring!

The sudden ringing of the phone jolted Tamarra from her thoughts. She'd been letting both her home phone and cell phone go to voice mail all week. She'd wait a few minutes after the ringing, then pick up her phone to check for messages. If it was Paige or someone from church, she'd call them back immediately. She knew better than to go MIA up at New Day. Them saints would do a drive by to come see about her in a heartbeat. So versus having to literally face anyone, she'd rather put on a happy face over the phone. Certainly that would keep them at bay, for a little while anyway.

She lay on the couch staring at the ringing living room phone, wondering if it were her mother calling again. Mrs. Evans had left her a couple of messages, which were the only ones she hadn't returned.

"*Baby, it's Mom,*" her first message had said. "*I know you were probably a bit caught off guard. I'm sorry. But please call me back. Your brother and I need to talk to you.*"

Her second and last message had said, "*Tamarra, it's Mom again. I figured I'd give you a couple of days to gather your thoughts and return my call. It's now day three, and I still haven't heard from you. Please call me, honey. I know things between us were just starting to get back on track. I'd never forgive myself if I've ruined any chances of a full reconciliation. But please, Tamarra. Call me back. Your brother—*"

The time allotted for callers to leave a message had run short, cutting off her mother before she could finish speaking. Tamarra was glad of that considering she was about to bring up her brother again. Her brother. It was amazing how Tamarra had lied so much about being an only child over the years that she'd convinced herself of it. No one from her adulthood knew about Raymond, not Maeyl, not Paige, not even Pastor. That's the way she wanted to keep it too.

After several more rings the caller was sent to voice mail. Tamarra got up from the couch and walked over to the phone. Without checking voice mail, she looked at the caller ID first. Her stomach knotted when she saw her mother's phone number on the caller ID.

"Why don't you just leave me alone?" she found herself yelling as tears flooded her eyes. "No no no. I'm not going to cry," she told herself as she began to pace away the tears. "I've dealt with this for far too long to be crying about it now. No, I'm not going to do it." She briskfully and harshfully rubbed her hands across her eyes just as the phone rang again.

She'd had enough. She couldn't hide behind the threat of a ringing phone forever. How crazy was that? If she kept it up, she thought she might go crazy for real, end up in a room with four rubber walls. Her brother had already taken so much from her. She refused to hand him her sanity on a silver platter.

With every ounce of courage she could muster up, she walked over and picked the phone up, placing it to her ear. "Yes, mother," she answered. Just then, it felt like every ounce of bravery she had just moments ago had evaporated into thin air. She thought of her brother being on the other line with her mother via three-way, and it sent a chill through her veins. She completely froze when she thought of something even worse. What if he weren't on the three-way? What if he were right there with her mother? In the very same house on the very same phone line? What if—what if he had been released from jail?

Chapter Fifteen

For the past couple of weeks, both Mother Doreen and Bethany had been walking around the house on egg shells. With Uriah back on the road and the children involved in school and extra curricular activities, it always seemed to be just the two of them in the house. Constantly being around someone and not speaking to them had taken its toll on Mother Doreen. To her, it just didn't seem Christ-like. She wanted to sit down and talk with her sister, perhaps continue the subject matter they had touched upon back at the restaurant. But God hadn't yet given Mother Doreen the words she needed to speak into her sister's life, and anything other than that would have been flesh. So as difficult as it was, Sister Doreen remained silent and waited on God.

Even today as they sat next to each other in church receiving the Word, when instructed by Pastor Davidson to touch their neighbor and tell them that they are blessed, they both made it a point to touch the neighbor opposite of one another. When instructed to touch their other neighbor, they were forced to speak.

"You are blessed." Neither one of them sounded convincing. And other than those three words, the two didn't share anymore with each other. They just sat through the remainder of the Word, altar call, and then the benediction.

Mother Doreen had noticed that Bethany was one of those church folks who always made her way to the altar after service to shake her pastor's hand. Normally, Mother Doreen would be by her side, but she didn't want to be transparent in front of Pastor Davidson, fearing he might call the two sisters on the clear distance between them. So Mother Doreen decided to go on and head to the car.

"Mother Doreen!"

She turned to see Pastor Davidson waving her down. Her plan of escape had failed.

Mother Doreen huffed under her breath, and then made her way to Pastor Davidson. She stopped momentarily and huffed even louder when she saw Pastor Davidson wave down Pastor Frey as well. Everything in her wanted to turn around and pretend she hadn't even noticed the pastor's summons, but she'd already made clear eye contact with him.

"Pastor Davidson, you preached a mighty powerful word today," Mother Doreen complimented. "Didn't he, sis?" Mother Doreen looked to Bethany and smiled.

Bethany appeared to be like a cat in its kitty litter trying to cover up a mess.

"Why thank you, Sister Doreen. I'm glad you received it." Pastor Davidson smiled, not taking note of the fact that Bethany slightly rolled her eyes at her sister and didn't respond. "You know, membership usually goes down whenever I preach about hell and damnation, but hey, I have to be obedient to the Master."

"Amen to that," Mother Doreen agreed.

"But anyway, I haven't gotten a chance to speak with either you or my assistant pastor here." Pastor Davidson patted Pastor Frey's back. "How did your dinner date go a couple of weeks ago?"

Bethany twisted her lips.

"You mean our meeting?" Mother Doreen was precise in her annunciation of the word meeting.

"Uh, yeah, well, you know." Pastor Davidson laughed it off. "Was Pastor here able to enlighten you on the different ministries here at Living Word, Living Waters? I understand that eventually you'd like to return to your hometown in Ohio and continue your ministries there, but while you are here, I don't see why you can't bless us with your gifts, talents, and time. You know, God's work is never really church work. It's kingdom work, which means your ministries should be able to go wherever you go. God will make room for them, you know. But I'm sure I don't have to remind a woman of God such as yourself about God's Word. Do I?"

If Mother Doreen wasn't mistaken, it sounded almost as if Pastor Davidson was trying to convict her for not being active in his church.

"Oh, I'm sure you don't have to remind her," Bethany said, not making a very good attempt at covering up her sarcasm. "She knows everything, about the Word that is."

Pastor Davidson let out a nervous chuckle, and then continued. "Nonetheless, that's why I asked my assistant pastor here to sort of mentor you, or counsel you if you will, on the vision and mission of our church." Pastor put his hands up in defense before Mother Doreen could say a word. "Now I know what you are thinking, that Pastor Frey is younger than you." He patted Pastor Frey once again. "Oh, but he is wise with wisdom of the Word. Loaded with biblical knowledge. Besides, age ain't nothing but a number." He looked to Pastor Frey. "Ain't that right, brother?"

Pastor Frey discretely looked at Bethany before his eyes focused on his shoes. "That's what I hear, Pastor. That's what I hear."

"Good, then it's all settled. Until Mother Doreen receives a revelation on what she's called to do while here, I'd like for the two of you to meet weekly, and then report back to me." Pastor Frey looked at Mother Doreen. "Over dinner of course. And of course, I'll be flipping the tab. That way, even if you decide not to be a part of the ministry, you'll still at least get something out of it." He winked, then looked to Pastor Frey, and then back at Mother Doreen. "Maybe even more than you both ever bargained for." He looked at Bethany and winked at her, accompanied by a nod. "Now if you all will excuse me. There are a couple of visitors I'd like to go say hello to before they get away." On that note, Pastor Davidson walked away.

Reading between the lines, it was now pretty clear to the three parties left standing there that Pastor Davidson had something up his collar. It was more than just seeing to it that Mother Doreen became a part of the Living Word family. It appeared more as though he wanted her to become a part of Pastor Frey's family.

Mother Doreen had to admit that after having dinner with Pastor Frey a couple of weeks ago, he wasn't that bad at all. She was glad that she'd declined Uriah's invitation for them all to have dinner together. This enabled her valuable time alone with Pastor Frey in order to discern his true intentions with her sister. Surprisingly enough, after she'd returned from the restroom where she had a minor altercation with her sister, the two had a pleasant time.

At first, Mother Doreen had studied his actions closely. She wanted to see if he acted funny with Bethany having dinner with her husband a mere few tables away. She studied his eyes closely, figuring she would find them wandering off to observe Bethany and her family, but they never did. His eyes, instead, stayed steady on Mother Doreen as he held conversation with her. She looked for all the tell-tale signs; his looking downward, over her shoulder, at her chin, doing anything at all cost to keep from looking her in the eyes for fear she'd see right through him. But again, none of that happened. Not once did he seem distracted from his mission at hand, his assignment from his superior to share with her the different ministries at Living Word and where she might be able to assist.

Pastor Frey wasn't the only one doing the talking over dinner. Mother Doreen had found herself sharing information about her ministries back at New Day Temple of Faith, including the Single's Ministry.

"We don't have a Single's Ministry here at Living Word," Pastor Frey had informed her. "Perhaps that's something you could lay the foundation for while you are here," he suggested.

"Well, it was fairly new, too new to really see whether or not the vision, mission, and bylaws we had set up were actually effective," Mother Doreen replied in between bites of her French Onion Soup. "Anyway, I need to call back to Ohio and get with the new leader that was left in charge to see how things are going. Prayerfully the ministry is growing."

"Oh, if you planted the seed ordained by God, I'm sure He's watering and doing a wonderful work with it indeed. Which is why you should maybe pray that God would have you do the same for Living Word."

"Hmmm." Mother Doreen's spoon rested over her soup. "You might be right, Pastor Frey." And she didn't even stutter when agreeing with the man. "I never thought of that. I guess God could have some other work for me lined up down here besides watching out for—" Mother Doreen halted her words, and then quickly shoved a spoonful of soup in her mouth. She couldn't believe she'd almost said what she was about to say, that God had something for her to do in Kentucky other than watch his sneaky behind. "Anyway, I'll pray on it."

"That's all we can ask." Pastor Frey smiled and winked. The smile was charming to Mother Doreen. The wink made her blush, only she didn't realize that she was blushing. But Pastor Frey noticed.

"So I hope you don't mind me asking, but with God putting it into your spirit to start a Single's Ministry, can I assume that you are single and in the market for a husband?"

"I wouldn't go as far as to say that. I mean, I am single, but in the market for a husband? I mean, I follow the lead of the Holy Spirit. Whatever God has for me, I want it. But I can't honestly say starting that ministry had anything to do with me wanting to find a husband. After all, any man God sent my way would have big shoes to follow after my Willie." She looked up. "God rest my Willie's soul." She drew an invisible cross across her heart with her index finger, and then continued. "He was a mighty fine husband indeed. Flaws and all." A light bulb went off in Mother Doreen's head as the breeze from the door of opportunity swiftly opened and brushed across her face. "So tell me, Pastor Frey, have you ever been married?"

"Once or twice," he winked. Mother Doreen kept a steady face that made Pastor Frey change his mind about the smile that was going to follow the wink. He cleared his throat and got serious. "I'm once divorced, once windowed. My first marriage, I was young and fresh out of high school. Trying to be too big for my britches. We never even made it through our honeymoon before she ran off with a fellow high school classmate who went pro ball-first round draft pick." He shook his head. "I knew I shouldn't have quit the basketball team junior year."

"God's plan is always better, so I'm sure some good came out of the situation."

"It did, it did," Pastor Frey agreed. "Then there was Jean, my second wife. Virtuous woman of God she was. She lost her life in a car accident."

"I'm sorry to hear that, Pastor." Mother Doreen gave her deepest of sympathy.

"I just thank God that He saw fit to give me seven years with her, even though He took her away in an instant."

"That must have been difficult for you and your children."

"Oh, I don't have any children, not technically. After the accident we learned that Jean was with child. That was a double whammy because we had tried for years to conceive." He looked up to heaven. "Though He slay me, still will I trust Him." He cited the scripture from the book of Job.

"Amen. Hallelujah," was all Mother Doreen could say before finishing up her soup. "How come you never thought of starting a Single's Ministry?" Mother Doreen got back on track and started picking. For some reason, Pastor Frey's genuine sincerity had a way of throwing her off her path. "You are single after all. Aren't you?"

"Uh, yeah, you know how it is. I really don't have the time it takes to dedicate to develop a relationship."

"I see." Mother Doreen paused momentarily. "I'm sure if God has that special someone out there for you, He'll make it so that you have the time."

"Yeah, I guess you're right. He always seems to make time for everything else. For instance like right now. I can't remember when I was last able to fit a night out to dinner into my busy schedule, but what do you know? It's just like you said, Sister Doreen, God made a way."

Mother Doreen couldn't help but stand there at the altar and reflect on those words that Pastor Frey had spoken at dinner two weeks ago. If she weren't mistaken, it was almost as if he were inadvertently trying to flirt with her. She blushed at the thought, not realizing that she was blushing. But as Pastor Frey stood there, he noticed. And Bethany noticed too.

Chapter Sixteen

"Your clients must be writing you blank checks to have you catering events on Sundays now," Paige said as Tamarra followed along side of her down the buffet line at the Golden Coral. Since Paige hadn't had the pleasure of enjoying Sunday dinner with her best friend in quite some time, she invited (insisted after Tamarra had initially turned her down) that they meet at the Golden Coral Buffet. The line moved swiftly as it wasn't nearly as crowded on Thursdays as it was on Sundays.

Although the last thing Tamarra had on her mind was food, she'd been glad a few days ago when she sat on her couch screening her calls, and then finally decided to answer it, that it was Paige. Her mother had just called, and she'd let the call go to voice mail, so when the phone immediately rang again, she had assumed it was her mother. She let out a deep breath when it was Paige's voice she'd heard on the other end of the phone instead of her mother's.

"No, it's not that. When I booked the catering affairs, I must have been looking at the wrong month or something, not realizing the dates fell on Sundays."

"And back to back Sundays no less." Paige shifted her head and her slicked back ponytail swung from side to side.

Tamarra tried to detect whether or not Paige was insinuating that she wasn't being truthful, but she couldn't tell. But what if, in fact, that's exactly what Paige was getting at? It wasn't like it was the truth. Tamarra had lied to Paige, telling her the reason for her absence the last couple of Sundays at church was due to catering events she had to tend to. Thank goodness for Tamarra that Paige didn't really go to Bible Study on a regular due to her work schedule, or else she would have questioned her on being absent from Bible Study as well.

"I know. I have no idea what I could have been thinking."

"I do," Paige said with confidence.

Tamarra froze at the thought that someway, somehow Paige had learned the ugly truth about her having a brother and what he'd done to her. Had her mother somehow managed to reach out to her best friend and fill her in on all the filthy details? That wouldn't have surprised Tamarra as it wouldn't have been the first time she felt her mother had betrayed her.

Learning her lesson about jumping to conclusions, like she'd done so many times in her and Maeyl's relationship, she decided to act nonchalant. "You do?" Tamarra put a couple of pieces of lettuce on her plate as the foundation for her salad.

"Yep. It's Maeyl and that woman, isn't it? Sasha's her name?"

Relieved and willing to go with the lesser of the two evils that had been plaguing her thoughts, Tamarra agreed. "I guess you could say that."

"Tamarra, girl, I can't believe you haven't talked to him about it yet." Paige shook her head.

Tamarra couldn't believe it either. She couldn't believe that in the past two weeks, Maeyl and Sasha had actually been the least of her worries. For all she knew, the two of them had been secretly seeing each other behind her back.

Tamarra simply shrugged her shoulders at Paige's comment and the two women continued down the buffet and returned to their table.

Paige's plate was practically full, while Tamarra had barely placed anything on hers. Scarfing down a few bites of her meal, Paige noticed Tamarra's half naked plate and her sparse appetite.

"Are you sure everything is okay?" Paige asked Tamarra. "The last time we came here and you barely put anything on your plate, it had to do with you and Maeyl."

Paige was referring to the time when Tamarra was dealing with all the gossiping and whispers that were floating around church regarding a picture of her and Maeyl that had been posted on the church website. The picture was misleading, making it appear as though Tamarra and Maeyl were in a compromising position. Tamarra had initially thought Maeyl was responsible for posting it, but she later learned that it was Helen. And the thought of Helen and Maeyl being in on it together had only briefly crossed her mind.

Tamarra was fit to be tied when instead of kicking Helen out of the church, Pastor ended up giving her a leadership position in children's church. Sometimes Tamarra felt as though their pastor wasn't nearly as hard on members for their actions as needed to be, but that was something she and some other members were praying on, that the New Day pastor would walk in holy boldness and put the smack down when need be.

"It doesn't have anything to do with Maeyl," Tamarra answered.

"Oh, then something is wrong then." Paige said it as though she'd tricked Tamarra into confessing.

Tamarra knew she couldn't hide the truth from Paige (the truth that something was wrong that is) because she'd done a great job in hiding the fact that she even had a brother. So now, even though she knew she needed to talk about what was truly bothering her, she couldn't. So she decided to follow up one lie with another. "Oh, I can't fool you. I guess the thing with Maeyl is bothering me." She didn't feel like she was really lying because now that Paige had brought the issue back up, it was bothering her.

"You really love that man, don't you?" Paige asked as if she'd just had a revelation about her best friend and the man she was dating.

"I really do, Paige. I really do." Tamarra said it in a sigh as she picked around at her food. "After my divorce, I never thought I'd know love like this, a love so honest and true." Tamarra wrapped herself up in thoughts of how much Maeyl loved her. Outside the love of God Himself, Maeyl's had been the love that made her feel safe and protected. Now the one thing that threatened that security, she couldn't share with him either. And how could he protect her from something he knew nothing about? She felt so torn.

Seeing the look of confusion on her friend's face, Paige all of a sudden felt torn too. It ached her heart to think that another man might hurt her friend. Tamarra had already survived a divorce that she hadn't wanted. She'd all out begged her husband not leave her for his other woman and the child that the two of them had out of wedlock. Paige couldn't sit quietly knowing that there was a chance that the scene could replay itself.

"Tamarra." Paige set her fork down on her plate. "There's something I need to tell you. It's about Maeyl, Maeyl *and* Sasha and something I witnessed on Sunday."

Chapter Seventeen

"Are you en route?" Lorain asked her mother over the phone.

"I am indeed," Eleanor replied into her cell phone as she drove down the highway.

"I figured as much. When I called your home phone, and it went to your answering machine, I knew you were probably on your way to my house."

"What do you mean on my way to your house?"

Lorain could hear the confusion in her mother's voice. "Uh, hello, it's Saturday . . ." Lorain looked at her watch, "at one o'clock. I thought you said you were going to come over and help me put the information bags together about the Single's Ministry," Lorain reminded her mother as she sat in her living room with dozens of plastic bags, flyers, scriptures, and personalized items she'd had made up with New Day Temple of Faith Single's Ministry printed on them.

At her and Unique's last planning session, Lorain had come up with the idea that the ministry should prepare bags of information regarding the ministry. These bags would be distributed to current members, but more importantly, they would be readily available to other interested singles that might need more information.

Lorain had spent hours upon hours on the Internet working with printers and designers to create a logo, etc. She'd submitted all the necessary paperwork to the financial board for approval and payment to the various vendors and companies she'd used. She'd also found several entertaining Christian fiction books to include in the bags, books that she thought might be appropriate and relevant reads for Single's Ministries such as *The List* by Sherri Lewis and *The Single Sister Experiment* by Mimi Jefferson. She found it to be favor able that the books that had originally come out in trade paperback were now in mass market at very economical prices.

Immersed in the project, even missing Bible Study last week to work on it, Lorain was proud of all she had accomplished. Since she had done most of the leg work, her mother had agreed to come help her stuff the bags this Saturday at one o'clock. Lorain was excited about killing two birds with one stone, completing the bags and spending mother-daughter time. Now her excitement was starting to fade as it appeared as though her mother was bailing out and all the remaining work would be left up to her as well.

"Chile, I thought I told you that I have a movie date this afternoon with a fella who's courtin' me," Eleanor stated in more of a bragging manner than one of regret for having to leave her only child hanging.

"No, you did not tell me that." Lorain sighed. "Who are you going out with anyway? Brother Joseph again?" Lorain asked, referring to the gentleman whose phone number her mother had gotten when she'd visited her church a couple of months ago.

"Oh, no! That old fool couldn't keep up with me. I done met me somebody else. Broady's his name. He's a retired principal, and daughter, the man is fine. He gon' be ya step-daddy, just watch and see." She chuckled.

Lorain just shook her head and smiled. She couldn't even be mad at her mother. If she had the option, she, too, would rather be out on a date than sitting in her living room on a Saturday afternoon stuffing bags. Come to think of it, it wasn't that Lorain didn't have any options, it's just that her options no longer lined up with her Christian walk.

It wasn't too long ago that Lorain was being wined and dined by rich doctors and lawyers, that is, of course, when they weren't wining and dining their wives. Then there were times when she had even more options than she cared to have. Those were the days when she'd double-dip date, which meant go out with one man Saturday afternoon and go out with a different one come Saturday night. After one too many trips to the pharmacy for penicillin and the ultimate HIV scare, Lorain had changed her ways, her heart, and her mind. Everything, especially her body, now belonged to God.

Those two weeks of waiting on those HIV results after learning that a past lover of hers had died from AIDS nearly killed Lorain before any disease might have ever had a chance of doing so. She hated to admit it, but the prayers she'd sent up during those two weeks were the first she'd ever prayed to God. She'd begged God to make it so that she didn't have the disease that she had compared to a death sentence. She promised Him that she would turn from her wicked, promiscuous ways if He spared her, not even knowing back then that when her test results had read negative, that it was only by God's grace and mercy.

Unlike many other people who find themselves between a rock and a hard place and make all types of promises to God if He brings them out, Lorain kept her promise and gave her life to Him. She kept praying, then when prayer wasn't enough, she started reading the Bible. And when she couldn't understand some of the things the Bible was saying, she began going to Sunday School to learn more about His Word. From there, she started going to Sunday service and eventually got saved, baptized, and now served as head over a ministry.

Lorain had come a long way. Although the HIV scare was devastating, even causing her to lose five pounds, she knew it had taken that circumstance to make her realize that she had abused her body long enough. She'd allowed men to abuse her body long enough. It was God and His love for her that finally made her realize that it was that initial abuse of her body that she'd suffered as a young girl that had initiated her down such a path of destruction. But now, once again thanks to His grace and His mercy, she was headed down a path of righteous.

"If you knew like I knew, you'd get you some business and go out there and find you a man too," Eleanor stated. "I mean, how you gon' be running the Single's Ministry and it keeps you so busy that you can't find a man? It sounds to me almost like it's a curse. The head of the Single's Ministry is almost obligated to stay single, right? How they gon' have somebody with a man telling single people how to cope? That's just like a childless person being a child therapist, wouldn't you agree?"

Eleanor didn't even allow time for Lorain to respond before she continued ranting on. "Besides, didn't your pastor appoint you an assistant? Get that child to help you."

"Puhleeze." Lorain rolled her eyes and sucked her teeth. "The last time I got together with Unique, she wasn't any help at all. All she did was bring her kids up in here to eat up all my food, which is why I haven't even bothered to waste my time by including her in anything else."

"Ha! What food?" her mother laughed. "Any time I've ever been over to your house, there ain't never been no food there. That child must have created a miracle up over there."

"I see you aren't going to be of any good use to me today, so tah-tah," Lorain spat.

"Don't be hating on me," Eleanor huffed.

"I'm not, Mom." Lorain sighed, then looked at the mass of items around her. All of a sudden her head started to spin. She'd done her best at making sure everything was organized, but now that it looked as though she'd have to do the most tedious part of the task alone, it all just seemed overwhelming. "Anyway, you just go on out on your date. Have fun and don't worry about me over here."

"I will go on out, and I won't worry about you." Eleanor ended the call.

Lorain took a deep breath in the place where she sat Indian style in her living room. As she exhaled, she fell backward onto a pile of personalized ink pens and folders that were behind her.

Life just didn't seem fair right about now. Her mother was getting ready to spend her day at the movies having fun. Unique was probably at home with a bag of microwave popcorn watching a TV marathon or something. And here she was stuck, all alone with a mound of work that needed to be done. Lorain thought back to her mother's words. What good was having an assistant who didn't assist? As she started stuffing the bags, Lorain made a mental note that she'd have to have yet another word with the pastor regarding Unique.

Keeping true to her word, Lorain had phoned Pastor that Saturday afternoon and agreed to meet a half hour before Bible Study to discuss her issues with Unique. Although she wished she could have spoken with her pastor that very next day prior to church service, she knew better than to deposit anything negative into her church leader's spirit before Pastor had to preach the Word of God. So she had waited until now, four days later, to diplomatically tell her pastor that she believed there may have been some static on the lines of communication when God gave instructions to make Unique her assistant.

"Humph, I should have known."

Lorain looked up to see Unique standing in the doorway of the waiting area outside of Pastor's office. "Unique," she stood and greeted.

"Yeah, hello to you too." Unique sounded anything but sincere.

"So it looks as though once again we've both asked to speak with Pastor regarding the Single's Ministry."

"I guess it does." Unique walked over next to the chair where Lorain had been sitting and sat down.

"Ladies," Pastor said, entering the same doorway that Unique had just walked through. "Sorry I'm late, but I had to go to Manor Care nursing home in Westerville and pray with Sister Lana."

That was one thing the members of New Day Temple of Faith loved about their shepherd. Instead of just praying *for* folks, their pastor prayed *with* folks; teaching them that all had access to God's ear in Jesus' name.

"Oh, that's okay, Pastor." Unique stood. "I'm just getting here myself."

"So, women of God, would you like to join me in my office?" The Pastor proceeded to unlock the locked office door.

The women shot each other uncomfortable looks. It was as if they were both thinking the same thing. Lorain spoke up first.

"Well, Pastor." She fidgeted. "I was hoping that I could speak to you alone."

"Yeah, me too," Unique stated.

Pastor looked confused. "Well, Sister Lorain, when you called me you said that you needed to speak to me concerning Sister Unique's involvement in the Single's Ministry." The Pastor looked to Unique. "Unique, when you stopped me after church service this past Sunday, you said that you needed to speak to me concerning Sister Lorain's involvement in the Single's Ministry. Once again, I figured since both of you each wanted to speak about the same subject matter, we'd all meet together. That saves me time, allowing more time to go out here and pray for folks. After all . . ." Pastor looked back and forth from one woman to the next, "neither of you would say anything about the other to me that you wouldn't be able to say in the other one's face, correct?"

Both women appeared to be caught off guard, all of a sudden wrestling with purse straps and shirts that didn't seem to be all the way tucked in.

Getting no verbal response, Pastor continued. "Now, if there is a personal matter either of you would like to discuss, then by all means we can do that on individual basis; otherwise, I'd like to kill two birds with one stone, if you saints don't mind." Pastor smiled at both women.

"Sure," Unique said through a light huff, "I don't mind."

Pastor opened the office door wide and stepped aside as Unique walked in, then nodded for Lorain to do likewise.

This time, instead of sitting at the shiny, mahogany desk that rested in the office in front of a matching credenza, the Pastor took a seat on the leather sofa and instructed the women to do the same in whichever seat they pleased. Lorain sat on the sofa while Unique sat in a chair across from the sofa.

"Sister Lorain, how about you open in prayer?" Pastor asked.

"Certainly," Lorain replied. They all bowed their heads, and she proceeded with a quick prayer.

"So I know last month's Single's Ministry meeting was cancelled due to Brother Haggie's Friday evening wedding ceremony," Pastor stated. "So this upcoming Friday will be the first time you two will jointly run the meeting. How have you prepared? Do you have an agenda, and have you each agreed on who will cover which parts of the agenda?"

"That's what I wanted to talk to you about," both women said.

Lorain looked at Unique. "You go first."

"Oh, no, you go right ahead," Unique insisted, obviously feeling as though she was the defense and wanted to save her closing arguments for last.

"Well, Pastor—" Lorain started.

"Oh, if it's about Sister Unique, feel free to address her as well." Pastor smiled.

"Well, uh, okay," Lorain shrugged. "Well, Pastor, and Sister Unique, I feel as though even though I've been assigned an assistant, I'm doing all of the duties myself. And if that's going to be the case, then I don't believe I need an assistant." Lorain sat back and rested her hands on her crossed legs.

"Sister Unique, how do you feel about what Sister Lorain just stated?" Pastor asked.

"I find it ironic that what I wanted to discuss was Sister Lorain's lack of delegation," Unique fussed. "She just took over like I wasn't even the assistant. Like she's on some power trip and wants to prove that she can do it all herself."

Lorain was offended. "Well, you could have jumped in and helped anytime. I would not have been mad." Lorain rolled her eyes. The Holy Spirit tapped Lorain on the shoulder and shook His index finger at her, reminding her that getting out of character would be the wrong thing to do. She adjusted her attitude. "I mean, I would have really appreciated any help you could have offered."

"Really now?" Unique's tone was that of disbelief.

"Yes, really, but it's evident that you'd rather just sit back and allow me to do everything."

"I only let you do everything because I didn't seem to have a choice in the matter," Unique said in her own defense. "I mean, from day one you made out the agenda for our meeting, you had all of the ideas and suggestions, so you did all the talking. It was like you were in your own little world, in your element. I just thought you liked taking charge and being in charge. Heck, I figured I was doing you a favor by letting you. I mean, not once did you ever ask me for my input in anything. You already had the blue print engraved in stone, Moses." Unique knew darn well she could have kept that last slick comment to herself.

Lorain was silent as she took in Unique's words.

"Is that true, Sister Lorain?" Pastor looked to Lorain for some sort of confirmation.

"Well, I guess, I, uh," Lorain stammered, not realizing before now how on point Unique was. If Lorain was going to be honest with herself, then she had to admit that she had, in fact, taken control. Not once had she even asked Unique for her opinion regarding anything. She had just laid down the law so to speak. But by the same token, Lorain didn't want to carry the burden alone. "But I still don't see why you couldn't have just taken the initiative to even offer some assistance." Lorain directed her words to Unique. "And you have to admit, I did call you up this past Saturday and ask for your help." Lorain felt a little vindicated in the fact that after her mother stood her up and after stuffing ten bags, she decided to call Unique up and ask for her help.

"You called me at the last minute, and I had other plans," Unique reasoned.

"Oh, let me guess; another marathon of the series *The Game* was airing on *BET*, and you couldn't tear yourself away from it long enough to do a little bit of work for the Lord," Lorain snapped, the alignment on her attitude apparently still a little off balance.

"Actually, if I may interrupt," Pastor said, "This past Saturday I had Sister Unique volunteering to read to the children at Reynoldsburg Public Library." Looking at Unique, the preacher asked, "How did it go anyway?"

Unique's eyes lit up. "Oh, Pastor, me and my children had a blessed time. Thank you for recommending that I participate in the New Day Let's Read Ministry. Not only did I feel good about giving my time, but by accompanying me, my children are learning how to give their time as well. Doing the Lord's work is one thing, but being able to do it with my children is just something special."

Unique's entire face was now lit up. Lorain noticed it did that every time Unique interacted with or spoke of her children.

"I'm glad to hear that, Sister Unique," Pastor stated. "I know it's hard sometimes for these mothers with young children to give of their time, so I figured this would be perfect for you and your children. So should I let Brother Hammond know that he can count on you to be a part of the Let's Read Ministry in the future?"

"I'd love that." Unique smiled. Her grin then faded as she looked over at Lorain. "That's if the duties don't interfere with those of the Single's Ministry. Because 'spite what Sister Lorain thinks, I do want to be a part of it. I just didn't want to step on her toes and make it seem like I was trying to take over or anything. But I do want to be used." Sadness seemed to cover Unique's face. "People think I'm not capable of anything just because I didn't go to college, and I have all these babies. I admit that sometimes I myself start to agree with them, so I just fall back and go with the flow. But I have some pretty good ideas about things that I'd like to say the Lord put in my spirit."

Now this was a side of the woman Lorain had never seen. Lorain felt sad for Unique. She would have never guessed that with such a bold personality, Unique had any doubts about herself and her abilities. Lorain could really relate to that, for over the years she had felt that the only thing she was good for was a roll in the hay. There were plenty of times when she had felt that her worth was underestimated. Like when she'd get passed up for promotions on the job because her supervisors thought there wasn't any more to her than a big butt and a smile like she had no substance. People wouldn't even give her a chance. Now, thinking back on her own past, she realized that she'd treated Unique the same way people had treated her, not giving her a chance.

Lorain felt even more horrible because as part of her defense, she had wanted to use the fact that Unique had declined to come help her do the work on Saturday. She had just assumed Unique preferred to sit around and watch television all day instead, but all along, she had been out doing kingdom work.

"Oh, you do have plenty of good ideas," Pastor assured Unique. "Sister Helen told me how you suggested she teach the kids in children's church how to learn the books of the Bible the same way you taught yours, by having them rap them. She said that almost all of the children already know the books of the Old Testament."

"Praise God." Unique clapped as both she and Pastor gave out a few shouts unto the Lord.

"Anyway," Pastor said after calming down, "it seems as though you two really don't have an issue with the duties of the Single's Ministry, you just had a few misconceptions is all. Do you both agree?" Both women nodded. "So how about we touch and agree on better communication between the leaders of not just your ministry, but all the ministries at New Day. Amen?"

"Amen," the women agreed.

"Good. Now, Sister Unique, how about you close us out in prayer?" Pastor stood and signaled for the women to stand as well so that they could all join hands.

"Heads bowed, eyes closed, and minds cleared," Unique instructed after they had all stood and joined hands. "Heavenly Father, we come humbly to your throne of grace on this blessed day that you have made. Father, we are rejoicing. Father, we are glad in this day for we have entered these very gates with thanksgiving in our hearts."

Lorain had to open her eyes and look at Unique to make sure she wasn't reading from a piece of paper. Her words flowed like a melody that was reaching the very ears of God. She was clear and precise, and even quoted scriptures during her prayer, feeding back to God His very Word. Lorain was shocked. She had no idea that Unique knew how to go to the throne. She was moved and touched by Unique's powerful prayer to guide and instruct not only their ministry, but New Day as a whole.

By the time Unique concluded the prayer, one of the New Day ministers had begun Bible Study without them. The prayer ended up being a half hour long, even though it felt like mere seconds. All three were in the Spirit, shouting, dancing, crying, and giving praise. Unique had taken them to another level with her words. Lorain couldn't deny it. Walking out of Pastor's office, Unique was not the same person she'd seen her as upon entering it. More importantly though, Lorain wasn't the same person either. Just think, the words of her so-called nemeses were what had changed her.

Lorain's mind was clear, and her heart was light. She'd seen the errors of her ways as the Holy Spirit dropped the story of Mary and Martha into her spirit. Had she been Martha, doing all the labor, and then running to complain to Jesus how Mary hadn't helped her with it when all along she should have been over with Mary at Jesus' feet?

It had been Lorain's prayer that a change take place. It turned out, all while she was praying for God to change Unique so that she could deal with her, Unique wasn't the one who needed changing. Lorain was grateful for God working on her, but little did she know, God wasn't done with her just yet. He needed to make a lot more changes in her. Her heart needed to be prepared like never before in order to receive the blessing He was about to bestow on her. But Satan was gearing up to do everything in his power to block it.

Chapter Eighteen

"Is there something going on between you and Pastor Frey that I should know about?"

There. She'd said it. She'd asked the million dollar question.

"Tuh! Shouldn't I be the one asking you that same question?"

Mother Doreen couldn't believe that the question she'd been wanting to ask ever since she arrived in Kentucky had been asked. She knew that it was only a matter of time before the words sauntered around in thin air before evaporating away while an answer was thought upon. Only thing is, she thought that she would have been the one asking the question first and that her sister would have been the one answering. Instead, she found herself on the opposite end. It was almost laughable. Even to the point where Mother Doreen thought her sister might be trying to use reverse psychology, asking her the question before she could get around to being asked the question herself, beating Mother Doreen to the punch so to speak.

"Oh, don't you dare try to answer a question with a question," Bethany snapped, letting out a frustrated chuckle. "That's the oldest trick in the book."

"Oh, child, please." Mother Doreen shooed her hand at Bethany and continued snapping the fresh green beans in the kitchen sink like she'd been doing prior to Bethany interrupting her.

"Don't 'child, please' me. As if you haven't noticed over the years, I'm all grown up now, Reen. I'm not a child, which means I don't need you here just to be some type of watch dog over me the way you did with Ester, Clarice, and me when we were younger." Bethany then mumbled under her breath, "I can see why our two sisters went to college as far away as they could and never came back. They didn't want you hovering over their every move. God bless their sweet, sweet souls."

"Excuse me? What was that?" Mother Doreen asked, not able to make out her sister's words.

"Look, Reen, now I agreed to you coming here when I thought you were genuinely here because you cared about my health and wanted to see after me," Bethany said, ignoring Mother Doreen's request for her to repeat the words she'd mumbled under her breath. "But now I'm not so sure that was a wise decision."

Mother Doreen paused before snapping a green bean in half. "How dare you question my motives? You know how much I care about you. I've already lost two siblings to disease. Do you think I want to lose you too, Beth?"

Flaring her hands in the air she sat down. "Oh don't call me Beth. You know Uriah calls me that." She said it with such disdain. Like the word Beth was tainted.

"And just what in the world is so wrong with that? Any other woman would be glad to be given a pet name by her husband."

"Yeah, well, I'm not any other woman."

The door was wide open, so Mother Doreen walked through it. "Okay, perhaps you are not any other woman, but tell me this, sis, is Pastor Frey the other man?"

"There you go insinuating things again." Bethany looked down, fiddling with her wedding ring.

"Well, I wouldn't have to insinuate anything if you'd just speak the truth and shame the devil."

There was a few seconds of silence. Mother Doreen looked at her baby sister and could tell that there was a mental tug-o-war going on in her head. She decided to come at Bethany with a more civil tongue. After all, the Word of God had already told her that she'd accomplish more with a sweeter tone than that of a bitter one. Snapping the ends off a green bean, she placed it in the bowl next to the sink, dried her hands on the apron she was wearing, and then walked over and sat down next to Bethany.

"Look, sis," Mother Doreen said, placing her hand gently atop Bethany's. "You may think I'm old, and you may think I'm a fool. But I'm a wise old fool." Mother Doreen let out a peace making chuckle, then folded her hands in front of her. "I know what I see, sis, even with my eyes closed." Bethany didn't speak, but noticing the moisture forming in her eyes, Mother Doreen knew if she kept walking around the wall, it would eventually crumble. "I guess what I don't understand is why. I mean, I don't know exactly what has gone on between you and Wallace, but I can see what's going on now and what it could lead to. Besides, God done blessed you with such a good man that—"

"Wallace?" Bethany cut Mother Doreen off. "You called him Wallace." She rose to her feet slowly as she glared at Mother Doreen accusingly. With hands on hips she spat, "Since when do congregation members call their pastors by their first names? That's a sign of disrespect."

Mother Doreen found herself chewing on the very same words she'd posed to Bethany not too long ago. She was at a loss for words, not knowing when she'd found it appropriate, when she'd gotten to a point with Pastor Frey where she now referred to him by his first name, outside of church. Perhaps it was at their brunch meeting earlier that day when he'd told her, "Please feel free to call me Wallace in these settings." Mother Doreen had asked him just what setting he was referring to. "This type of setting," he'd responded, "when it's just you and me on a more personal level. Because for some reason, when we meet, it just don't feel like church business."

Mother Doreen blushed at that recollection of how much she'd blushed when he'd actually said the words. But she couldn't get caught up in the snare of the devil, which is what a wee bitty part of her thought Pastor Frey might be trying to do, avert her attention, distract her from her true mission in Kentucky. Only thing was, in all honesty, the man didn't seem to have a manipulating bone in his body. He seemed so sincere in every way.

"And besides," Bethany continued, "what good is it for a woman to have a husband who gives her pet names if he ain't gonna be around to pet, if you know what I mean. Even if something was going on between Wall . . . Pastor Frey and me, could anyone blame me? It's been three months since Uriah has even touched me."

"Well, what did you want the man to do for God's sake, get freaky in the intensive care unit? Girl, you been in the hospital more than you've been out."

"Now don't you go making excuses for him too," Bethany said. She implied that either Uriah himself or someone she'd confided in about her and her husband's lack of intimacy had defended Uriah as well. "I've been out of the hospital a good while now. The only thing is, he's never home. And when he does drop in for a spell, the man is too tired to . . . pet." She flopped back down in her chair exasperated.

"I know it must be rough for both you and Uriah." Mother Doreen once again tried to speak in a gentle tone while placing her hand atop her sister's. "But turning to another man for comfort is just not the godly thing to—"

Bethany snatched her hand from up under Mother Doreen's. "Don't you dare sit there and try to judge or convict me of anything. Just because your Willie chased after every skirt in the Midwest, and you were dumb enough to go chasing behind him doesn't mean I—"

Mother Doreen slammed her fist on the table and stood. "Don't you ever let my Willie's name," she looked up. "God rest my Willie's soul." She drew an invisible cross across her heart with her index finger, and then continued, "come out of your mouth in that fashion again. You hear me?"

Bethany jumped in, and the women began to talk over one another, pointing, accusing, and offending.

"Mom, Auntie. Please stop it! Hudson and I can hear you guys all the way from the study in the basement," Sadie informed the two women as she stood in the doorway of the basement.

Both Mother Doreen and Bethany looked embarrassed to see the young girl's presence. They each secretly wondered how long she'd been standing there. And if they'd been so loud that the child deemed it necessary to come upstairs and order the two to quiet down, then exactly how much had been heard?

Sadie looked from her mother to her aunt, then headed back down to the basement, closing the door behind her. She left both women feeling naked and exposed.

Mother Doreen cleared her throat, then walked back over to the sink to finish up the green beans. She said a silent prayer to God as she snapped away, repenting for her previous actions. She was grieving because she knew she had grieved God with her actions. He'd trusted her enough to send her there on assignment, and she couldn't keep it together long enough to minister to anyone. She felt like a complete failure by having to ask God to forgive her and to give her one more chance. Trusting God's Word and knowing that He'd forgiven her instantaneously, Mother Doreen knew she now had to seek forgiveness from her sister as well. Forgiving her sister for anything she said that Mother Doreen's flesh might have wanted to hold against her.

"Bethany?" Mother Doreen turned from the sink to see her sister hunched over, holding her stomach. "You all right?"

Bethany nodded her head, but it wasn't convincing. This was the second time this week Mother Doreen had witnessed her sister having stomach issues. She started to beat herself up all over again, wondering if she'd worried her sister sick with all this business about Pastor Frey. She felt that she might be doing more harm than good, and she didn't want God to think that He couldn't use her.

"We're calling your doctor first thing in the morning," Mother Doreen told her sister as she walked over to her. "But first, we're going to get you to bed so you can rest. You've probably just been working yourself up. I promised God that I would see to it that you walked in your healing, and no matter what, that's exactly what I'm going to do."

Bethany, willingly and appreciatively, allowed her sister to lead her to her bedroom. Mother Doreen helped Bethany get comfortable in the king size bed she mostly slept in alone.

"God, please have your way in this house," Mother Doreen found herself praying as she tucked her sister in bed. "We surrender our ways for your ways, Lord. Please, God, have your way."

Exhausted, Bethany closed her eyes and seemed to fall off to sleep before Mother Doreen could even exit the bedroom. Mother Doreen smiled at her resting sister, convinced that God was already at work making things better. Little did she know though, things would get a lot worse before they would get any better.

Chapter Nineteen

"Are you trying to make me look like a fool or something?" Tamarra yelled as soon as Maeyl opened the door to his apartment. It was Saturday afternoon and she'd driven at least twenty miles over the speed limit trying to get to his house. What should have been a twenty minute drive had only taken her ten minutes tops.

Tamarra knew that obedience was better than sacrifice, but she prayed God's grace and mercy would keep her from the sacrifice of getting a speeding ticket for disobeying man's traffic laws. God's grace and mercy had surely served to be sufficient this time.

She was still sick to her stomach with the information Paige had shared with her at the Golden Coral about Maeyl and Sasha this past Thursday. She had quickly lost her appetite and hadn't eaten a full meal since. Before Paige could stop her, Tamarra had barreled out of the restaurant like a woman on a mission, leaving a trail of smoke behind her. And where there was smoke, there was fire, so it was time to see who was going to walk away with third degree burns.

On the day at the Golden Coral when Paige had enlightened Tamarra with the information about seeing Maeyl and Sasha together, Tamarra had gone straight to Maeyl's place to confront him. Fortunately for Maeyl, he hadn't been home. At the time, Tamarra figured that was a good thing. She had been so fired up that her flesh might have gotten her into some real trouble. But after two more New Day members called her on the phone repeating the same information that Paige had shared with her (that Maeyl and Sasha had been spotted together in the waiting area outside Pastor's office holding hands) she couldn't take it any longer. She'd grabbed her purse and keys and drove straight to Maeyl's house. A phone call was not in order. This deserved a face to face on every level.

It angered her even more that Maeyl hadn't even tried to call her all week to explain his sorry behind. But enough was enough as she stood at his doorstep again, this time finding him at home, ready to confront him about himself.

"Tamarra," I was just about to call you.

"Like—" Tamarra caught the expletive before hurling it from her tongue. A lot of Christians justified their explicit use of the "D" word and the "H" word by saying that they were in the Bible. Some Christians even went as far as grouping the "A" word for donkey in that category as well, but Tamarra was determined not to be one of those Christians. "Like heck you were," she stated instead.

"But I was. Honest," Maeyl proclaimed. "I know I haven't called you all week, but you wouldn't believe the things that have taken place, which is exactly why I was about to call you."

"Sure you were. And *honest*? What do you know about being honest?" Tamarra folded her arms and stood on the doorstep.

Maeyl let out a sigh, then closed his eyes. "I guess you heard." Maeyl shook his head as he opened his eyes again. "Those busy body—"

"A busy body don't have nothing to do with you getting busy with Sasha's body."

Maeyl's mouth dropped wide open. Tamarra couldn't tell whether the expression he wore on his face was one of shock or embarrassment.

"Whoa, hold up!" Maeyl put his hands up in defense. "I don't know what you heard, but—"

"Enough, that's what I heard," Tamarra said as she brushed Maeyl out of her way, barging into his place. "Enough to know that once again, I've been made a complete fool of when it comes to me and Maeyl Ruebinstein."

Tamarra threw her car keys on the coffee table and fell onto Maeyl's couch, tired and broken. Tired of being the bearer of a broken heart. When Paige had told her that after church service she'd witnessed Maeyl sitting next to Sasha outside of Pastor's office, Tamarra thought she'd just die right there on the spot. But when Paige added salt to the wound by telling her that the two were holding hands, Tamarra thought she had died. Unable to catch her breath, she really thought she had died, or was dying, one of the two. She felt as though she'd held her breath on the entire ride there. And now here she was in the living room of the man that she loved wondering if she'd ever breathe again.

Closing his front door, Maeyl slothfully joined his woman on the couch. Tamarra, like a child would do, scooted away from Maeyl when he sat next to her.

"Look, Tamarra, I don't know what you heard," Maeyl started to explain, "but Sasha is someone from my past that I hadn't seen in years up until recently. Don't you think you at least owe it to me to tell you the whole truth of the matter? You know where your jumping to conclusions has gotten us before."

Tamarra could admit that in the past she'd come up with her own conclusions before seeking the facts. Doing so had caused even more heartache and troubles for everyone. But this time she honestly felt as though she'd come to a true and factual conclusion. The information she'd received had come from a reliable source, someone who would never lie to her or set out to purposely sabotage her relationship. No, Paige was Tamarra's best friend. What she'd told her was pretty much Bible. Tamarra could see that in the agony in Paige's eyes as she'd told her. She could tell poor Paige had been agonizing over whether or not to share what she'd witnessed with her own two eyes for fear of hurting her best friend.

"I'd rather hurt you now with this information," Paige had told Tamarra back at the Golden Coral buffet, *"than allow you to be hurt later; when it's too late."*

"I know the truth, Maeyl," Tamarra said, looking dead into his eyes. She immediately turned away. Those dark brown eyes of his weren't about to hypnotize her and make her forget all about him and Miss Sasha. "After church service last Sunday, you and that woman, Sasha, were sitting outside of Pastor's office holding hands like two lovebirds."

"That's not true," Maeyl said.

"Oh, so are you calling my best friend a liar?" Tamarra snapped.

"Yes, no, I mean . . ." Maeyl's words trailed off as he tried to organize his thoughts.

"That's what I thought." Tamarra dropped her face into her hands. "Maeyl, how could you? I mean, I know I haven't really been there for you these last couple of weeks, and prior to that, you hadn't been there for me either. But still, I thought the bond that we shared was stronger than that, one that some hussy couldn't just walk right up and tear through."

"Please, Tamarra." Maeyl was getting frustrated by not being able to share his side of the story. "Just let me explain."

"What's there to explain?" Tamarra stood up. "You were caught red handed holding that woman's hands. You don't even hold my hands in church."

"That's not how it was," Maeyl insisted in a pleading manner as he stood.

"So you weren't holding her hands?"

"Yes, we were holding hands, but it's not what—"

"Oh, no wait." Tamarra put her hands up and put a forced smile on her face. "I know this game. I can play along. It's called finish the sentence." Tamarra paced back and forth in a sarcastic manner as if she were having to rack her brain. "It's not what I *think*. Oh no, it's not what it *looked like*. Huh? Is it one of those, Maeyl? Tell me, huh, is it? Don't they teach you men any other lines besides those?" Now Tamarra forced out a chuckle. "Oh, yeah, that's right. They do teach you men another line: 'It was just that one time. It didn't mean anything.' Tah, are you kidding me? That's what *Lifetime* movies are made of, buddy." Worn out from all the fast talking and pacing, Tamarra, once again, retreated back to the couch. "I can't do this again. I love you, Maeyl, but I can't . . ." Tamarra's voice broke up as tears fell from her eyes.

She was so overwhelmed. Not just by the situation with Maeyl, but the situation with her family as well. So much was happening and all at once. She just wanted to go crawl up under a rock and die. If Sister Deborah's life was anything like hers, she could see why her fellow church member had gone on a sabbatical. Now, Tamarra wished she'd joined her.

"If you'd just let me explain everything to you about me and Sasha, then you won't have to go through this three ring circus thing you put yourself through whenever something gets misconstrued."

"No, that's not what I mean. I can't do this again . . . Us." She pointed to her chest and then to Maeyl. "I can't do this my-man-leaving-me-for-another-woman thing again. I just can't do it, Maeyl. So before I let you walk out on me to go be with a blast from your past, please, allow me to save you the trouble." Tamarra picked up her keys off of the coffee table and made her exit through the door, but not before saying, "Good-bye, Maeyl. It's been real."

Chapter Twenty

"Lorain, child, are you paying attention to anything that I'm saying to you?" Eleanor snapped at her only child, at the same time snatching a dinner plate from her hand as the two stood in the dining room. It was Lorain's task to dress the table. "I told you to use your grandmother's good china to set the table. Broady ain't the kind of man you use everyday dishes for, he's a bring-out-the-good-stuff kind of man." Eleanor rolled her eyes and collected the other two everyday plates Lorain had placed on the table.

"Oh, sorry, Mom," Lorain apologized, scooping up the everyday bowls.

"Oh, child, you done set out the wrong silverware too?" Eleanor began scooping up the eating utensils as well.

Eleanor was reaching her boiling point with her daughter. First Lorain had showed up a half hour late with the ingredients her mother had asked her to pick up. When she did show up, only half of the ingredients were in the bag. She'd forgotten the other items, and since they were already running behind schedule, Eleanor decided to make due.

"My bad, Mom." Lorain followed her mother into the kitchen, both their hands full of place settings.

"My bad?" Eleanor asked. "What the heck is *my bad?*"

Lorain let out a chuckle. "Oops. I mean, I'm sorry. I think that Unique is starting to rub off on me. That girl is something else." A smile covered her face as she shook her head, recalling the time she'd spent with Unique and her three children earlier that morning at her house. They'd met up to plan a dinner for the Single's Ministry like the one Mother Doreen and Sister Deborah had planned. Their hopes were to increase membership even more by inviting New Day singles who hadn't yet joined the ministry. Free food had worked for the past leaders, so it was Lorain and Unique's hope that it would work for them too. On top of that, their fellow member, Tamarra, had even landed her a man as a result of the dinner. Word of that indeed would be an added bonus for their efforts.

Ever since her meeting with Pastor and Unique, Lorain had stayed in prayer on the situation regarding Unique and the Single's Ministry. She'd spoken into her own life, reminding herself that it was all about Jesus. It wasn't about her relationship with the folks she had to operate with in the ministries. It was about her relationship with God. She prayed that God would change her own heart and her own ways. That God would change her mindset toward Unique, and that God would give her patience with things that ordinarily might test her. She prayed that God would use her as the solution for any issues that might arise between her and Unique. She found that praying that God change her versus God change someone else had a much better result.

Lorain hadn't been the least bit surprised at how well the meeting had gone. She'd called up Unique a couple of days before and asked her to put the agenda together this time and to include any ideas she had for the ministry. Lorain could hear the excitement in Unique's voice over the phone.

"Are you sure you want me to do it?" Unique had double checked. She'd heard Lorain ask her for her help and ideas, but had she really meant it?

"I'm certain," Lorain had assured her with pleasure. Lorain was glad to rid herself of some of the hands on tasks, as she wanted to spend some time in the Word seeking scriptures for the ministry. She realized that both Mary and Martha's duties were very important to the kingdom, and that it would be beneficial if she and Unique switched up every now and then.

Unique had even managed a way to include her children by coming up with the idea of having a special event every now and then for singles with children. She expressed to Lorain how difficult it could be for a single person with children to do the dating thing. There were issues of finding babysitters during the courting process, issues of finding a partner who was willing to accept the children, and then there was the issue of when to introduce the children to the mate. With the children being a major factor in the single parent's life, Unique felt that they, too, should be a factor that the Single's Ministry began to focus on.

Lorain couldn't relate since she had no children and didn't plan on having any to call her own. But for those who did, she welcomed Unique's suggestion. She encouraged Unique to pray on the matter for confirmation from God and what He'd have her address and how He'd have her address it. Unique felt as though her worth in the ministry increased each and every time Lorain cheered her on to take the lead, unlike their last meeting in which she felt muzzled by Lorain's authority as leader.

The two women had gotten along better than either of them could have ever imagined. They were strictly about their Father's business, not wasting any time on seeing who could throw the lowest verbal blow. Although at one point Lorain did find herself out of line when Unique's cell phone kept ringing.

"I'm so sorry," Unique had apologized while she and Lorain worked in the living room. The children were in their usual place in the kitchen with their coloring materials. "I don't know why all my babies' daddies wanna call me at the same time."

No sooner had Unique apologized did her phone ring again. She looked down at the caller ID. "Shoot, this is Man-Man's daddy again. I gotta take it because he's supposed to be dropping some money by to me later on before he drives out to New York."

Lorain didn't give her the fake and phony, "Oh, that's okay, girl," because it wasn't okay. She was sick of that phone ringing off the hook with all those babies' daddies. They had a lot of ground to cover, and how could they do so if she were constantly on the phone?

Although Unique had only been on the phone less than a minute, it felt like ten to Lorain.

"My bad," Unique had apologized after ending the call. "Sometimes it gets crazy with all of my sons' fathers calling and stuff, but I can't complain. At least them fools do call to check on thangs. They make sure they always with their sons on Father's Day."

"Whoo, then I bet I was right about you having to install a revolving door on Father's Day for when all of them come through to pick up their kid." Lorain briefly chuckled at her own insulting joke before she was convicted in her spirit. "But I guess that's good though. At least they are trying to be good daddies," was her attempt to clean up her comment, but from the look on Unique's face, she didn't know if it was too late.

The hood in Unique had already risen up as her fist balled and she prepared to flex on Lorain. Yep, she wanted to beat girlfriend down right there in her own living room. She'd had enough of her slick comments regarding the status with her children.

"Look, Mommy," her middle child interrupted as he entered the living room waving a picture he had drawn. "It's you and Miss Lorain." He handed his mother the picture of two stick figured women holding hands and each holding a Bible. Each character donned a cross necklace around her neck.

"Oh, thank you, baby," Unique said as her eyes lit up at her child's work. "I'm hanging this one up to shine as soon as we get home."

Lorain watched as a genuine proudness covered Unique's face. Her heart almost melted. "Yes, that is a beautiful picture," Lorain complimented the child.

"I'm gonna make you one too, Miss Lorain," he said, "that way you can have something to hang up until God gives you some kids of your own to make stuff for you. Then you can take mine down and put up theirs. And I won't get mad either."

"I'd love that," Lorain smiled, as the child walked away, promising to return in a few minutes with a picture for her.

Unique didn't forgot about the comment Lorain had made prior to her son coming into the living room, but the scene that just played out before her had softened her heart tremendously. The last thing she wanted was for her sons to witness her mopping the floor with Miss Lorain, and then being hauled off to jail.

"Yeah, their daddies would be fools to miss out on their lives," Unique continued the conversation, but on a much lighter note than she had planned to less than five minutes earlier.

"I must say, Unique, you do a wonderful job with your boys. They are so well mannered. Always clean and cute as little buttons." Lorain called herself shelling out a compliment, but almost sounded like Mrs. Millie talking about Sophia's kids in the movie *The Color Purple*.

"Yep. I try to keep them looking decent and in order with the money their fathers let me hold. You know, throwing me some change here and there to take care of the kids."

"What do you mean throwing you some change here and there?" Lorain was confused. She might not have had a child of her own, but she had surely heard of that little something called child support. "Don't the courts tell them what they have to pay, and then it comes right out of their paychecks?'"

"Ha!" Unique laughed. "In the perfect world, I guess that's how things are done. But honey, where I come from ain't that same kind of world, and it sure ain't perfect. Most of my sons' fathers hustle for a living. They ain't seen the likes of a paycheck. They set their own wage by how hard they grind out there on them streets."

"But what if something were to happen to them out there on them streets? If they aren't getting paychecks, then that means that they are not paying into social security, which means that their kids wouldn't receive a dime of social security benefits if they died or got hurt or something and couldn't work for the rest of their lives."

Unique pondered Lorain's statement momentarily. "Hmm. I never thought about that."

"And not that I'm trying to be all in your business because this conversation is about the welfare of your children right now, but do you even work? Are you even working a job where you are paying into social security? You know Pastor always reminds us that tomorrow ain't promised."

Once again, Unique pondered Lorain's statement. Shaking her head, Unique replied, "I just get assistance from the State." She shrugged her shoulders. "You know, I guess I just been living for today, and all this time I was thinking that I was living for my children's tomorrow." Unique shook her head again, and Lorain thought she saw tears form in her eyes.

"Well, that's just something to think about," Lorain told her. "Like my mother used to tell me, 'Be who you want your children to be.' And since I don't plan on ever needing that advice, I'll give it to you." Lorain winked, and the two proceeded with the business at hand, not even taking a second thought to how a conversation that could have ended up ugly became a beautiful, enlightening situation.

Just then Lorain had a sudden thought. Perhaps she could

help Unique get set up in running her own Mary Kay Cosmetics business like she did on the side. Who knows? She could eventually end up with a pink Cadillac. God was good like that. In addition, she could use training her as an excuse to teach the child how to apply make-up correctly and how to determine the right amount.

Lorain had been so engrossed in thoughts of Unique that she hadn't even heard the doorbell ring or noticed her mother hurry from the kitchen to go answer the door. As a matter of fact, as she exited the kitchen with the good china in hand, she had no idea that the dinner guest had even arrived.

Upon entering the dining room she'd placed the dishes down on the table, and then looked up to see both her mother and her mother's date standing with their arms intertwined. Her mother was wearing a huge Kool-Aid grin on her face like she'd been fishing for hours and had finally reeled in the big catch of the day.

"Sweetie," Eleanor said to Lorain, "I want you to meet Broady. Broady, this is my only child, Lorain."

"Nice to meet you, Lorain." Broady extended his hand. Lorain just stood frozen. There was silence with the exception of the shattering sound of the china dishes clinking against one another as Lorain's hands trembled.

"Honey, aren't you going to say hi?" Eleanor let loose of Broady's arm and slowly approached her daughter. "Sweetie, are you okay?" Lorain placed her hand atop her daughter's chilled and sweaty forehead. "Lorain, honey?"

Lorain remained frozen with her eyes locked on Broady. She was unable to respond to her mother.

Eleanor followed Lorain's eyes to Broady, and then looked back to Lorain. "Sit down, Lorain, darling. You look as though you've seen a ghost."

Eleanor walked Lorain past Broady and into the living

room where she sat her down on the couch. Lorain couldn't speak. She might have appeared as though she'd seen a ghost, but she hadn't. In her mind, she had seen the devil himself.

Chapter Twenty-one

"Reen, this cake is beautiful," Bethany complimented as she placed the birthday cake Mother Doreen had made for Hudson on the center of the table.

Both Bethany and Mother Doreen had been attempting to be cordial to one another these days. Embarrassed from when Sadie had walked in on them arguing, they wanted to make sure that it didn't happen again. Even this past Sunday at church when Pastor Davidson told them to hug three people and tell them they love them, the two sisters performed the act on each other.

"Thanks, sis, I just hope my nephew likes it," Mother Doreen stated as she prepared a nice green salad.

"Oh, Hudson is going to love it."

"Well, you know how these kids are nowadays. He's turning seventeen, so he might be insulted by a birthday cake. Might think it's for babies."

"Well, like I tell him all the time, he is a baby, my baby. And he always will be."

"Well, your baby is growing up. And it is a Friday night. I know we mean well by preparing him a surprise birthday dinner, but he might have other plans, you know. I mean, he's even got himself a girlfriend," Mother Doreen told her.

"Girlfriend?" Bethany was none the wiser that her oldest child had been dating someone.

"Yep," Mother Doreen confirmed. "I was walking through the house praying last week. You know how God sometimes pulls me from my sleep at ungodly hours to just walk around and pray? Well, as I was walking by his bedroom praying, I heard some mumbling. I finally came to the conclusion that it was Hudson on the phone with a girl."

"And how did you come to that conclusion?" Bethany shot her sister a peculiar look.

"By pressing my ear up against the door and listening to him try to smooth talk her." Both women laughed.

"Ain't nothing changed about you, Doreen, has it? I remember when you used to do that mess to me, and then blackmail me with telling Mama or Daddy on me for sneaking and talking to boys. And now history repeats itself."

"Umm hmm. And you better keep an eye on that child. The boy's got game." Once again, both women laughed. "But seriously, he does. Reminds me of my Willie." She looked up. "God rest my Willie's soul." She drew an invisible cross across her heart with her index finger, and then continued. "Now that man was as smooth as butter."

"Indeed he was, and I didn't blame you for following him across the states to be with him." Bethany paused for a minute. "I'm sorry for what I said that day about Willie."

"It's water under the bridge, water under the bridge." Mother Doreen smiled. "But let's just hurry up and get this dinner prepared before the kids and Uriah get home. I just can't believe God made it so that he can be here to celebrate his son's seventeenth birthday. Hudson is going to be so surprised, 'cause it's important for a boy's daddy to be around for occasions like this you know." Mother Doreen stared off for a minute. "I take that back. I can believe God did it because that's the kind of God we serve. He can make anything happen."

"Yeah," Bethany stated. "It's crazy that Uriah's load got cancelled and he's able to come home."

"For three whole days no less," Mother Doreen added. "Hudson's birthday ain't but one day." Mother Doreen walked over to Bethany, bumped her elbow, and then made googly eyes. "I bet God made it so that them other two days is for Uriah to be here for his wife."

"Oh, Reen, now stop." Bethany rolled her eyes and her face flushed with embarrassment.

"Girl, we grown women. And you're a married grown woman, so don't be embarrassed about doing the nasty."

"Reen!" Bethany gave Mother Doreen a sisterly whack on the shoulder. "Stop it now, before I send you packing back to Malvonia, Ohio."

"Please, you'd miss my cooking too much to send me away."

"Don't flatter yourself. Just 'cause I don't be in the kitchen cooking full course meals every night don't mean I can't burn. How you think I hooked Uriah in the first place?"

"Well, if you hooked the man by switchin' in the kitchen, then I suggest that's how you keep him, by taking notes from me," Mother Doreen boasted as she placed the finished salad in the fridge to keep it chilled.

"Oh, so I guess you think you're Chef Ramsey now, huh? You can burn, Reen, but don't get all puffed up about it. If you were that good, you'd have your own cooking show on the Food channel."

"Ohhh, look at jealousy rearing its ugly head," Mother Doreen teased. "I must be doing something right," she said as she walked over to her sister and pinched more than an inch on her waistline, "because you look as though you done picked up a few pounds here lately."

Bethany quickly brushed her sister's hand away in a nervous, uncomfortable manner. "Now stop it, and let's check on that lasagna you got cooking up. Hopefully it's done so I can get that garlic toast in the oven."

"Oh, shoot, my lasagna." Mother Doreen slipped on some

oven mitts. "Messing around with you, I done almost forgot about it." She opened the oven and pulled out her masterpiece, then placed it on the stovetop. "Yep, looks done to me." Mother Doreen sniffed the air and inhaled the homemade sauce, while admiring the four different cheeses bubbling that had browned just right. "Umph, umph, umph, looky here."

Bethany walked over to the lasagna, one of her favorite dishes. Ordinarily she could have stood over it and inhaled the aroma like it was a vapor. But today, as she inhaled deeply in an attempt to take in the delicacy, her stomach began to churn. The smell that had once been like a sweet fragrance floating through her open bedroom window on a summer morning was now like a whiff of fertilizer.

Grabbing her stomach, Bethany made a quick exit from the kitchen, barely making it to the bathroom in time.

"You all right, sis?" Mother Doreen called out, her feelings slightly hurt by her sister's reaction to her lasagna pie. When Bethany didn't reply, she made her way to the bathroom Bethany had treaded to. Knocking on the closed door, Mother Doreen asked once again, "You all right in there, sis?"

Finally, Bethany was able to speak from the other side of the door. "Yeah, Reen, I'm fine." A couple of minutes later, Bethany reappeared from the bathroom. Mother Doreen still stood outside the door with a worried look on her face.

"You sure you're all right, Bethany?"

"Yeah, sis, I'm fine," Bethany assured her as she walked slowly, rubbing her stomach. "I guess that breakfast I made this morning didn't agree with me." Bethany let out a nervous laugh. "Suppose I do need you around to do the cooking after all." Once again, Bethany allowed a nervous laugh to escape her mouth. Mother Doreen didn't return the laugh as she stood stone faced. "Oh, don't look so worried, sis. I'm sure I'll be just fine. It ain't nothing that a ten minute catnap can't fix. So if you don't mind doing the garlic bread for me, I'ma go lay down for a spell. All right?"

Mother Doreen nodded. "Yeah, sure," she said as she watched her sister climb the steps and disappear into her bedroom. "You go right ahead and lay down," Mother Doreen mumbled to herself. "I'm sure it ain't nothing a ten minute nap can't fix." This had been the second time this week Bethany had needed a ten minute cap nap to make things all right. Mother Doreen walked back in the kitchen, keeping her last thought to herself, the thought that perhaps it was going to take more like nine months to fix what was wrong with her sister.

Chapter Twenty-two

"Umm, I don't know about this dress either," Tamarra said with her nose turned up. She had her back toward the full length mirror, looking over her shoulder to see how the long, chocolate brown gown looked from the rear. She'd stopped counting how many size twelve dresses she'd tried on after the first one.

Paige sucked her teeth. "Tamarra, this is the last of the five maid of honor dresses that I picked out for you, and you've given each of them the thumbs down. Now my ego is a little bruised. I'd like to think that I have halfway decent taste."

Tamarra sighed. "You do, friend. It's not you or your taste, it's just me."

"Maybe you're right. Some of those suits you wear to church are a little out dated, and those hats."

"Tamarra sighed again. "Yeah, you're probably right. A little outdated. And those hats." Tamarra turned to face the mirror. She looked at herself one last time before frowning with slumped shoulders.

"As a matter of fact, I think I'm just going to have Sister Lorain be my maid of honor. I'm sure she could work any of these dresses out." Paige was testing her best friend to see if she were really focused on the task at hand.

"Yeah, Sister Lorain," Tamarra agreed with a nod and sigh. "She'd work any of these dresses out."

"Okay, that's it," Paige snapped. "You're not even really paying attention to anything I'm saying. Your mind is a million miles away. Perhaps we should just do this another day. I thought picking out the maid of honor gown with my maid of honor was going to be fun, but it's been about as fun as watching paint dry."

"I'm paying attention, Paige, really," Tamarra tried to convince her friend. She didn't want to do it another day. In being honest, she hadn't wanted to do it today, but she knew she had to get it over with, and get it over with was what she wanted to do. How could she possibly enjoy - how did her best friend think could she could enjoy doing anything that had something to do with a wedding when her relationship with her man was pretty much history? Heck, if she were back in the world, she and her girlfriends would have been downing Apple Martinis somewhere and having an "All Men Are Dawgs" male bashing session. And it would have taken God's grace and mercy to get them back home safe and sound without wrapping their vehicles around a telephone pole or jeopardizing someone else's life. It was times like these that Tamarra was so glad she was saved.

"If you're paying so much attention, what did the first dress that you tried on look like?" Paige stood with arms folded, resting her weight on one side of her leg while Tamarra failed to recall any details. "Okay, what about the second dress?" Same result, Tamarra couldn't even recollect the red satin bow that wrapped itself around the chocolate brown gown and rested on her hind end. "The third? The fourth?" Paige walked over to Tamarra and covered her eyes. "What about the one you're still wearing."

Tamarra felt ashamed. She was busted. She'd just stared at herself in the mirror for practically ten minutes in that dress and could only blurt out one final detail. "It's brown?" And she even said that with uncertainty.

"Just take it off." Now it was Paige who sighed with great disappointment. "I'll just start from scratch and look for more dresses next week."

"No, Paige, honey, I'm sorry. I can get into this dress shopping thing. Really I can. I'm sure all of these dresses are truly lovely. I just need to focus. I've got so much on my mind in dealing with my brother and Maeyl and all."

"Brother? You don't have a brother." Paige was confused. For the little over two years she'd known Tamarra, she knew of her to be an only child.

"Did I say brother?" Tamarra let out a nervous chuckle. "I meant mother," she lied, hoping Paige would buy it. She'd never shared the fact that she had a brother with anyone because she herself never wanted to acknowledge his existence. But now it seemed as though her mother was going to force her to. But at least her mother had stopped calling her. It took her a minute, but she finally got the hint that Tamarra didn't want to talk to her or her brother.

"You're having issues with your mom? But I thought you two had really been getting along."

"Yeah, we had been." Tamarra dropped her head. "But turns out she's the same old Mom."

"You should have told me what you were going through. We could have done this some other time. Or I could have been like any other bride-to-be and picked the dern dress out myself without even giving you a say."

"Point taken, smarty pants." Tamarra cracked a smile. "I know you were just trying to include your best friend in the process of one of the most special days in your life. And I don't want to ruin it. I just need to get my head right is all."

"Well let's not let this day be a total bust. How about just for the fun of it we go looking for your dress at the mall? You never know what we might stumble upon. And if all fails, we can at least hit up the food court." Paige bumped Tamarra's shoulder. "What do you say?" Paige's deep dimples sunk in her cheeks as she smiled.

"Why not?" Tamarra stated with a forced smile. She'd wished she'd just chosen one of the dang on gowns because all she really wanted to do was to go crawl in bed and sleep the day away.

"Let's just go to Tuttle Mall. Even if we don't find you a dress, we can still look for shoes. They have some cute ones here, but some of the prices are crazy ridiculous."

"Sounds good." Tamarra retreated to the dressing room and changed back into her street clothes before she and Paige headed to the mall. Twenty minutes later, the two friends had found themselves heading straight for the food court versus doing any shopping at all. They figured they'd be more enthused on full stomachs.

"I must admit, almost nine dollars for half a sub sandwich, an order of fries, and a drink isn't something I'd expect to pay for a meal at a mall food court," Tamarra confessed, "but dang, it's good."

"See, I told you," Paige said with a mouthful of food, glad that she'd talked her friend into trying something she'd never had before.

"And being that I cook for a living, you know this must be good. I don't eat just anything you know."

The two women managed to gobble down their lunch. They then stood up, gathered their trash to place on their 'for here' trays, then walked them over to the trash bin. The women dumped their trash into the bin, and then placed their brown, plastic trays atop it on a stack that already existed.

"After we shop, I'm coming back for some cookies," Paige said.

"You sure aren't the typical bride," Tamarra chuckled. "I didn't eat for months before my wedding, all in the name of fitting into my wedding gown. It was a wedding gown that I'd gotten two sizes smaller than I actually was just to motivate me to lose weight."

"Well—" Before Paige could reply, she was interrupted by a familiar voice.

"Sister Paige, Sister Tamarra? What a pleasant surprise!"

Both Paige and Tamarra turned around to find New Day's church secretary standing behind them with both arms loaded with shopping bags.

"Praise the Lord." Paige hugged the elderly woman.

"Praise the Lord." Tamarra nodded and smiled at the woman whom she secretly deemed a busy body. If ever anybody wanted to confirm a rumor or something that was going on around the church, they knew to go to her. Because nine times out of ten, she was the original source in the first place.

"Praise the Lord," the New Day secretary replied. "I would hug you both, but as you can see, my arms are full." She boastfully raised the bags as high as she could.

"Looks like you are getting your shop on big time," Paige told her.

"Well, you know I loves Pastor. There's nothing like having a spiritual parent," the secretary stated. "Pastor's birthday is one of those occasions where I can go all out to show how grateful I am for the years of being fed God's Word." She observed both Paige and Tamarra's empty hands. "I take it that you two are just getting started with your shopping for Pastor's birthday."

It was then that the women remembered their pastor's birthday was only three days away. With Tamarra's mind occupied with family and relationship matters, and Paige's mind occupied with wedding matters, the fact that New Day's pastor was about to celebrate a forty-seventh birthday had slipped their minds. That was another thing about the church secretary that bothered Tamarra; instead of doing what any other church secretary would have done and simply collected money to purchase a group gift from the church as well as discretely pass a card around for the congregation to sign for Pastor's birthday, she wanted to stand out as being one of the few who remembered and showed up bearing gifts. It was little things like that that often made some of the congregation members question whether or not the New Day church secretary was serving God and seeking His approval, or serving and seeking the approval of man.

"Uh, yeah, actually, we are just getting started," Paige pretty much lied, and then looked to Tamarra to back her up. Tamarra didn't respond.

"Okay then, well, I'm gonna grab me a bite to eat. I'll let you two go ahead and get started. Have a blessed day," the church secretary said as she began to walk toward an Asian food spot.

"You have a blessed day too," Paige said as she started off, Tamarra right behind her.

"Oh, and sweetheart."—the secretary grabbed Tamarra gently by the arm. She then whispered in her ear, while she rested her hand on Tamarra's shoulder. "Don't let that situation with Brother Maeyl and Sister Tasha get you down," she said, mispronouncing Sasha's name. But Tamarra knew who she was referring to. "Pastor is doing everything under God's authority to help the two of them to get to the bottom of things so that you and Brother Maeyl can get on with a life that I know the Lord has ordained to be."

Tamarra remained silent. It was obvious that the church secretary knew something that she didn't know. She figured she'd let her do all the talking while she listened, in hopes of perhaps learning something new herself.

"Now don't go thinking Pastor is putting y'all's business out there like that. I assure you that Pastor hasn't spoken to me, or anybody else, but God that is, about what's going on. But last Sunday, after church, the two of them were holding hands and praying. I could hear them praying from my office, which is right next to Pastor's you know. "They went into prayer before they went into Pastor's office for counseling. From the gist of Brother Maeyl's prayer, I pretty much figured out what was going on. Oh, and it was a powerful prayer indeed. Had me in tears. He wants God to take care of the situation speedily so that he can move on with the life he has planned for you and him." She moved even closer to Tamarra. "I hope I'm not spoiling anything, but it sounded to me like the plan included marriage." She winked, and then stood erect, as tall as her four foot seven inch frame would allow her to. "Well, I've probably said enough." Now she was speaking loud enough for Paige to hear as well. "You two go on and enjoy your day. And stay blessed, ya hear?"

Paige and Tamarra watched the woman walk away, struggling to keep a firm grasp of her bags.

"So, where do you want to head first? Nordstrom? How about that one store that—No, let's get Pastor's birthday gift first. That way I wouldn't have been completely lying to—"

"I don't mean to cut you off, Paige, and please don't be mad." Tamarra had the most regretful look on her face. "There's something I really have to do first. I know my mind hasn't really been into this all day, and now it's really not into it. I promise on everything that I'll make it up to you. We'll do this another day, and I'll be much better company."

Paige had to admit she expected shopping with her maid of honor for a dress and shoes to be much more exciting and happy, yet Tamarra had been a total drag. But by the same token, she had been able to put a pretty clear scenario together from the words she'd overheard the secretary spill into Tamarra's ear. She completely understood Tamarra's urgency to make things right with Maeyl, but didn't want their day together to end either. Paige's face now mirrored Tamarra's and was just as regretful, if not more.

"I had truly been looking forward to this day, so I hope you don't get mad at me when I say—" Paige turned her frown upside down and smiled at her best friend before saying, "Girl, go get your man!"

Paige didn't have to tell Tamara twice.

"Thank you for understanding," Tamarra said excitedly. "And I'll make it up to you, Paige Robinson. I promise, I really will. I'll even cater your rehearsal dinner if you'd like," Tamarra exclaimed while she fumbled for her keys, glad that she'd met Paige back at the bridal shop instead of them riding together like Paige had originally suggested.

"Oh, just get out of here already before I change my mind and make you try on ugly shoes." Paige rolled her eyes playfully.

"Thanks again for understanding, Paige." Tamarra was now headed for the exit. "Oh, and will you pick Pastor something up for me? I'll pay you back."

Paige gave her a stern look. "You're pushing it, girlfriend."

"Okay, okay. I'm gone." And just like that, Tamarra was gone, out the mall doors and headed to her car. Once in her vehicle, she drove just as quickly to Maeyl's house to restore their relationship, as she had on the day to sever it. But this time, just like always, she hoped that he would be forgiving and make amends with her.

About a half hour later, Tamarra pulled up to Maeyl's place. She was glad to see his front door open since she hadn't bothered to call to make sure he was home. Upon knocking on the screen door, she waited patiently. The multiple voices inside let her know that she wasn't the only company Maeyl had. The high pitched giggle let her know that she wasn't the only female company that Maeyl had either.

A few seconds passed when Tamarra looked through the screen door straight into the kitchen and saw a little body appear in the kitchen doorway. It was that little girl, Sasha's little girl. But the words that flew from the child's mouth told Tamarra that she was someone else's little girl as well.

"Daddy?" the small child called out.

"Yes, dear?" Tamarra heard Maeyl's voice, but she didn't see him.

"That woman from church is at your door."

Chapter Twenty-three

Lorain literally had to drag herself out of bed in order to prepare for the Single's Ministry meeting that was less than two hours away. She'd already called off work that Friday morning, in addition to having called off Monday as well. She thought the three days in between would have allowed her to recuperate from the sudden shock and anxiety attack she'd suffered on Saturday. She was wrong, dead wrong. Now today, almost a week later, she had the right mind to just lie in bed until canker worms began to nibble away at her flesh. But she wasn't in her right mind. She hadn't been since last Saturday after storming out of her mother's house without even saying so much as a good-bye.

She'd left her mother's house in a complete trance. She didn't even know how she'd made it home she was so shaken up after seeing Mr. Leary standing there in her mother's dining room in the flesh. After all the years of never even bumping into him in the grocery store, post office, or anything, she had been so sure he was dead by now, or perhaps even in jail if there was such a thing as justice. But she could see now that he was alive and well. The only consolation Lorain got out of that was that now he was wooing older women, women his own age, instead of young, vulnerable girls like she had been twenty-three years ago.

The man her mother referred to as Broady, Lorain knew as Mr. Leary, her middle school counselor back in the day. She'd never known him by his first name, only his last. It was normal for kids to only know their school superiors by last names since, out of respect, that was the way they were taught to reference them.

Why hadn't she asked her mother the last name of the man she was dating? Perhaps knowing both his last name and the fact that he was retired from the school system, she would have been able to put two and two together. That way she could have prevented her mother from taking her relationship with that man any further. But even so, how would she have possibly done that without having to tell her mother something she should have told her years ago? If she couldn't tell her then, how could she tell her now? And maybe Mr. Leary had been right, maybe it was all her fault. After all, she was the one who used to sneak and change into those short little mini skirts once she got to school and plaster cherry blossom lip gloss on her lips, making sure she wiped off every trace before returning home.

She wanted someone to notice her. She wanted the attention, which is why she would transform herself from the Plain Jane look Eleanor would send her off to school in. So once Mr. Leary started showing her special attention, as he called it, because she was a special student, her mission had been accomplished. Lorain couldn't lie; at first everything about the way Mr. Leary treated her made her feel special and grown up. But she was a child. She wasn't supposed to feel grown up. And she certainly wasn't supposed to be engaging in the grown up things she eventually found herself engaging in with Mr. Leary.

Seeing that man again struck up a sheet of guilt that covered Lorain like she was a king sized bed. She didn't so much feel guilty for the acts she'd performed with the man, she felt guilty just thinking about how many other young girls he'd probably done the same thing with all because she never told. After several months of him pulling her out of her various classrooms for their special meetings, she informed him that it was time she told her mother about the two of them. He nearly went insane, grabbing her by her arms, shaking her and telling her how that would be the biggest mistake she could ever make.

First off, he told her that other people wouldn't understand how special she was, why he'd chosen her. He told her that instead they would be jealous and brand her as just a ho, a title that would follow her all the way to high school. He told her that if she told anyone, there was a chance he could go to jail and it would be all her fault. He made her feel as though she was even more to blame by accusing her of deliberately wearing those revealing clothes.

By the time Mr. Leary finished putting the blame on her, there was no way in the world Lorain could tell anyone about what her young mind had conceived as her and Mr. Leary's relationship. He was right, no one would understand. No one could ever know. There could never be any proof that she had been *one of them fast girls*, as her mother used to refer to some of the other neighborhood girls. And several months after that day in Mr. Leary's office, the one thing that threatened to be a tell all for sure, she'd gotten rid of.

With no proof of what Mr. Leary had done to her, even if she did tell her mother what had happened all those years ago, how could she make her believe her now? She could hear Eleanor now being upset with her for making such an accusation when she'd finally found her a man. As a matter of fact, she could still hear her mother's loud ringing voice in her ears from when she had fussed her out on the phone last Saturday.

When her mother had gone into the kitchen to retrieve a glass of water for her, Lorain had made a David Copperfield escape.

"How you gon' have me cook up a mess a food and you

leave without saying good-bye, let alone taking a plate with you?" Eleanor had spat a few days ago into the phone receiver. It had been only seconds after Lorain had gotten into her car and driven away.

At the time, Lorain thought she'd accidentally put her cell phone on speaker because Eleanor's voice was booming so loud through the phone. "I'm sorry, Mom, I just—" Lorain hadn't even had the strength to finish the lie.

"Sorry? Is that all you have got to say for yourself? Runnin' out of here lookin' like a fool. Even worse, making me look like a fool for raising a fool."

"Mom, I'm sorry. I just wasn't feeling well all of a sudden." That had been the truth. She'd become almost sick to her stomach at the sight of her old school counselor. Although he'd aged, she recognized him well. But he appeared not to recognize her at all.

"I said I was going to get you a glass of water," Eleanor had reminded her. "Child, I been coming up with instant remedies for your illnesses since you were born. What made you think I couldn't have done the same this time around? On a day that was supposed to be so special? All I had to do to that water was add a drop of—"

Lorain had sat with the phone to her ear, no longer attentive to her mother as Eleanor began to rattle off all types of concoctions she could have mixed up with items right there in her kitchen. Lorain knew there was no use in listening. She knew that there was nothing her mother had in her house that could cure what had come over her. There was nothing she could go out and buy either, except maybe a .22 automatic. Lorain had quickly shook that violent thought from her head the minute she was convicted by the Holy Spirit for even allowing it to infiltrate her mind. So once again, she had tuned back into her mother's words.

"We'll since you don't have nothing to say, I'm not going

to sit here on the phone wasting my time begging and pleading for you to come back," her mother had told her. "But you owe me, Lorain. You owe me big time for making me look like a fool in front of the man that's going to be your step-daddy."

The phone went dead. Eleanor had hung up in her daughter's ear.

For the next hour, Lorain had driven around, searching for a gun store that might waive the two week waiting period.

Chapter Twenty-four

"Three months my foot!" one woman called out. "Three months is three months too long to wait to introduce your children to the person you're dating."

Just as Unique had suggested during her and Lorain's meeting at Lorain's house, they'd decided to discuss the matter of single parenting at the Single's Ministry meeting. The topic at hand was how long a person should wait before introducing their children to the person they are dating. It seemed to be getting quite heated.

"If I had kids," the woman continued, "the first time the man came to pick me up for a date, when I opened the front door, my kids would be standing right there beside me, ready to meet him."

"But what if it's just that, a date? What if nothing else comes of it, and the very next week you're out on another date?" Maeyl asked as he sat next to Tamarra who had been silent during the entire discussion, flipping through her Bible, pretending to be searching out scripture. "Are you just going to keep bringing all these men to your doorstep and going out with them for your children to witness? I mean, what type of impression would that leave on them?"

"Yeah, he's right," someone agreed.

"I don't want my kids seeing me going out with a different man every other week," Unique chimed in. "I feel that by three months, a person should know whether or not the relationship has potential to grow, and if it does, at that point, the children should be weaved into the scenario. If not, three months is still early enough for everyone to cut their losses without anyone getting hurt."

"More importantly, the children don't get hurt," an older woman added. "Because single folk have to realize that when they date someone and they bring their children into things, the children, in essence, are dating this person too. The children have feelings and could really grow to like this person. So when you break up with them, the children have to break up with them too."

"I still say three months is too long to begin to include the children," the woman who'd replied first said, standing her ground.

"I'm going to have to agree with Sister Unique," Lorain stated. Everyone looked at her as though she was Chris Brown showing up at Rihanna's birthday party. Thanks to the church secretary, everyone was pretty much privy to Unique and Lorain's issues with one another. The last person they expected to agree with Unique was Lorain. Even if she did feel the same way, they still never imagined she'd vocalize her agreement, even if not doing so was just to spite Unique. But it was time for Lorain to be an example at New Day, to show her fellow saints that it was just as easy to love each other as it was to love God. At least it should be.

Of course, for Lorain, it had taken praying and fasting to be able to get to that point, to realize that God had to change her, not the people she came into contact with. If she couldn't tolerate and get over herself in order to deal with her neighbor, then how on earth was she going to be able to deal with the devil? And if her mother truly had intentions on getting serious with Broady, she knew she'd be battling the devil face to face. So she couldn't waste her energy cat fighting with Unique. She had to save her strength for the real enemy.

"I just don't think it looks good for a man or woman to

be dating all kinds of people and introducing them all to their children," Lorain concluded, looking at Unique, who smiled, feeling good to have Lorain's support. Lorain only hoped to have that kind of support from her mother once she informed Eleanor that she didn't want her seeing Broady anymore, without actually telling her why.

"Who said anything about going out with these men?" the woman continued in her own defense. "See, children are the true test of character. I promise you all that God must have given them some kind of sixth sense, because children know a good spirit from a bad one a mile away. You can always tell the type of person you're dealing with by how a child reacts to the person. I guarantee that when your date shows up on your doorstep, you'll know by your child's reaction toward them whether or not you should even waste your time going out on a date in the first place."

There were a few chuckles and giggles throughout the room. There were even a couple of Amens.

"Um, hmm, y'all know I'm right," the woman nodded. "Either the child is going to be all standoffish and won't even say hi, want to hurry up and get out of the room and away from them, or, if you're dealing with a good spirit, even the shyest child on earth will at least let out a pleasant 'hello' and might even blush or giggle a little bit. Am I right about it?" she asked as chatter began to wave across the room from people recalling situations that confirmed the woman's theory. "Y'all know I'm telling the truth." She spoke as if she were speaking a scientific theory.

Unique even had to agree to some degree. "You might have a point, sista, because I know my kids won't even entertain someone with an ugly spirit. So if ever any of y'all greet my kids and they don't have no holler for you, now you'll know why."

There was laughter throughout the room. There were two

people who weren't laughing though. This sudden topic regarding single parents dating was just too soon for Maeyl and Tamarra to entertain. Too soon.

Tamarra sat there wondering why, of all the topics, God had decided to drop this one into the spirits of the ministry's leaders. She wasn't ready to talk about kids. She wasn't ready to talk about dating a man with kids. More specifically, she wasn't ready to even acknowledge that she now fit into that category, that she now found herself dating a man with a kid.

It wasn't fair that she would now have to learn an entire new set of rules. She had enough going on in her life. Why did God always have to pile everything on her all at once? Was God ever going to let her walk at least a mile weight free? She felt as though all of her life she'd had to carry a cross, sometimes not even her own. Now here she was again with the one her mother was making sure she carried, as well as the one Maeyl was now, in so many ways, asking her to carry.

Tamarra sat in the Single's Ministry meeting attempting to block out the discussion going on. She shifted from left to right every now and then as if she were uncomfortable. There was no ifs about it. She was uncomfortable. She was uncomfortable each and every time Maeyl's participated in the discussion at hand. She was afraid that people would start to wonder why he was so interested and involved in a topic that really didn't relate to him, well, as far as they knew. He rarely ever dialogued when at the meetings, and now all of a sudden he had plenty to say. Tamarra was afraid that someone would put two and two together and call him on it. As Maeyl added his last two cents, Tamarra's fear was about to come to pass.

"I think every one has a valid point, but I'm still going to support the idea of waiting at least three months to get to know someone before introducing them to your child," Maeyl insisted, and then rested his case by resting his folded hands across his lap.

"Well, well, well," the woman who felt there should be no waiting period stated. "You all heard brother Maeyl. Sounds like three months it is." It was clear that the woman was perturbed about not getting everyone to side with her. She looked to Maeyl. "Hmm, and you're quite passionate about it too, Brother Maeyl. One would think you had a kid running around here." Knowing that Maeyl and Tamarra were dating, the woman then looked to Tamarra. "Sister Tamarra, do you know something we don't know?"

By now Maeyl was livid by the way the sore loser was coming at him—and his woman. This was why he hadn't wanted to join the Single's Ministry in the first place, but nooooo, Tamarra just had to be persistent in talking him into it. He'd heard that the ministry was nothing but a bunch of women sitting around male bashing and gossiping, but figured if God had a resource for him to stay holy while he dated the woman he was in love with, he'd make the sacrifice.

Maeyl had to admit, outside of the tit for tat the women sometimes engaged in while trying to get their points across, he'd taken in a great deal of wisdom and knowledge. The information had definitely helped both him and Tamarra to date one another in a manner that was pleasing to God. Now, yet again, God was blessing him with some timely information. But for Tamarra, none of this seemed like a good time.

"Come on, Brother Maeyl, you can tell us," the woman persisted, turning her attention from Tamarra back to Maeyl. "You got a child running around somewhere that we don't know about it?" She chuckled.

Maeyl's jaws tightened, his mouth salivated and his heart rate increased dramatically when he realized that the woman's question wasn't rhetorical. She, along with everyone else in the room, was waiting for an answer. Some just thinking the question was a joke and that Maeyl would quiet her up with a hand swoop and a playful, "No." But as all eyes stayed glued on Maeyl, he knew he had to do something.

This, by no means, was how he'd intended on sharing the news with his church family of his three-year-old daughter. He wanted to give the woman the hand swoop and playful "No" that many were expecting, but something in him simply would not allow him to deny his daughter. He could deny the child no more to the mass of people that surrounded him than he could have denied her to Tamarra that day she showed up on his doorstep and heard the child refer to him as Daddy—and him reply.

That morning of the day Tamarra had come to his apartment, Maeyl had received the test results from the DNA test Pastor had suggested they take. It had been Maeyl's idea to counsel with Pastor the Sunday Sasha finally decided to acknowledge Maeyl as her child's father. She had told him that she'd known exactly who he was the moment she saw him standing in the center church aisle that day she went to the altar for salvation. Her intentions were never to hunt the man down whom she knew had fathered her child, but in her mind, it had to have been fate.

She shared with Maeyl how life had been a struggle for her in raising her daughter alone, but it was something she had prepared herself to do when she decided to keep the baby. It was a burden that she thought she was prepared to haul alone, but when her child was diagnosed with displaying signs of having autism, she knew it was more than she could bear.

As she sat in the lobby of the doctor's office crying after learning of her child's diagnosis, a woman just walked up to her. The woman, seeing Sasha clinging to her daughter, laid hands on both Sasha and her daughter and began to pray. She prayed that the devil's assignment on their lives be canceled. She also prayed that God would heal and deliver the child of any diagnostic or report from man that did not line up with the Word of God or His will for the child's life. Of everything the woman prayed, the words "Lord, your Word says that you will give this woman no more than she can bear," stuck out in Sasha's head. Never attending church regularly as an adult, or even the same church twice for that matter, Sasha felt that at that point in her life, the Lord was her only chance at help.

The way Sasha saw it, God was bound and determined to apprehend her. When she exited the clinic, she saw a sign stapled to the telephone pole inviting all, the sinners and the saved, to Easter Sunday service at New Day Temple of Faith. Sasha was a sinner who needed salvation. She almost hadn't been able to make it on Easter Sunday due to her car breaking down with a flat tire, but she eventually made it after a Good Samaritan helped her change her flat. Upon arriving at New Day, she realized that it was one of the few churches she had visited in the past. When she saw Maeyl standing there that day in church, even though she didn't have a relationship with the Lord before walking down to that altar and giving her life to Him, she knew her help had come from the Lord in the form of her baby's daddy.

Now faced with the dilemma of denying or proclaiming proudly his daughter, Maeyl chose the latter.

"As a matter of fact," Maeyl puffed out his chest and declared, "I do have a child. A daughter. Her name is Sakaya."

Chapter Twenty-five

"Come on in and take a seat, Uriah," Pastor Davidson instructed as he led Uriah into his office. "I'm so glad that the Lord made it so that you were in town this weekend and able to come fellowship with us."

"It is indeed a blessing to be able to hear you give the Word live and in person, Pastor Davidson. Bethany makes sure I get a copy of the CD of your preachings when she can. I listen to them faithfully while on the road, but there ain't nothing like being right here to hear them in the presence of the Lord amongst the saints," Uriah declared as he took a seat at the chair across from the pastor's desk.

After service today, Pastor Davidson had made a beeline straight to Uriah. It was odd because one of the church members had invited a slew of her unchurched family members to attend, yet Pastor Davidson bypassed them all, giving them a simple handshake and wave along with a "Thank you for coming, God bless you, good-bye." It was the church version of what Russell Simmons did at the end of every episode of his *Def Comedy Jam*.

Pastor Davidson appeared overjoyed to have his brother in Christ in the building. Forsaking all new visitors and his attempt to greet them, ultimately getting them to join Living Word, he asked Uriah if he could have a few minutes of his time to chat it up in his office. Now the two sat in Pastor Davidson's office doing just that.

"Well, I do hope those sermons have been a blessing to you while on the road," Pastor Davidson stated.

"I assure you that they have."

There was a moment of awkward silence before Pastor Davidson spoke again. "So Bethany must be beside herself to have you home." Pastor leaned back in his chair and offered Uriah a knowing look.

"Surely not as happy as I am to be home, and for three whole days straight. I just couldn't believe that for some reason I wasn't on the log for any runs. Right on time to celebrate my son's seventeenth birthday. God is awesome. I know it was Him who orchestrated all of this. At first, I was a little disappointed to hear that I wouldn't be hauling for three whole days. No hauling means no money. But like you preached today, Pastor, I'm going to trust in the Lord that He'll make a way for all of my family's needs to be met. God's bigger than any paycheck I could ever receive," Uriah testified, on the verge of letting out a Holy Ghost shout. "Being able to be here with my family is priceless."

"That's good to hear," Pastor Davidson said. "I, too, am glad that you were able to be here at church and also at home with your wife and kids. I know it must be difficult for Sister Bethany sometimes to have a husband who is always away from home. I know that even though I've been in the ministry for years, First Lady Davidson still gets a little lonesome when I have to go away to conferences and whatnot. But there ain't nothing like the warm welcome I get when I return home, if you know what I mean." Once again, Pastor Davidson gave Uriah a knowing look. This time he added a wink.

"Uhh, well, uhh yeah," Uriah stammered with downcast eyes. He was a little uncomfortable with the direction in which the conversation was now going.

Pastor Davidson anxiously leaned in, trying to read Uriah's expression. He couldn't tell if Uriah was looking away out of the embarrassment of his pastor's innuendo about his and his wife's bedroom life, or if he were looking away out of embarrassment that he and Bethany perhaps didn't have a bedroom life. Pastor decided to dig deeper. "You do get that warm welcome, don't you, brother?"

"Well, uhh, in all honesty, Pastor, I really haven't had the time." Uriah was almost ashamed to say it.

"Haven't had the time? You've been home three days, and you're leaving this evening, right?"

Uriah nodded. The look of shame had not erased itself.

"And you mean to tell me you and Sister Bethany haven't— you know—welcomed one another in the proper fashion in which husbands and wives do?"

"Well, when I got in on Friday, all we did was celebrate Hudson's birthday. I'd driven all the way in from Atlanta just to get home, so by the end of the night I was dead tired. I didn't wake up until after two o'clock in the afternoon the next day. I only got up then because I'd promised Pastor Frey I'd join him on his visits with the sick and shut in."

"What?" Pastor Davidson's tone was that of anger. He almost jumped up out of his chair. Realizing he'd almost come out the pocket, he relaxed back into his chair. "I mean, how could Pastor Frey ask you to do such a thing knowing you'd need to spend time with your family?"

"Oh, he didn't ask me," Uriah corrected, "I offered and insisted. After all, that man has made it a point to be there for my family. He was faithful with visiting Beth while she was sick and shut in. He allowed God to use him without murmur or complaint. I wanted to do God's work too while I had the opportunity."

"I see," Pastor Davidson's mouth said, but Uriah could tell by his demeanor that he didn't understand. More than likely had a bone to pick with Pastor Frey. "I guess by the time you got finished running with Pastor Frey you were wore out."

"No, not really, but after I got home and ate up that wonderful meal Doreen made for the family, I couldn't move. Fell asleep right there on the living room couch and didn't wake up until it was time for church this morning. My sister-in-law can burn. Doreen ain't no joke in the kitchen."

"Yeah, Sister Doreen," Pastor said as if his mind had wandered off. He seemed disappointed and at his wits end. He thought for a moment before saying, "Well, like I said, I know what it's like when you have to be on the road. Trust me, it can't be easy for your wife either, especially with all that she's been through. What do you say that your kids join me and First Lady for dinner tonight? Sister Doreen can join us too. I even think Pastor Frey is going to be there. That way you can have some alone time with your wife before heading out."

"Oh no, Pastor, we couldn't impose like that. Besides, Pastor Frey already has dinner plans with us. Doreen invited him to share in my farewell dinner before I hit the road again. As a matter of fact, I'd like to invite you and First Lady to join us. There's plenty. With the spread Doreen's got warming in the oven at home, she probably had to have been up cooking since five o'clock this morning. What do you say, Pastor? How about it?"

Pastor Davidson sighed, and then accepted Uriah's invite, all the while with a look on his face the read, *"If you can't beat 'em, why not join 'em?"*

Chapter Twenty-six

"How could you not tell me?" Paige spat as soon as Tamarra opened her front door. She brushed by her, threw her purse on the couch, and then turned to face her best friend. "I thought we were friends–best friends. I thought we could share any and everything with each other."

Paige began pacing the floor. "How long have you known? When did you find out?" A horrified look covered Paige's face. "Don't tell me you found out along with the rest of the world during the Single's Ministry meeting." Paige snapped her finger. "Ooohhh, I knew I shouldn't have agreed to fill in at work for Norman. I should have brought my tail on to that meeting like my gut had told me to do. I am still officially single you know," she said matter of factly. "I'm not married yet. And I promise you I would have told that Maeyl about himself. Humiliating you like that. That's something he should have at least have had the decency to share with you in private. Don't you think?" Paige stopped pacing long enough to look toward Tamarra for agreement.

Tamarra's eyes gazed down toward the floor as she nibbled on her bottom lip. It was a tell tale sign that Maeyl had told Tamarra before the fact.

"So you did already know?" Paige threw her hands on her hips. "And you didn't tell me." Paige allowed her hands to drop to her side in defeat. She immediately began pacing again. "I guess you took it well. Guess you didn't need my little ol' shoulder to cry on, or my little ol' ear to vent into it." She stopped pacing and looked at Tamarra. "I mean, did you know how stupid I felt when Sister Noel mentioned it, and I was clueless? I should have known before that walking and talking *New Day Tell All* book knew."

Tamarra could tell that Paige was hurt. But she couldn't tell if she were more hurt because Tamarra hadn't come to her at all, or if it were because other church members had found out first. Either way, Tamarra didn't blame her friend for being upset with her. In the past two years of their friendship, Paige had entrusted Tamarra with a great deal of things and situations she had gone through. All Paige seemed to have wanted was a little reciprocity here.

Having truly wanted to tell her best friend, and knowing she should have told her before she heard it through the grapevine, Tamarra felt bad too. On Friday night, after the single's meeting was adjourned, she knew that it would only be a matter of time, minutes to be exact, before word would get out about Maeyl's confession of being the father of Sasha's daughter. It was inevitable that word would eventually get back to Paige. Tamarra was surprised it had taken this long, and she knew there was no way they were going to get through a Sunday at New Day Temple of Faith without somebody telling somebody else's business.

The right thing for Tamarra to do would have been to call her best friend and share it with her on the day she had showed up on Maeyl's doorstep and found out first hand. But she'd been way too humiliated to do just that. It was already hard enough for her to get that small child's whiny voice out of her head; "*Daddy?—That woman from church is at your door.*"

Upon hearing those words, Tamarra's heart had dropped down to her feet as she stood outside of Maeyl's door as frozen as a Popsicle in a deep freezer. Even his warm, loving voice, when he made his way to the door to greet her, didn't unthaw her immediately. He had to call her name a couple of times, eventually coming outside onto the porch to give her a nudge.

"Tamarra, honey, are you okay?" he'd asked her.

"Uhh, yeah, uhh, fine—I guess," she said, slowly coming out of her daze. "Did that little girl just call you Daddy?" There was no beating around the bush on Tamarra's end, not today. She'd played games with Maeyl long enough trying to get him to tell her the real deal about him and this Sasha woman, the real deal of which her spirit had already tried to tell her about. But no, she didn't want to trust the voice within her. She just had to hear it from the horse's mouth. So God gave her exactly what she wanted.

"Yes, she did call me Daddy," Maeyl had confessed, looking Tamarra in the eyes, waiting for her reaction.

A nervous chuckle escaped Tamarra's lips. "And why, might I ask, would she be calling you that?"

"Because I am," Maeyl said without hesitation. "And I have a DNA test to prove it."

Tamarra turned as pale as a ghost and almost lost her balance.

"Are you okay?" Maeyl asked her, supporting her by the arm. Tamarra was too beside herself to even reply. "I'm sorry, Tamarra. This isn't how I wanted you to find out. But you weren't really speaking with me and—"

"Then you should have spoken to me!" Tamarra snapped, raising her tone.

Maeyl looked over his shoulder to make sure his houseguests weren't witnessing the brewing argument. "I tried, but you wouldn't take any of my calls since the day you stormed out of here."

"Then you should have left me a message!" Her tone was even louder.

"This isn't really the type of thing you leave your woman a message about over the phone."

"Then you should have driven to my house."

"Without calling first? You wouldn't take my calls."

"Oh, enough already!" Tamarra yelled at the top of her lungs, frustrated that Maeyl seemed to have a comeback for everything she said. "You're just full of excuses, aren't you?" Tamarra looked him up and down. "I just wonder what your excuse is for being a whoremonger!"

"Daddy?" There was that little whiny voice again. "What's a whoremonger?"

Both Tamarra and Maeyl were startled by Sakaya standing in the doorway.

"Come on, baby, I think we better come back and see Daddy another time." Sasha had appeared in the doorway behind Sakaya, swooping her up in one arm while carrying her purse and an American Girl doll that resembled and was dressed identical to the child in her other arm. She gave Maeyl a remorseful look as she exited the apartment. "I'm so sorry, Maeyl." She looked to Tamarra. "We're sorry." She began to make her way down the steps.

"Sasha, wait, you don't have to go," Maeyl called out.

"Actually we do." Sasha looked from Tamarra to Maeyl. "I think you two need to talk." She looked at her daughter. "In private and without virgin ears around."

"Mommy? What's a virgin?" The child was full of questions. She didn't miss a beat. Autistic she wasn't. Either the doctors had originally misdiagnosed, or when that woman laid hands on the child and both prayed for a healing and rebuked the doctor's reports, it worked. Because when Sasha took the child to another doctor for a second opinion, no signs of autism were detected. Either way, Sasha had given God all the glory for her daughter being a normal, healthy child.

"I'll call you later, Maeyl," Sasha stated. "Good-bye, Sister Tam—Tamarra?"

Tamarra was surprised to see that this woman knew her

name. That only meant one thing; Maeyl had been discussing her with that woman. It burned Tamarra up to know that Maeyl had been discussing her with another woman. "Yes, that's right. It's Tamarra. But best you believe, I am no sister of yours." There was a gasp from both Maeyl and Sasha's mouth. Not even Tamarra could believe she had spoken the words she'd only meant to think. Served her right though, for even thinking something so ugly. Especially after Pastor was always preaching about how everybody is God's children. How everyone are brothers and sisters in Christ.

Knowing she was dead wrong for the way she had come off at Sasha, Tamarra wanted to apologize, but her pride wouldn't let her. Her woe is me attitude wouldn't let her. As far as she was concerned, she was the victim in this situation. It was understandable if she said a thing or two that wasn't Christlike, wasn't it? She couldn't have apologized if she wanted to, as Sasha quickly made her way to her vehicle, strapped Sakaya into the backseat, and drove away.

After watching Sasha peel off, Maeyl had insisted that he and Tamarra take their conversation inside. The neighbors had already heard more than they needed to. It was inside that Maeyl explained to Tamarra how Sasha had been conceived, how he never knew the child even existed, how it was God's doing that the child's mother and he even crossed paths again. Maeyl insisted that this didn't change the way he felt about Tamarra and that things wouldn't change between them. It was then that Tamarra decided she'd sweep her pride up under the rug and pretend that love conquered all. All the while, deep inside, this was the one instance in which she felt that the Bible had perhaps been in error when it stated that love could cover a multitude. For some reason, as much as she loved Maeyl, she just didn't feel as though it could cover the circumstances she now found herself in.

Why she had been so surprised, so stunned, at hearing the

child refer to Maeyl as Daddy she didn't know. Her spirit had already told her such from the moment she'd looked into the little girl's eyes. The girl's words were nothing more than further confirmation. Now Tamarra realized that as agonizing as not knowing was, sometimes knowing was even more agonizing. Darn that Eve for eating from the Tree of Knowledge!

After bumping into the church secretary and hearing what she had to say about Maeyl and Sasha, Tamarra knew she had previously jumped to conclusions the day she stormed out on Maeyl All she'd wanted to do was to apologize to him. She had showed up seeking forgivness, not baby mama drama. And on top of everything else, it was the child's mouth Tamarra had to hear the news from first. In her opinion, she should have been the first person Maeyl called once he got the test results. With that being said, Tamarra truly could understand how Paige felt about her not coming directly to her. But just in case she didn't, Paige was going to make sure she did.

"I have to hear it through the grapevine that Maeyl has a daughter—with Sasha."

"I'm sorry, Paige," Tamarra apologized. "I wanted to tell you, but . . . but." Tamarra became choked up.

Seeing her friend in such pain made Paige realize that this wasn't about her. "No, I'm sorry," Paige said, walking over to her friend and comforting her with an embrace. "It was selfish of me to even come here and try to make this all about me. I can't imagine what you must be going through knowing that yet another man—" Paige immediately stopped her words from coming out.

Tamarra slowly separated herself from her friend. "Go on. Say it." She looked at Paige. Paige became a big watery blur as Tamarra's eyes became completely full with tears. "Say it, Paige. Knowing that yet another man, a man that I'm in love with, has gotten some woman pregnant outside of our relationship, has a child and is going to run off and live happily ever after with his baby's mama. See, this is why I didn't want to say anything to you, to anybody, because I knew you'd all be thinking the same thing."

"Tamarra, that's not true." Paige tried to rub Tamarra's arm, but Tamarra snatched it away.

"What do you mean it's not true? You just said it yourself." Tamarra tightened her lips. "I knew I shouldn't have shared my testimony about me and my ex-husband in that stupid Single's Ministry meeting. Now everyone knows my business and it's going to do me more harm than good. Now everyone is going to know that something is wrong with Tamarra," she began to rant in third person. "Tamarra can't keep a man. She must be cursed or something." She walked over to her couch and flopped down. She looked upward. "I don't blame you, God. I guess since I can't give these men babies, you've got to make sure they get them from somewhere."

There was awkward silence. In all of her murmuring and complaining, Tamarra had said something, yet another thing that she hadn't shared with her best friend.

Paige swallowed, then slowly walked over and sat down next to Tamarra. "I could pretend like I didn't hear what you just said, but I won't."

Tamarra didn't reply.

"Do I need to ask you about it, or are you just going to tell me?"

Again, Tamarra didn't reply.

"You always made it seem as though you were happy you'd never had a child with your ex-husband, Edward. You made it seem like it was just something the two of you never sat and decided you wanted to do. So now, are you saying that it wasn't that you didn't want to have kids, but that you can't have kids, Tamarra?"

Tamarra still remained silent.

"Well, it's evident that the two of us aren't as close as I

thought we were. I mean, I thought I was a good friend to you." Paige's voice began to tremble as she held back tears. It hurt her deep inside that Tamarra hadn't trusted her the way Paige had trusted Tamarra. "I thought I was the type of friend that you could trust and share anything with, but I guess I was wrong." Paige stood. "I guess I was wrong about you too, about us—this entire friendship. I mean, I honestly don't know how well I know you after all." After making her way to the door and opening it, before exiting she turned and said, "And don't worry about us finding a maid of honor dress for you either . . . you read between the lines."

Paige disappeared to the other side of the now closed door before Tamarra could stop her. In all honesty, Tamarra didn't know if she even really wanted to stop her. The way she felt, she just wanted to crawl under a rock somewhere . . . anywhere where she could cut herself off from the world. She knew she should be hurt that Paige no longer wanted her to be a part of her wedding, but in fact, it was a relief. As far as she was concerned, Paige getting married was probably the worst mistake she could make. But she wouldn't dare tell her friend that. No, if Paige had said it once, she'd said it twice: *This is the man I prayed to God for, so I know our marriage is going to be blessed.*

"Humph.Been there prayed that," Tamarra said out loud just thinking about her friend's naivety. What made her think Blake was so different than any other man? All she was doing was setting herself up to be hurt, truth be told.

The phone rang, and immediately Tamarra thought it was Paige calling to apologize for booting her out of her wedding.

"Poor girl didn't even make it out of the driveway," Tamarra said as she got up to retrieve the phone. "She knows I love her," Tamarra said before answering the phone. "I'm sorry, Paige. You are my best friend. I do trust you, and I know that I can share everything with you. As a matter of fact, I really do need to talk, not just about me though. But about you and Blake—this whole marriage thing—just everything, girl—"

"Tammy?"

Tamarra froze mid-sentence.

"Tamarra, honey. It's your brother and me," her mother chimed in. "Thank you for finally answering the phone, sweetheart. We really need to talk to you about—"

"How dare you, Mother!" were the only words Tamarra could muster up. Her mother could not have picked a worse time to call. "How dare you after all of these years try to bring my brother back into my life? You and I barely had a relationship, Mom. We were just starting to get things back on track, and now you feel as though things are going so great that you can invite Raymond to join in on the so-called reconciliation? This was all a trick, wasn't it, Mother? You were just trying to get back in good with me so that you could, once again, manipulate me regarding Raymond. Well, guess what? I don't want anything to do with you or my brother. From this day forward, not only do I not have a brother, but I don't have a mother either."

Tamarra slammed the phone down and made a quick turn to go back to the couch. Upon turning around, she froze in her tracks.

"Brother?" Paige said to Tamarra with a look of confusion on her face. She'd returned to retrieve her purse that she'd left on Tamarra's couch. She didn't bother knocking, figuring since she'd only been gone a few seconds, Tamarra probably hadn't bothered to lock the door yet. But when she walked right in, she had no idea she would be walking in on such a conversation. She was flabbergasted. But even more so, she was confused. She was now almost totally convinced that the woman standing in front of her wasn't who she thought she was. "You have a brother, Tamarra? Just how many secrets are you keeping?"

Chapter Twenty-seven

"I don't care what you say, if you ain't feeling no better in the next couple of days, I'm personally driving you to the doctor's office," Eleanor said as she carried a pot of chicken noodle soup through Lorain's doorway.

"Mom, you didn't have to come all the way over here. I'll be fine," Lorain assured her mother as she closed the door, and then followed Eleanor into the kitchen area.

"Where's your thermometer?" Eleanor asked, setting the pot on the stove. "I need to see how high your fever is."

"Mom, I don't have a fever." Lorain sucked her teeth. "Like I told you, I'll be fine. I just need to rest."

"Oh no, I'm not buying it. There is no way you can be fine," Eleanor insisted as she made a beeline toward the bathroom to search the medicine cabinet for a thermometer. Lorain stayed on her heels. "You have to have a fever. Never in your life have you turned down a trip to the mall when I'm buying, so I know you're sick—delirious even."

Just two hours ago, once Eleanor figured church had let out, she called Lorain to invite her to go shopping. When Lorain had first declined, stating that she didn't have the money to go shopping, Eleanor then offered to buy her daughter a pair of shoes if she agreed to tag along. Lorain knew how much her mother hated shopping alone, but still, she declined, this time stating she still wasn't feeling one hundred percent herself. Lorain was a shoe diva, had over 100 pair stacked in her closet, but she didn't want to spend time with

Eleanor for fear she might bring up *him*. And she just wasn't quite ready to talk about *him* yet.

"Mom, please. Now you know it's not that serious."

"Like heck it ain't." Eleanor paused for a moment, then turned to her daughter and asked, "Did you even go to church today? Because you didn't call me to come visit with you this Sunday. Even though you know half the time I'm going to say no, you still ask all the time." She turned back toward the cabinet and began digging through it. "I couldn't have come visit New Day no way. I visited Broady's church today."

"That man goes to church?" Lorain asked. Her tone revealed a mixture of both shock and disgust.

"Well, yes, he does." Eleanor ceased her search and faced her daughter again. "You asked that like the man is one of Satan's imps. Yes, he goes to church." She continued her search. "Loves the Lord. As a matter of fact, he helps oversee the Youth Ministry."

Lorain lost her balance as her body flushed with heat. She grabbed hold of her mother to keep from falling.

"That's it; we're going to find an urgent care that's open on Sundays," Eleanor said, now completely putting an end to her search, closing the medicine cabinet. She grabbed her daughter by the elbow in an effort to lead her out the bathroom door and straight out the front door.

"Mom, no! I'm not sick. Not physically anyway." Lorain pulled her arm from her mother and then went and sat down on the couch.

"What do you mean, 'not physically'?" Eleanor raised her eyebrows. "You trying to tell me you're going mental on me or something? Oh Lord, don't let it be," Eleanor began to plea with raised hands. "I promise for now on I'll go to church to see about you, not to find no man and not to please no man. I'll make sure it's all about you, Lord, just don't let my baby be going crazy. I need her to be my maid of honor in my wedding soon."

"Oh Lord!" This time it was Lorain crying out to the Lord.

This was the second time her mother had made reference to marrying Broady. The first time she brushed it off as her mother exaggerating her interest in the man. Her mother was a sucker for a nice looking gentleman and had claimed many men as her future husband merely by seeing them in the grocery store line. Lorain had to admit, although she'd only laid eyes on Broady for a hot second, he had aged quite well. His salt and pepper hair that was a cross between both wavy and straight was very becoming of him. His full matching beard and thin mustache was simply GQ. The casual button up shirt he wore with his dress pants and leather loafers defined his six foot two inch, medium build frame. So she could see why her mother would be so quick to want to become Mrs. Broady Leary. Even so, she was willing to bet her tithes and offerings that if her mother knew the truth about Mr. GQ's past, she'd feel otherwise.

Lorain certainly wanted to, but couldn't find the words to tell her mother about Broady; what he'd done to her. Now she felt as though he was abusing her all over again by dating her mother. He had to know the torment she would feel. Or did he? Did he even recognize her? Her mother had gone back to using her maiden name while Lorain still carried her father's last name, so the name thing alone wouldn't have rung a bell with Broady.

Nonetheless, just the thought of the entire scenario is what was making Lorain sick. Right now, it wasn't even just the fact that her mother was dating the man that made her sick, it was the fact that he was somewhat in a position of authority at his church to do to other girls what he'd done to her.

How could God let that man be the overseerer of a youth ministry, any ministry for that matter, but especially one that gave him authority over young kids, young girls. Just like he had been in a position of authority over her. He'd abused that authority once, what made God believe that he wouldn't do it again?

Lorain couldn't help but wonder how many girls like her he'd abused at the church all in the name of Jesus. How many girls he had posed to merely counsel or pray with, but then took it a step further. It tore Lorain's soul apart knowing that these girls may have had to suffer all because of her keeping quiet about what he'd done to her. Her brain could barely obtain all of the thoughts that were traveling around it. She felt that if she didn't do something, she just might go crazy. But for now she would just thank God for keeping her mind thus far and pray for Him to continue to keep it.

"No, Mom, I'm not going crazy or anything like that. It's just that—" Lorain's words trailed off when she looked into her mother's eyes. *Tell her. Tell her*, her inner thoughts urged. "It's about Broady." Lorain paused and dropped her head.

Eleanor sighed, and then joined her daughter on the couch. "I know already, sweetheart."

Lorain was stunned. "You do?"

Eleanor shook her head. "Yeah, Broady told me."

Lorain's voice got caught in her throat. After one hard cough though, she was able to release it. "He did?" There was both surprise and shock in her tone. She didn't know which kind of way to feel right about now. A part of her wanted to commend the old man for stepping up to the plate and telling her mother about his past—their past. Another part of her wanted to knock her mother upside the head for still wanting to be involved with the man.

"Yes, he did." Eleanor lifted her head and looked into her daughter's eyes. "I didn't believe it at first though. I guess I was just waiting to hear if from you. I mean, you're at the age now where you could have just told me. Back when you were younger, I could understand. But you're not a little girl anymore, sweetie."

Lorain's eyes watered. "Mom—I–I don't know what to say." Lorain had to admit that there was a feeling of relief that she didn't have to fix her mouth to tell her mother about what Broady had done to her. She didn't know exactly what to say and how to say it, but now she didn't have to worry about that. Now all she had to worry about was how her mother would see her from this point on. Would she think she played a part in it? Would she blame her in any way? Would she be hurt that Lorain didn't feel she could come to her about it?

"You don't have to say anything, and I won't make you say anything." Once again, Lorain felt relief. "All that matters now is that I know what's going on, and I'm going to do everything motherly possible to help you get over it." Eleanor wiped the tear that was now running down her daughter's face. "I just need you to know that I'd never put Broady before you, any man before you."

"So does that mean you're going to stop seeing Broady?" Lorain didn't hesitate to ask the million dollar question.

"Child, no," Eleanor was quick to say, as she brushed her daughter away. "I said I'm never going to put the man before you. I didn't say I was going to give up the man for you."

"Mom, are you serious?" Lorain exclaimed as she stared at Eleanor with dropped jaws. Surely she was missing something here, or had her mother just informed her that she was going to continue seeing the man who'd taken advantage of her when she was just a young girl in middle school?

"I'm dead serious," Eleanor informed her, confirming that she'd heard her right the first time. "I'm not going to stop seeing Broady. As a matter of fact, I didn't want to go shopping today just to be shopping. I wasn't going to buy you no any old pair of shoes." A huge, proud smile covered Eleanor's face as she placed her left hand on her chest and fluttered her fingers. "I wanted to shop for dresses for us to wear for my wedding ceremony, and shoes to match."

That's when Lorain saw it. Never mind the words that had
the nerve to escape her mother's lips—that's when she saw it,
the bling-bling diamond engagement ring that rested on her
mother's ring finger. She jumped to her feet like a Jack-In-
The-Box. "What? You mean after what he told you, after what
I just confirmed, you're going to marry that man?"

"I reckon I am, and you shouldn't be so selfish about this.
Your mother ain't no spring chicken you know." She ran
her hands down her thighs that still stuck out in all the right
places. "I may look like a spring chicken, but Lord knows I'm
not. I may never get a proposal again. Don't you want Mama
to be happy?"

Lorain just stood there shaking her head in awe. "I can't
believe this."

"Look, dear, like I said, you're older now. You can get over
these types of things."

"These types of things? You act like this is something that
happens all the time."

"Well, it does, doesn't it?" Eleanor had a confused look on
her face. "I mean, Broady said it happened all the time with
the girls at the school he retired from."

Lorain grabbed her stomach. She thought she was going to
be sick. She needed that thermometer more than ever now.
Certainly it was her mother who had the fever. She was the
one who was delirious. If not that, then her mother had certainly drunk the Kool-Aid, recipe compliments of Jim Jones.
Or had she been just flat out brain washed by Broady? Lorain knew he had the capability to brain wash young girls, but
grown women too?

"So there are others besides me?" Tears began to pour from
Lorain's eyes.

"Honey, don't cry." Eleanor raced to her daughter's side to
comfort her. "Broady says it's natural for a girl to feel this way.
I know you learn in church that jealousy is not a spirit of the
Lord, but you're only human."

"Jealousy?" Lorain had no idea why her mother thought these words would be comforting to her.

"Yes, jealousy. Isn't that what's going on here? You're jealous that for so many years it's been just me and you, and now that Mama has a new man in her life, you're feeling jealous, scared that he's going to replace you in my life? Broady told me that you'll get over it eventually, once you see that a husband and wife's relationship could never take the place or come between a mother and daughter relationship."

Lorain just stood there with her mouth agape.

"I know, I know, sweetie." Eleanor hugged her daughter and pat her back like she'd done so many times when Lorain had been a child and needed comforting. "You don't have to say anything. Like I said, at first I wanted to hear it from you. I wanted to hear from your mouth that you were afraid you'd lose me to Broady, but I won't make you say it. You must feel silly being a grown woman having to admit that you are jealous that your mother has a new man, especially with you not having one. It must be an even bigger embarrassment considering you teaching your Christian folks how to get one as leader of that Single's Ministry. But it's nothing to be embarrassed about. Broady said he's seen it a thousand times over the years with the young girls at school, some of the boys too—"

As Eleanor went on and on, Lorain blocked the sound of her mother's voice out. When her mother had said the words, *"Broady told me,"* Lorain had thought he'd told her about what he'd done to her. She had no idea that all this time, all throughout her mother's and her conversation, that they'd been on two different pages.

"Now we haven't exactly set a wedding date, and I know all of this seems so soon," Eleanor continued, "but we both agreed that there is no need in us dragging this engagement thing out like you young folks do. Besides, at our age, tomorrow definitely isn't promised. So if I have things my way, we'll be married in the next couple of months."

Lorain was listening again. "Mom, I . . . I," she stammered, still at a loss for words as a result of the confusion that had just taken place. "You can't marry him!" Lorain just flat out said in a stern tone.

Eleanor was stunned by her daughter's tone toward her. "Excuse me, young lady?"

"I mean, you can't marry him because—because you just met the man. You can't possibly know everything about him." Lorain was certain her mother didn't know everything about him.

"I know enough, thank you very much." Eleanor's displeasure with her daughter's attitude and tone was evident. "Look, I don't have to stand here and take this." Eleanor headed for the door. "You can stay over here and act jealous and play sick all you want to. That's on you. But Mama is about to become the new Mrs. Broady Leary, like it or not."

Eleanor had exited the house and slammed the door behind her before Lorain could say another word. "The next Mrs. Leary," she repeated. "Oh, he's creepy all right." He was creepy enough where Lorain just couldn't let her mother do it. She couldn't let her mother marry that man. She had to give her a reason to return that engagement ring, even if it meant finally telling her what she should have told a long time ago.

Chapter Twenty-eight

"Father God, we thank you for the time you allowed us to fellowship as a family," Mother Doreen prayed. She, Bethany, Uriah, their two children and Pastor Frey stood in a circle in the living room, holding hands, as they said a prayer before Uriah headed back onto the road.

Mother Doreen prayed for a few more minutes before closing out prayer in Jesus' name by asking the Lord that travel mercies be upon Uriah across the highways and the byways.

"Amen," all said in unison behind Mother Doreen.

"You got everything?" Bethany asked her husband as she grabbed his leather jacket he wore no matter the season. Since he traveled all over the map, he never knew what the weather was going to be like. He figured he couldn't go wrong with a leather jacket.

"Yep, I reckon I do." Uriah looked around the room to make sure he wasn't leaving anything behind.

"Wait a minute, Dad," Sadie said as she made a mad dash for the kitchen, and then returned with a foiled plate in hand. "You left the plate for the road Aunt Doreen fixed for you."

"Oh, son, you don't want to leave that," Pastor Frey said as he eyeballed Sadie hand the plate to Uriah. "That sister-in-law of yours has some of the best cooking I've ever tasted, and remember, I was twice married."

There were a few chuckles.

"Pastor and First Lady will be sorry they couldn't make it to enjoy some of that delicious food," Pastor Frey said.

"Yeah, when I invited him and First Lady, he was excited to be able to come, but then he called Beth and told her that something came up," Uriah said with a bewildered look on his face.

"Yeah, I know how it can be," Pastor Frey said in his senior pastor's defense. Some of these saints think can't nobody pray them out of a situation but Pastor, so they call on him any day, anytime, never once thinking that he might just need some time for himself."

"The devil is a liar," Mother Doreen declared. "Folks better start learning to pray for themselves, to lay hands on themselves, to encourage themselves, to speak into their own lives. Didn't they get anything out of Jesus' relationship with the disciples? He taught them how to—"

Pastor Frey stood there with a proud smile on his face as he listened to Mother Doreen finish making her point. "Mother Doreen, I tell you, you are a mighty woman of God. The way you can always seem to bring biblical knowledge to any situation never ceases to amaze me. You sure you ain't got a calling on your life to teach? Because you break it down plain and simple, my sister."

Mother Doreen had no idea that she was blushing as a result of Pastor Frey's comments when she replied, "Well, I do believe that has been prophesied to me a couple of times," she admitted.

"Then, sister, you better walk in that prophesy," Pastor Frey insisted. "Remember what happened in the Bible to the man given the talents and he didn't' use the—"

"Ahem." Bethany clearing her throat cut off Pastor Frey's thoughts. It was then when both he and Mother Doreen remembered that they weren't the only two standing in the room.

For the first time, Uriah noticed the somewhat brewing attraction between his sister-in-law and Pastor Frey. He looked over at his wife and winked. It was the type of wink Pastor

Davidson would have given. Bethany simply rolled her eyes up in her head.

"I guess I'll walk you out, Brother Uriah," Pastor Frey said, patting Uriah on the shoulder. "Where are you headed to anyway?"

"Sunny California," Uriah replied.

"Oh my, what a drive," Pastor Frey stated. "Are you sure you're up to that?"

"That's exactly what the receptionist of the company who gives me my assignments asked when I called in. Asked me was I feeling okay enough to go on the run. Are y'all trying to tell me I'm getting old or something?"

Pastor Frey nervously cleared his throat, and then offered to drive Uriah to his truck that was parked in a vacant store lot a few blocks up.

"Thank you, Pastor, but I think I'll walk some of this food off," Uriah said to him, grabbing his packed bags that sat by the front door. "And again, thank you for coming over."

"Oh, anytime, Brother Uriah. Anytime."

After everyone said their good-byes to Uriah, he and Pastor Frey exited the house.

"I miss Daddy already," Sadie said as she walked over and put her arm around Bethany. "Don't you, Ma?"

"Sure, honey, sure," Bethany said as she pat her daughter's arm. "Anyway, we better get the kitchen cleaned up." Bethany quickly turned to head to the kitchen.

"Mom, are you okay?" Hudson asked when he saw what looked like his mother stumble.

"Uh, yes, dear, I'm fine," Bethany said as she balanced herself long enough to go into the kitchen. Once in the kitchen, after failing at her attempt to balance herself by gripping the counter, she then headed down the hall to the restroom. About ten minutes later she opened the bathroom door to find her sister standing right outside the door with her hands on her hips. "Reen!" she exclaimed, putting her hand over her heart. "You scared me."

"And you're scaring me," Mother Doreen replied.

"Oh sis, please, it's nothing. Probably just some bug."

"Well, it ain't the twenty-four hour bug because you been sick longer than twenty-four hours." Mother Doreen stood there waiting for her baby sister's comeback. She had none. "Uh-huh, just as I thought."

"I don't know what you're—"

". . . talking about." Mother Doreen finished her sister's sentence. "Oh, you know darn well what I'm talking about," she said as she leaned into her sister while pointing an accusing finger right in her face. "As a matter of fact, you know what I've been talking about since day one."

Realizing that there was no way around the truth, or Mother Doreen for that matter, Bethany took her usual defensive stand. "Look, Reen, you've been meddling since you got here, and I'm sick and tired of it. You been picking and prodding me like I'm some lab rat. When that didn't work, you now call yourself trying to do the same thing with Wal—Pastor Frey." Bethany crossed her arms. "So you mean to tell me with all the time you've purposely been spending with Pastor Frey, he hasn't told you what you've wanted to hear?"

"What do you mean by *purposely?*"

"Oh, you know just what I mean. Acting like you're stealing time away from Pastor Frey doing his ministerial duties when all you're really doing is taking him off my hands. You always have been a jealous ol' somethin'."

"Ooooh, I got a right mind to snatch you up by your arm with my one arm and then wear you a new hide with my free arm, just like I used to do when we were little." Mother Doreen seethed the words through her tight lips as she squinted her eyes like Esther from *Sanford and Son*. It was a surprise that the words "You fish eyed fool," didn't spill from her lips next.

Intimidating as her big sister was, as her big sister had always been, Bethany didn't back down. "Well, I'm not a little girl anymore, Reen, and it's about time you stop treating me as one. I'm a forty-year-old woman, a wife, a mother of two with one on the—" Bethany's words trailed off once she realized what she was about to say.

"Oh, don't stop now." Mother Doreen smiled with victory. "See that's the problem. When you were little, I never had to snitch on your behind too often because I knew you'd run your mouth just long enough for you to tell on yourself."

"Tell what? There's nothing to tell?"

"Then why'd you stop? What were you about to say? Huh, sis?" Bethany turned her nose up and looked away without responding verbally. "You are a mother of two with one on the what?" Mother Doreen began to antagonize her sister by putting her hand to her ear as if she were listening loud and clear. "Come on, say it." Still Bethany didn't reply. "Look at you standing there. You're even ashamed to say it. How I see it, a woman ain't ashamed to declare she and her husband are about to be parents unless, that is, if she and her husband ain't about to become parents, if you know what I mean."

"Doreen Nelly Mae Tucker!" Bethany spat in shock.

"Bethany Lou Ellen Tyson!" Doreen shot back.

"Mother, Auntie Doreen!"

For the second time that month, Sadie's voice had interrupted an argument between the siblings. Once again, both Mother Doreen and Bethany looked embarrassed to see the young girl standing there. And yes, once again they each secretly wondered how long she'd been standing there. How much she'd heard.

"Yes, Sadie," both women said in unison sing song voices as if they hadn't just been yelling loud enough to wake the dead.

"What is it, honey?" Bethany asked her daughter.

Sadie answered with a trembling voice. "It's the police. They're at the door."

Chapter Twenty-nine

"I don't know what to say." Paige sat at Tamarra's kitchen table with Tamarra sitting directly across from her. For the first time ever, Tamarra had actually shared with someone the fact that she had a brother and why she had denied him all these years. She even informed her of the role her parents had played in it. "I mean, I know what to say. I have lots of things I want to say. I just don't know how Christlike they are. I mean, your parents—" Paige shook her head in disgust. "They should be in jail too, Tamarra. I know that's an awful thing to say, but my God." Paige continued shaking her head.

"I know," were the only words of agreement Tamarra could utter.

After a few more moments of silence, Paige stood. "You're better than me. I couldn't have played along with the whole thing about your parents pretending to divorce and all that mess. I would have been on *Oprah* and everything telling this story. Somebody would have had to pay, that's for sure." Paige was steaming for what had happened to her best friend as a young, innocent child.

"Well, Raymond paid. He went to jail," Tamarra sighed.

"Yeah, but not for what he did to you," Paige reminded her.

Tamarra shrugged.

"Like I said, you're better than me," Paige repeated.

"Should I take that as a compliment? That I'm better than you?"

"You most certainly should, because if it were me, either that brother of yours would be serving time for the crime he committed against me, or I'd be serving time for the crime I committed against him after the fact."

"Vengeance is mine saith the Lord." Tamarra recited the scripture that had kept her from doing something insane for all of these years. A scripture that had kept her from blowing her brother's brains out with her daddy's shotgun, kept her from sprinkling rat poisoning on his pizza, kept her, while he slept at night, from cutting off his—just kept her. She'd stood on God's Word long before she even knew she was standing on it. She'd been kept by the strength of Jesus long before she even knew just how strong Christ was.

Paige allowed her body to relax back in the chair. "Girl, you're right," Paige told Tamarra. She then looked upward. "Lord, I repent for having those thoughts. In Jesus' name, forgive me." Once again, there was silence. "So what are you going to do?" Paige finally asked. "You can't dodge your mom forever—or your brother. I mean, like you said, you really don't even know if he's still in jail. He could be out and show up on your doorstep."

A look of fear flushed over Tamarra's face. "You think so?" She stood and frantically began checking the kitchen windows to see if they were locked. She then headed to the back and then front door to make sure they were locked.

Paige got up and followed her. "Look, Tamarra, I don't mean to speak the spirit of fear into you. Just call your mother. I mean, maybe this is why you go through so much; you keep running. Stand up and face your giants or demons or whatever you want to call them. Just stop running. You're not supposed to turn your back on Satan when God has equipped you with every ounce of armor needed to defeat him. As a matter of fact, that rascal is already defeated."

With her hand on the lock after double checking to see

that it was, in fact, locked, Tamarra turned around to face her friend. "You're right."

"I am?" Paige had even surprised herself. Usually it was Tamarra who was giving her all the right advice. It was Tamarra who had been walking with the Lord far longer than she had. She never imagined that she had what it took to minister to someone who'd been a Christian much longer than she had.

"Yes, you are. I've lived a lie almost all of my life when it came to my brother. Well, the lie ends here." After speaking with such authority, Tamarra walked over to her house phone, picked it up and dialed her mother's number.

"Do you want me to go? Leave the room or something?" Paige whispered.

"No. You stay put. I may need your support like never before when all this is over." Tamarra listened through the receiver as her mother's phone rang in her ear.

"Hello."

Her mother's voice choked up Tamarra.

"Hello," her mother repeated.

Tamarra looked at Paige who was standing there with her hand on her shoulder. Paige gave her a reassuring nod.

"Mom?" Tamarra said.

"Honey, I'm so sorry." Her mother immediately began apologizing. "I'd told Raymond how well you and I had been getting along lately. We both figured that since you were in a forgiving mode after all these years, that perhaps it would be best if he came to you sooner than later. Raymond said he prayed every night in his jail cell, before we ever made the call to you on the three-way, that God would touch and soften your heart. He's a changed man now, Tamarra. Really he is. But perhaps it was just too soon. I'm so sorry. I really didn't want to mess up things between the two of us."

"It's okay, Mom," Tamarra told her mother, also relieved

at the fact that Raymond was still incarcerated. She was glad to hear her mother confirm that they'd been reaching out to her via three-way, that he wasn't out of jail living with her parents or anything. She didn't know if she could deal with the fact that her brother was out free walking the streets. It had very little to do with walking in fear and everything to do with her feeling as if he never deserved to be free to walk the streets again.

"It's not okay. I pushed you. It was too soon. I should have just been blessed by the fact that you had forgiven me and left that alone."

"Did you say blessed?" Tamarra asked her mother, confused. She'd never known her mother to use that type of talk in reference to herself, church talk that is. Her mother didn't even attend church.

"Yes, I did. I said blessed. It may sound strange for you to hear me talk like that, but your forgiving me was nothing short of a blessing. I knew the day you decided to forgive me that there must be a God. No force on this earth could have gotten you to do that after all of these years. I knew this God you served must have been a mighty force if He could get you to forgive me. I felt as though I needed to thank Him personally. So that following Sunday morning, I found me the nearest church house to go give my thanks in. I've even visited the church a couple more times since then. I don't go every Sunday, but I did finally crack open that Bible that's been sitting on my coffee table for show all these years."

Both Tamarra and her mother let out a chuckle.

"Grandma would be proud, God rest her soul," Tamarra said, knowing that Bible had been a gift from her maternal grandmother to her mother as a wedding present. The inscription on the inside stated such. But not once had Tamarra ever witnessed her mother read it.

"Yes, she would," her mother agreed.

Tamarra and her mother spent the next two hours or so on the phone chatting like old girlfriends catching up. They talked about things they'd never talked about before. Tamarra even shared with her mother the situation with Maeyl and his newly discovered daughter.

It wasn't until Tamarra had gotten off the phone and retreated to her master bath to take a shower that she realized Paige had left. She had been so engrossed in her and her mother's conversation that she didn't notice Paige tip-toe out of the door. Not sure how much of the conversation Paige had heard, she made a mental note to call her in the morning to update her. If she could help it, she never wanted to keep any more news from her best friend again, good or bad. And as private as she'd kept the tales of her childhood, she had to admit that finally sharing the gist of her story with Paige had been like therapy, a release.

As the water droplets made their way down Tamarra's body, she was glad that she and her mother had gotten on good terms again. As for her brother, she still didn't want any parts of him—not yet—not now. Little did Tamarra expect, though, there was one part of him that was about to surface whether she wanted it to or not.

Chapter Thirty

It was Saturday afternoon as Lorain and Unique sat inside McDonald's watching Unique's children play on the indoor playground equipment. They hadn't met to discuss Single's Ministry business or anything like that. Lorain had just decided out of the blue to call Unique and ask her if she could take her and the children to lunch at McDonald's.

With so much going on in Lorain's life right now with her mother marrying Broady and all, she needed to get her mind off of that situation and focus on happier things. For some reason, the interaction of Unique and her children made her happy. Just watching those kids with their bright, well-behaved selves, seemed to put a smile on Lorain's face and allow her to lose herself in her own childhood, the days of playing with cousins. Besides that, Lorain's conscience had been bothering her regarding the time she refused to front Unique the money to get the children McDonald's meals for lunch. At least now that was one thing she could get off of her conscience.

"They are so cute," Lorain said to Unique, eating a French fry while admiring the children. "I can't believe they are so well-mannered, the way they talk and pray."

Unique looked at Lorain as she sipped on her strawberry milkshake. In all honesty, she didn't know whether to take Lorain's words as a compliment or not. "Why do you act so surprised? I mean, how did you expect them to act?"

Hearing the edginess in Unique's voice, Lorain made an

attempt to clean up her statement. "Oh, I didn't mean it like that. It's just that I expected them to be—well, you know how kids like that act. Single mom, different daddies, grew up in the projects, now living with an auntie. Just seems like a cha-otic life, so I guess I just expected them to reflect it."

It was a failed attempt on Lorain's part by Unique's stan-dard. Unique slammed her milkshake on the table. It caused Lorain to jump, then turn her attention from the children and to Unique.

"Why do you do that?" Unique said in a soft, broken tone. Her initial thoughts were to get loud and ghetto, like she sometimes did—okay, often did. But she suspected that that was the type of behavior Lorain expected out of her, out of her children, so she restrained herself and refrained from act-ing in such a manner.

"Do what?" Lorain shrugged as if she hadn't just, in so many words, put Unique and her children down. Although that had not been Lorain's intentions, she had, in fact, insulted Unique.

"Act like you're better than me and my kids," Unique an-swered. "You act like you are some high and mighty Mary the virgin just because I have all these kids and stuff and you don't have any?" Unique didn't wait for Lorain to reply before she continued as she stared over at her children playing without a care in the world. "So what that we're living with my sister while you're living in a nice little condo, townhouse, whatever you call it. Is that why you think you are so much better than us? Or do you really think you are better than me? Perhaps you don't at all. Perhaps you just want me to believe that you are better than me by always trying to put me down. You're trying to make me feel inferior to you. Put me down while you're lifted up, huh? Well, sweetheart, it's not working."

"Unique, I—" Lorain started, but Unique was quick to cut her off.

"Do you think this is the life I wanted for myself? For my children?" Unique's voice was starting to crack. "I mean, what little girl really sits in front of her mirror playing dress up and tells herself, 'When I grow up I want three kids with three baby daddies, to be on welfare, living in somebody else's house?'"

Lorain opened her mouth to speak again, but Unique was quick to cut her off again.

"This here is a curse. It's a curse that I'm trying to break. When I'm up in New Day praising and worshiping and falling out at the altar, it's not for show. It's not for God to bless me with a new car and a house of my own. It's to break the curse. And before you get it twisted, it's not my children that are the curse, but just my entire lifestyle. I mean, my mama got a bunch of kids and we all got different daddies. My sisters and brothers have all kinds of kids by different baby daddies and mamas. Heck, my twenty-six-year-old sister is about to be a grandmother."

Lorain gasped as she looked at Unique with shock.

"Yeah, that's right, you heard me. But what would a diva like you know about that? With all of your clothes and designer shoes? You were probably born with a silver spoon in your mouth. If you found a food stamp from back in the day, you probably would have thought it was Monopoly money." Unique snickered. "So now, knowing what you know about me and my family, I bet you can really turn your nose down at me. That's the kind of stock I come from. Or at least that's the stock I got throwed away into." Unique had this far off look in her eyes.

"What do you mean thrown away into?" Lorain asked, curiosity probing her to do so.

"They ain't blood. The family I grew up with, they ain't my blood."

Unique gave Lorain a look, debating whether or not she should share with her the story she was about to tell. But after deciding she'd already told her too much anyway, she decided to go for the gusto, really give Lorain something to talk about.

"See, my moms used to babysit for the woman and her husband who lived next door to her," Unique started. "It was a double family housing unit. My mom lived on the left and the woman and her husband lived on the right. The couple was my foster parents. I got placed with them when I was four months. Before that I had been in the system since birth, after some man found me in a trashcan."

Lorain sat frozen, hanging onto Unique's every word, as Unique shared the details of her life with her.

"I stayed with them until I was three years old." Unique looked to the floor as if the details she were about to give were painful to recollect. "The woman and her husband paid my mom to keep me for two weeks while they went out of town to visit relatives in one of their hometowns. One of them, I can't really remember which one, landed a good job offer while they were there. It was an offer that evidently they couldn't pass up. After talking it over, the couple decided to make the move, to relocate, but they didn't want to take me with them. At first they were going to just give me back to the State, but by the same token, they didn't want so easily to give up that monthly check they were receiving to care for me. So they made a deal with my moms."

"What kind of deal?" Lorain was almost afraid to ask, but once again, curiosity had forced her to.

"Well, as luck would have it, their luck, they'd been assigned a new caseworker while they were away. It was some woman who was brand new on the job, who had never met my foster parents before. To make a long story short, the couple bribed my mom into keeping me by offering her a piece of the pie. So when it was time for the social worker to come check up on me, my moms pretended to be the woman. She watched for the social worker to show up the day of their appointment. She met her on the doorstep and convinced her that somehow the wrong address had gotten on the paperwork, that it was the unit on the left and not the unit on the right that she needed to be coming to.

"The social worker penciled in my moms's address and said she would change it in the system when she got back to the office. Well, she did, so a check steadily came to my moms's address. She, in turn, sent half of it off to the foster parents and kept the other half for herself. I don't know how many years that went on. All I know is that I got throwed away by the system too."

"How so?" Lorain asked.

"That social worker never came back. She called a couple of times because I remember my mom telling her that her husband was away working and unable to talk or whatever. Of course my mom didn't have a husband, so I knew it was just her lying to the social worker. So much time passed and everything appeared to be kosher, I guess, as far as the system was concerned. Eventually the social worker stopped coming or calling, got fired and another social worker was never assigned or something. But nonetheless, the checks still came and that's all that mattered to my moms." Unique shook her head. "I found out by my older sister that my moms had written my foster parents a letter telling them that the State had taken me back. That way she no longer had to send them half of the money anymore and was able to keep all of the checks for herself."

"How was it that your mother could even cash the checks? Didn't they have the foster mother's name on it?"

"Oh. Before the woman and her husband packed up and left for good, she let my mother use her social security card and birth certificate to get a picture ID with my moms's face on it. Cashing those checks wasn't a problem, especially at the little check cashing place my moms always went to to get it cashed. They welcomed government checks of any kind."

Lorain shook her head. "All that for a lousy monthly check. I can only imagine what you thought of your moms and the foster mother once you found out."

"Oh, I ain't got no beef with them," Unique said nonchalantly and to Lorain's surprise. "They found a hustle, and they freaked it. It's that dirty witch who threw me away in the first place that I have a problem with." Unique stared off into a daze as her jaw tightened. This was the first sign of anger Lorain had seen Unique express since she began confiding in her. "My life might have turned out so different hadn't she thrown me away in the first place. Coward!" Unique shook herself out of her daze, then stood up. "So you can see why I don't need someone like you always looking down your nose at my kids like they trash or something. It's their mama who is the one that's trash. Or at least my mama thought I was trash anyway. She threw me away like I was. So the last thing I need is someone like you making my kids feel like they ain't nothing." On that note, Unique walked over and gathered her children and headed toward the exit door.

"Wait! Where are y'all going?"

"Home," Unique said.

"Look, Unique, it's not like that. Let me just take you home, and we can talk. I really think we need to talk." Lorain started to gather her purse and keys. "I believe God—"

Unique put her hand up. "You can go play church with somebody else. Me and my kids would rather walk," Unique said in a snappy tone.

Before Lorain could insist on giving Unique and her children a ride home, they were out the door.

"You okay, ma'am? Should we call somebody?"

Lorain looked up to see the manager of McDonald's standing over her with a concerned look on her face.

"Here you go." The manager extended a few napkins to Lorain.

Lorain was confused as to why the woman would be handing her a handful of napkins until she realized that tears had been pouring out of her eyes and that her nose was running profusely. Unbeknownst to her, it had been ten minutes since Unique and her children had left the restaurant. She'd been sitting there the entire time in shock, crying and heaving.

"Thank you." Lorain accepted the napkins from the manager. "I'll be fine. Can you just tell me where your restroom is so I can go get myself together?" Lorain let out a nervous and embarrassed chuckle before the manager directed her toward the restroom.

She got up and made her way into the women's restroom. She stood in the mirror and began to wipe her face with the napkins given to her by the manager. As she looked at herself in the mirror, her face transformed into the scared little girl she remembered staring at in the restroom mirror at Crestview Middle School when she was only thirteen years old.

"God, I now know what this is about," she whispered as fresh tears fell down her face. For the first time, Lorain knew why God had allowed her and Unique to cross paths. Now she only hoped He would tell her what to do next.

Chapter Thirty-one

"Are you sure you can do this?" Mother Doreen asked her sister as she gripped her hand. "I can go in and do it if you'd like me to."

"No, no," Bethany said softy. "I can do it. It may be the last thing I ever get to do for him, but it's the least I can do for him. To stand up and say, 'That's my husband,'" Bethany said proudly. "I know I probably wasn't much of a wife while he was—" Bethany's words trailed off and her tears trailed down her face.

"Now, now," Pastor Davidson said as he and his wife stood with Mother Doreen and Bethany in the corridor of the lowest level of the hospital. Pastor Davidson said he'd tried to phone Pastor Frey because he knew he'd want to be there, but all he'd gotten was his voice mail. "It's not your fault that you were in and out of the hospital. You were the best wife you could be."

Bethany shot Pastor Davidson a look that could almost kill. "I wasn't, and you know it," Bethany replied, with disdain in her voice. "What good was I to him always laid up in the hospital?" She turned to face her sister. "Like you've always told me from the jump, I needed to walk in my healing." She buried her face on her sister's shoulder. "I should have walked in it. I should have walked in my healing and been a better wife to my husband," Bethany cried.

"It's okay," Mother Doreen said as she stroked Bethany's hair. "It's okay." After a few more moments, Bethany pulled away from her sister, and Mother Doreen asked the initial question once again. "Are you sure you can do this?"

"Yes, yes," Bethany said as she regained her composure. "I can do it." She looked up at the doctor and the two police officers who'd showed up at her doorstep less than an hour ago to tell her that her husband's truck had been in a fatal accident and that he was believed to be the fatality, the body pulled from the burning truck. After Bethany came to after a few minutes of being unconscious, the police asked if she could come to the hospital and identify the body. They warned her that it was pretty much burned beyond recognition, but that they'd retrieved items and belongings that might have been able to help her confirm that it was him. If she weren't able to confirm, their next and only option would be to retrieve his dental records. So now here she stood, prepared to do just that, identify the remains of her husband. "Where is he?"

"Right this way," the doctor said, taking Bethany by the elbow.

Halfway to the big glass window that was the final destination, Bethany stopped in her tracks and turned back to look at her sister. "Come with?" she said.

Mother Doreen smiled at the words. Se remembered her baby sister using those words more than once whenever Bethany was trying to get Mother Doreen to allow her to "go bye-bye" with her when they were younger. "I'll come with," Mother Doreen replied as she joined up with her sister. A few seconds later, Pastor Davidson and First Lady watched as Bethany cried and slivered down to the floor, yelling the word, "Nooooooooooooo!"

"Baby, aren't you up and getting ready for church yet?" Mother Doreen asked her niece as she peeked inside the cracked door to Sadie's room.

Sadie was lying in bed on her back, staring up at the ceiling. It had only been less than a week since Uriah's funeral, and Sadie had been taking her father's death quite hard. Although she hadn't yet returned to school, Mother Doreen thought it would be a good idea if the family at least went to Sunday worship. It was obvious since church started in less than an hour that Sadie thought otherwise.

"I'm not going to church today." Sadie's tone said that it wasn't up for discussion. "And to keep it real, I'm not going next Sunday, or the Sunday after that, or the Sunday after that either."

Mother Doreen sighed and entered the room. "Look, baby," Mother Doreen said as she walked over and sat down on the bed next to Sadie, "I know you miss your father and that you are probably asking that million dollar question: 'Why did God let my daddy die?' but I assure you that God doesn't make any mistakes."

"Tsk." Sadie rolled her eyes and turned her back to her aunt. Her vivid disrespect shocked Mother Doreen. "Maybe God doesn't make mistakes, but His children sure do make a heck of a lot of them—way too many for me to want to be one of His children too." Sadie sat up in bed. Before Mother Doreen could even ask what Sadie was referring to, Sadie freely gave her the answer. "Do you think just because I don't say anything that I don't see what's going on around this place?"

With raised eyebrows, Mother Doreen replied, "Look, I understand what you're going through, child, but don't be talking to me like I'm one of your little homegirls, a'ight?" Mother Doreen said with a sassy attitude to reflect that she was just hip enough to know that she was being disrespected by the way her niece was coming at her.

Ignoring her aunt's contempt, Sadie continued in her same disrespectful tone. "It's just like in church. Yeah, us younger kids might joke around, talk and pass a note here and there while pastor is preaching. We might even laugh at Sister So-and-So who's singing off key, but we hear and see everything that's going on. Us kids could tell you everything Pastor taught on while the grown ups thought we weren't paying attention." Once again, Sadie gave off a tsk sound. "You grown folks always talking about how God is in the midst of everything. Well, if He's been in the midst of everything that's been going on around here and in that church, then I don't want any parts of Him." She folded her arms adamantly and flopped back down on her bed. She then lightly mumbled, "No wonder Hudson got a girl pregnant."

"What?"

The loud voice forced both Sadie and Mother Doreen to turn their heads toward the bedroom doorway, the direction from which the voice had come.

"Did you say—" Bethany grabbed her two month baby bump and gasped, "—that your brother—" she gasped again, "—got a girl pregnant?"

Bethany had already shared with everyone the information she'd known since two weeks after she'd missed her last period, that she was pregnant. She couldn't have hidden it much longer anyway, even if she'd wanted to. Due to her small, petite, thin frame, even though she was only a little bit pregnant, it was still obvious that she was with child.

Of course, prior to Bethany letting the cat out of the bag, Mother Doreen had already suspected as much, but Bethany had refused to confirm it since a part of her hadn't known exactly what she was going to do about the pregnancy. She'd never been an advocate for abortion or pro-choice. She'd always been pro-life without wavering, that was until she turned up pregnant at a time and an age in her life when the last thing she wanted was another child. She understood perfectly that split second thought Sara Palin spoke of when learning she was pregnant with her last child. But with the recent death of

Bethany's husband, being the cause behind the loss of another life was something she was not going to be a part of. An abortion was out of the question.

"I think you heard her right," Mother Doreen replied to her sister's query. "I think we both heard the child right." Mother Doreen hadn't taken her eyes off Sadie since the words had escaped from her mouth. She prayed that if she stared at her long enough, the words would find their way back in. That it wouldn't be so; that she wasn't about to be a great aunt. That her sister wasn't about to become a grandmother.

Sadie threw her hands up in the air. That secret was out now too. Hudson had just shared with Sadie the night before the fact that he'd gotten the girl he had been dating pregnant. He made Sadie promise that she wouldn't tell anyone, but Sadie knew her brother. She knew Hudson well enough to know that he knew she couldn't keep a secret to save her life. He was only telling her because of the very fact that he knew she would blab. Sadie telling the secret would let him off the hook from having to tell their mother. He figured that this way, by the time his mother confronted him about it, she'd already have had her initial outburst of anger and would perhaps go a lot easier on him than she would have had he been the bearer of such news.

"Oh, Jesus!" Bethany cried out.

"Bethany, honey, sit down." Mother Doreen immediately ran to the aid of her sister, guiding her over to the chair at Bethany's work desk. "Are you okay? Can I get you some water or something?"

"Heck no, I ain't okay," Bethany said, breathing deeply, still rubbing her belly. "Did I just hear that my seventeen-year-old son is going to be a—going to be a—a—"

"A daddy?" Sadie finished her mother's sentence. "That's exactly what you heard. Looks like little Frey the second there is going to have a playmate around here." Sadie laughed sarcastically.

Both Bethany and Mother Doreen's mouths dropped open in complete shock.

"Like I said," Sadie snared at Bethany, "I know what's going on around here. Daddy might not have because he never stayed around long enough to figure things out, but I'm not a fool. I may not be the brightest bulb on the string of lights, but I'm smart enough to figure out that Pastor Frey has been sniffing around you, Mama, way more than Daddy has. So when you turned up pregnant, I did the math. Either that baby is Pastor Frey's, or you're another candidate for the Immaculate Conception, because it sure as heck can't be Daddy's."

Bethany covered her mouth with her hand and began to shake her head in shame. She'd been so tangled up in the covers of the messy bed she'd made for herself, that she never stopped to think for one minute that her children had an inkling of what was going on.

Sadie chuckled at the surprising look on her mother's face. "Yeah, I thought so."

It was evident that Sadie was directing her hurt at the loss of her father toward her mother. She had to blame someone, and from the sounds of things, Bethany and God were running a tight race. Mother Doreen was sympathetic with her niece's pain, but still, she wasn't having it.

"Do you think this is funny, little girl?" Mother Doreen spoke in a tone in which her niece had never heard her speak. Her voice was loud with much authority.

To Sadie, this was uncharacteristic of her Aunt Doreen. All of a sudden, there was something different about her aunt's demeanor; like she meant business. The woman she was looking at now seemed to have a no nonsense aura about her. "Do you?" Mother Doreen said sternly as she marched back toward Sadie.

"No, ma'am," Sadie said. She cowered down at first, but then it was like whatever had gotten into her aunt had gotten into her also. She lifted her head and puffed out her chest. Her shoulders were straight as she challenged Mother Doreen with her eyes. "But are you even surprised, Auntie, that Hudson's in the predicament he's in? I mean, look at the predicament his own mother is in."

Bethany gasped. "Sadie, trust me, you have no idea what you're talking about." She'd not wanted her daughter to know that her cruel words were getting to her, but the tears that dared to fill her eyes and roll over her bottom lid gave her away. Bethany was hurt. Mother Doreen was infuriated.

"Look, child, grieving or not, I will not allow you to disrespect your mother like that," Mother Doreen scolded. "The Bible says to honor thy—"

"Blah, blah, blah." Sadie covered her ears as if she didn't want to hear it. "I don't care about that Bible or God anymore. Look where it's all gotten this family! We're like some trashy chick lit novel turned *Lifetime* movie. Starring Bethany the whoremonger and co-starring Doreen, the Bible toting sister who—"

Before Mother Doreen knew it, her hands were on her niece's wrists, snatching her hands away from her ears. Sadie was in shock as her auntie gripped her wrists with a death grip. Sadie tried to snatch away, but Mother Doreen was locked down on her like a parking boot on a car with ten unpaid parking tickets.

"Reen!" Bethany said hysterically at the now physical altercation that was taking place between her sister and her fourteen-year-old daughter.

Mother Doreen and Sadie were so involved in their tussle, that they never even saw Bethany leap up from the chair, trip over the throw rug at the foot of Sadie's bed, and land flat on her stomach.

Chapter Thirty-two

"Daddy, can I get dessert?" Sakaya asked Maeyl as the two of them, along with Tamarra sat in Family Café.

"What do you think, Tamarra? Should I let her? Is she a clean plater?" Maeyl teased Sakaya. He was making every effort to include Tamarra in their little playful venture.

Tamarra subconsciously rolled her eyes in her head. While some women would have admired a black man doing everything he could to form a bonding relationship with his little girl, Tamarra was sickened by it, and embarrassed, and disgusted. She was ashamed as well, ashamed for feeling this way toward the little girl. Or was it toward Maeyl? Or was it toward the entire situation altogether? She didn't know. All she did know was that she was not doing too well coping with the cards she'd been dealt.

Tamarra had been pretty distant from Maeyl. He thought it was because of the developing circumstances of him finding out he had a three-year-old daughter that he never knew about. And indeed it was. But it was also the fact that Tamarra had been dealing with the situation involving her mother and jailed brother. Now that that situation seemed to be somewhat under control, she knew it was time she faced this one as well.

When she had called Maeyl yesterday and suggested the three of them catch the latest Disney animated flick and a bite to eat, he'd at first declined.

"Sakaya is just now getting used to having me as her daddy," he'd told Tamarra over the phone. "I don't know if introducing her to the woman in her daddy's life is such a good idea right now."

As soon as he'd said the words, Tamarra recalled his support in the Single's Ministry meeting of a single parent waiting three months before introducing their children to the person they are dating. She assumed the same applied in their situation. When she'd replied to the rejection with, "Then I guess I'll ask you again in what, three months?" Maeyl quickly sensed her hurt feelings. That's when he decided to go ahead and give it a shot. So now here the three of them were: Daddy, daughter and . . . the girlfriend.

"Tamarra, what do you think?" Maeyl repeated when he didn't get a response from Tamarra. "Tamarra, is Sakaya a clear plater? Tamarra?"

"Oh, huh? What? I'm sorry," she apologized. "What did you say?" Tamarra's mind had wandered off just that quickly. She'd been too busy looking around the restaurant to see who was in there, who was there pointing and laughing at her. Poor Tamarra keeps hooking up with all these men with these babies' mamas. She could just look at their moving lips and know those were the words they were speaking. And she didn't blame them. Heck, she was thinking it too. She was uneasy, uncomfortable, and embarrassed. She could have kicked herself for even making the suggestion that they do a group thing in the first place.

"You should do what my mom always tells me to do," Sakaya suggested to Tamarra. "You should put on your listening ears. My mommy takes her hands, puts them in her pocket, pulls them out, and then places them on my ears." The little girl demonstrated on her father. "I'm sure she has some extra ones that you can have. She has lots of them." Sakaya smiled at Tamarra. "I'm sure my mommy won't mind sharing her stuff with you. She's already sharing Daddy."

Even in trying to force a smile, Tamarra couldn't. Just the

thought of that Sasha woman created a brewing sensation in Tamarra's stomach. The idea of that woman sharing anything with Tamarra, even a set of make believe ears, let alone her man, made her temperature rise.

"Can you two excuse me for a minute?" Tamarra asked. "I need to go to the little girl's room."

"As big as you are?" Sakaya asked. "You should probably go to the ladies room. That's where my mom always goes."

Tamarra really did need to go to the bathroom now because if that child mentioned her mother one more time, she was going to puke."

Chuckling at his daughter's comment, Maeyl said, "Go on, honey. We'll be waiting out here for you. I'm going to order Sakaya some dessert."

Tamarra smiled and made a beeline toward the bathroom. She couldn't get inside soon enough. She leaned over the sink, balancing herself with her arms as she stared down into the face bowl. She closed her eyes and shook her head. "Lord, what am I doing?"

"Something you have no business doing," a voice replied, "and on top of that, something you don't want to be doing."

For a minute there, Tamarra thought she finally had proof that God was a woman, but then she opened her eyes and looked up to see that the female voice she'd just heard had come from Zelda.

"Excuse me?" Tamarra said.

"You just asked the Lord what you were doing," Zelda reminded her. "Well, I guess He decided to use a wretch like me to come on in here and provide you with the answer." Tamarra remained silent. "Yeah, I saw you out there." Zelda nodded toward the bathroom door. "You looked as uncomfortable as a plus size woman whose girlfriends haven't told her she's fat, so she's still shopping in the Misses department."

Tamarra couldn't help but let out a laugh. "Zelda, you sure

do have a way with words. I guess that's what's missing up in New Day now that you're gone. I used to love when you had altar duties. You'd make it plain, my sister, that's for sure. Sure do wish you were still attending."

"Oh, no. Don't you dare try to turn the tables," Zelda said, shooing her hand. "God sent me in here to minister to you, not the other way around." Zelda stood next to Tamarra, leaning backward against the sink. "So why is it that you're out there trying to play step-mommy when you just ain't got it in you?"

"Excuse me?" This time Tamarra was offended.

"Oh, girl, please don't act like I just offended your character. You know I'm speaking the truth. And believe me, ain't nothing wrong with it. Some of us women are just not cut out to be step-mama. It's either our children or nobody's children. Ain't no sin in it. You have to love that child because it's one of God's commandments, but you don't have to be her step-mommy. And you can still love Maeyl, but it don't mean you have to be his wife." Zelda paused to allow the words she had just spoken to sink into Tamarra's brain. "Ain't nothing wrong with y'all going back to just being friends."

As the words saturated her mind and heart, Tamarra lowered her head. "But I want so badly to be that man's wife." She pointed toward the door that separated them from the dining area of the restaurant. "He's a good man—a man that I love. And Zelda, I thought I'd never love again after divorcing my husband of fifteen years. I really felt that Maeyl was the man God had for me to take away all of my pain and bitterness."

"Then I guess that was your first mistake. See, God's Word says that He sent us a comforter by way of the Holy Spirit. The Holy Spirit is our piece of God here on earth and our peace in God. So you looked toward a man to restore you instead of the person the Bible says is a restorer. No wonder God's removing Maeyl from your life."

"What? What do you mean removing him from my life?"

"Don't be in denial, Tamarra." Realizing that her from the hip manners were probably too hard for Tamarra's fragile state right now, Zelda toned down her disposition. "Look, Tamarra," she placed her hand on Tamarra's shoulder, "you owe it to that man to be real. You don't want to deal with that daughter of his no more than Elizabeth Edwards wants to deal with that baby John Edwards is accused of fathering."

In the midst of wanting to break down and cry, Tamarra chuckled at Zelda's last comparison.

"You know I'm right, and you know it's wrong for you to pretend that you do. Girl, we can't all be Tina Turner and take in Ike's kids when the mamma drops them off on the doorstep. It don't mean we don't have a heart. It means we are following our heart. I know plenty of women who try to hide their true feelings for the sake of keeping the man, but it ain't right. It ain't fair, and it ain't right. Don't you be one of those women. Sooner or later your true feelings will surface, and it will hinder that man's relationship with his daughter. He'll be too busy trying to walk on eggshells around you to give that little girl all the love and attention she needs from her daddy. Too many step-mothers and girlfriends control their man's relationship with the children he had from other relationships. Now that is what should be the sin. So don't be ashamed or think that you are less than a loving Christian woman of God just because you don't want to take on a relationship with a man who has children by another woman. It's those women out there who are faking it who should be ashamed."

Tamarra sniffed as she took in the Rhema word Zelda was delivering. "God sure can use you in His ministry to do kingdom work. You should consider coming back to New Day, or any church for that matter," Tamarra said to Zelda as Zelda handed her a tissue to wipe away the few tears that had dropped from her eyes.

"Tamarra, yes I know what the Bible says about fellowshipping among those with like minds, etc. But think about it, I didn't have to be a member of New Day or any other church in order for Him to allow me to operate in His ministry. This right here, dear, is kingdom work. No offense, Tamarra, because I know you mean well, but it's Christians like you that make sinners like me believe the only place a sinner can get saved is in the church house and by the preacher man. God meets us in the very place of our need." Zelda looked around. "Even if it's in the toilet stall."

The two women cracked up laughing and embraced.

"Thank you, Zelda. Thank you so much," Tamarra smiled as she cleaned her face. "You told me exactly what I needed to hear. Exactly what I already knew inside. Now how am I gonna go out there and tell the man I love?"

Chapter Thirty-three

For the past week, Lorain had pretty much been estranged from her mother. With the new development involving Unique, she just couldn't deal with her mother, not right now. There were too many pieces of the puzzle that she had to fit together. If everything fit the way she thought it would, the facts of her life would definitely turn out to be stranger than fiction.

"God, this is too much," Lorain said in a low whisper as she surfed the Internet, something she'd been doing for the past three days. She'd keyed in her credit card number more times than she swiped it on a weekend shoe shopping binge in an attempt to find out the needed information to verify what she thought to be true.

Personally, her gut feeling was all she needed to go by, but if she were ever going to speak on what she felt to be true, she knew that she would need tangible evidence. She'd gone to the *Columbus Dispatch* website and paid for some archived news articles that could verify her claim. She'd even located a website that, for a modest fee, could give her personal information on individuals such as their current address, previous address, even their neighbor's address.

"Bingo!" Lorain exclaimed after finding the final nail in the coffin. Finally, after three days of online researching, not only had she been able to verify her own untold story, but she'd retrieved and printed enough information to verify how her life related to Unique's as well—and to Mr. Leary's.

Everything seemed to be coming together in a way that could

have only been orchestrated by God. And now that Lorain had all this information at her fingertips, she had no idea what to do with it.

"Now what, God?" she asked as she hit the button that would initiate the printing of the last document she had researched.

Lorain slowly stood up and straightened out her aching back. The pain was due to sitting for so many hours in her computer chair. She began walking it out by pacing the floor and thinking—and thinking—and pacing. Deep in her soul, she knew what she should do, what she would want someone to do for her, but there was a part of her that was too ashamed and embarrassed to have to face the details of a past she was regretful of. How could she even fix her lips to tell anyone, including the main person who truly deserved to know?

Lorain stopped her pacing, then walked over to the printer after hearing the last page print off. She retrieved the pages from the print tray, held it in her hands, and looked at it for a minute. The nail in the coffin indeed. She made her way back to her desk and picked up the blue three prong folder she'd labeled "My Life." She placed it inside the folder, and then flung it back on her desk. It slid to the back of the desk and onto the floor. With the soreness in her back, she didn't feel like bending over to get it, so she decided to leave it there until she needed it. It would stay there, along with the other papers she'd collected for the last three days, until God ordered her next steps.

Deciding it was time she'd finally eat a decent meal, Lorain headed for the kitchen. She'd been so glued to her computer the last few days that she'd hardly eaten. She had been unable to tear herself away from the computer as it continued to spit out one piece of the puzzle after the next. She grabbed a couple of grapes from the fruit bowl and popped one in her mouth. As she opened the refrigerator, her doorbell rang. Looking outside her front room window, she noticed her mother's car in the driveway. She sighed and her shoulders slumped. Another unannounced visit from her mother couldn't be good.

"Hey, Mom," Lorain tried to say in a perky tone as she opened the front door. Popping the second grape in her mouth, she looked up, swallowed it whole and began choking. She tried to cough it up, but it was stuck in her throat. She hunched over in a ball with her hands gripped around her neck like she was trying to squeeze the grape up. She couldn't breathe.

"Oh dear God!" she heard her mother cry out. "I'll call 9-1-1!"

Lorain didn't know how much time was passing by, but it felt like forever and a day. The very air she breathed had been ripped from her in a matter of seconds. Just before she felt as though she were going to black out, she felt a presence behind her. She then felt arms around her. She felt fists gripped under her breasts. Next she felt a repeating pumping pressure. The grape hit the floor. She felt the arms release her.

"Are you okay?" was all she heard before she blacked out, hitting the floor and squashing the poor little grape.

"What happened?" Lorain asked in a groggy voice after coming to.

"You choked on a grape, honey, but you're okay now," Eleanor told her daughter as she stood over her with a smile on her face. She was delicately brushing her hands through Lorain's hair.

Lorain stared at her mother momentarily as if it had taken her a minute to figure out just exactly who she was. "Ma?"

"Yes, honey, it's me," Eleanor confirmed.

Next, Lorain's eyes darted around the room. "Where am I? What's going on?" All Lorain saw were white walls. She thought for a moment about where she could possibly be, and then began to panic. "Ma, what have you done? "I told you I wasn't that kind of crazy. And you go commit me to the hospital, all because I didn't want to go shopping with you?"

Eleanor allowed Lorain to ramble on before she stopped her. "Lorain, what are you talking about? It's been almost two weeks since we had that conversation. You're talking like we just had it."

"We did, didn't we?" A confused look flushed Lorain's face. Eleanor could tell that something wasn't right with her daughter.

"Hello, I'm Dr. Levington, the ER doctor on duty," the tall woman said as she entered the room with a clipboard in hand. She looked like she should have made her career in the WNBA.

"Hi, Dr. Levington." Eleanor stood and quickly approached the doctor. "What's wrong with my baby? I know my baby, and something ain't right."

"That's what I wanted to talk about." The doctor began flipping through the files. We took some X-rays of your daughter's head and an MRI—"

"Oh Lord. It's her brain. She's got brain damage or something, doesn't she?"

"Now, sweetie, calm down." Broady stood up from the chair he'd been sitting in over in the back corner of the room. He walked over to Eleanor and embraced her. "Calm down and just listen to what the doctor has to say."

"Ma, what's he doing here?" Lorain asked as she watched her mother be comforted by the man that had asked her to calm down. "Who is he?"

"What do you mean who is he?" Eleanor asked her daughter. "You know exactly who this is."

"Lorain, it's me, Broady," he said as he released Eleanor and looked at her. "You only met me briefly the other day, but I'm—"

Eleanor cut her fiancé off while charging toward Lorain.

She was pointing an accusing finger. "Oh, I see what you're doing, young lady." She then spoke to Broady while still charging at Lorain. "Don't even bother telling her who you are, Broady. She knows exactly who you are. You are the person who saved her life. If it weren't for the grace of God and you being there to give her the Heimlich maneuver, because the Lord knows I don't know how to do it, that grape would have killed her." She was now speaking to her daughter again. "But I know what you're up to. And don't even think for a minute this little game of yours is going to—"

"Please, everybody, just calm down," the doctor intervened. The doctor looked to Eleanor. "Ma'am, your daughter took a pretty hard fall and has suffered a minor concussion. Now that she has come to, I'd really like to run more tests, especially after what I've just seen. So I'm going to take the patient for some more testing."

Upon doctor's orders, Lorain was taken from the hospital room. Both Eleanor, who was still skeptical, and Broady had lunch in the hospital cafeteria, then returned to Lorain's room where they waited. A couple of hours later, Lorain was returned to the room, the doctor returning shortly after that.

"So doctor, what's the verdict?" Eleanor didn't beat around the bush.

The doctor didn't beat around the bush either. "She's not playing a game," the doctor replied. "From the results of all the testing we've done, more than likely your daughter is dealing with a selective memory," she said to Eleanor.

"Selective memory?" Eleanor was confused.

"Yes, with selective memory, patients can remember certain things for the most part. It's usually traumatic events that they tend to forget." The doctor then looked over to Broady. "For some reason or other, she probably really has no idea who this man is."

Chapter Thirty-four

"Mother Doreen, I got here as soon as I could." Pastor Frey arrived at the hospital waiting area out of breath. "What's going on?"

"Excuse me for a minute, baby," Mother Doreen said to Sadie who she had been embracing and rocking in her arms the last half hour.

Sadie was a complete mess. All she kept saying the entire time she, her aunt, and her brother followed behind the ambulance was, "This is all my fault. This is all my fault." Mother Doreen was doing her best to comfort her niece and let her know that everything was going to be okay, and that no matter what the outcome, she had nothing to do with it. It was all in God's hands.

"Hudson, make sure you stay here with your sister," Mother Doreen told her nephew who was sitting next to them. "I need to go talk to Pastor Frey—" She paused and looked up at the partially distraught gentleman. While cutting her eyes at him, she said the word, "alone."

Mother Doreen got up and led Pastor Frey outside of the emergency room doors where the sun was shining and the birds were chirping on this beautiful, yet chilly, November morning.

"Mother Doreen," Pastor Frey pleaded while placing each of his hands on her shoulders.

Mother Doreen had to admit that there was something about Pastor Frey that she liked, his touch being one of them. There was something so sweet and gentle about him. For a minute there, she was even foolishly falling for him, but had prayed, gouged herself with blessed oil, and fasted for three days, asking God to remove the feelings she was having for him. Feelings that weren't part of the plan, she was sure.

She wanted God to keep her on the straight and narrow in order to fulfill her assignment there in Kentucky. It was clear that she suspected Pastor Frey of being up to no good with her sister, but for some reason, when the two of them were together, he acted like Bethany didn't even exist, never brought her name up or anything. But Mother Doreen knew she couldn't change her initial perception based on that. She was, in fact, wavering and doubtful, which is why she had to have the conversation she was about to have with Pastor Frey in order to clear things up once and for all.

"Please, tell me what's going on." Pastor Frey was frantic, as he had been ever since Mother Doreen called him on his cell phone just as he was about to enter the church. All he'd had time to do was wave down a fellow member and ask that they relay to Pastor Davidson what was going on; that he wouldn't be in church today in order to go see about Sister Bethany. "How is Sister Bethany? Is she okay?" All of a sudden a horrible thought entered his mind. "The baby—is everything okay with the baby?"

"I'm not sure if everything is okay with Bethany's baby," Mother Doreen said to him, considering no one had yet updated them on Bethany's condition. "Or should I say I'm not sure if everything is okay with Bethany's and your baby." She shook her shoulders free of his touch.

Pastor Frey turned beet red. But what Mother Doreen found most peculiar was the complete look of confusion on his face.

"Please, let's not play games, Pastor Frey. I'm way too old for that. And playing games is what you've been doing since I arrived. Playing games with my sister. Playing games with me. But I've figured you out. All you were trying to do was to be a distraction to me—get me all rallied up into thinking you had

an interest in me so that I wouldn't detect your interest in my
sister. Well, the game ends here, and from the looks of it, no
winner will be declared."

"You've got this all wrong," Pastor Frey said.

"Do I?" Mother Doreen leaned in close to Pastor Frey's ear.
"You and I both know that that baby ain't none of Uriah's,
God rest his soul. That's your baby, and you know it. I know
it too."

Just when Mother Doreen thought Pastor Frey couldn't
turn any redder, he did. He was as red as the devil is depicted
to be.

"Baby? My baby? Mother Doreen, what on God's green
earth are you trying to insinuate about me? Anybody who knows
me knows that I love the Lord. I delight in God's commandments." A stern and angry look covered Pastor Frey's face. "And
I abide by them. So for you to stand here and accuse me of
adultery, and even worse, creating a baby as a result of the act,
is nonsense!" Pastor Frey was all in Mother Doreen's case, but
she wasn't fazed.

"Humph." Mother Doreen rolled her eyes. She wasn't about
to fall for his well rehearsed act. Standing there acting like he
was none the wiser about what she was talking about. Versus
stand there and play that little game with him, she decided to
get right to the point, which is exactly what she'd intended to
do when she phoned him just forty-five minutes ago and told
him about Bethany's accident. It sure wasn't for him to run
up there to the hospital and act like he was there as part of his
ministerial duties. It was to finally lay the cards on the table,
which is exactly what she'd just done.

"Like I said, the game is over, Pastor Frey, and it's time for
you to follow the advice of John the Baptist and repent."

"You are making a mistake, a big mistake, Sister Doreen."
Pastor Frey said this with such conviction that Mother Doreen
almost believed him. "That baby your sister is carrying is not

mine. I would never do such a thing to Brother Uriah. He knew that about me."

"Well, he may have thought that all the sniffing you did around his wife was in the name of Jesus, but I know better."

"Believe me when I say I was only doing what God told me to do when it came to being there for your sister." A weird look suddenly appeared across his face as he hesitantly added. "What God *and* Pastor Davidson told me to do."

It was at that very moment when a spirit of discernment filled Mother Doreen like never before. Had she, in fact, been distracted? But not by the man whom all this time she'd thought had set out to do so?

Just then, Sadie, followed by Hudson, raced from the double doors.

"Mom's okay," Sadie cried out, "but the baby is gone!" Sadie fell into her aunt's arms, and the fight they'd had earlier had long been erased, washed away by each of their tears that fell and hit the pavement.

Chapter Thirty-five

"Hello," Tamarra answered the phone after seeing Maeyl's number on the caller ID.

"Hi, how are you?" Maeyl asked Tamarra in an upbeat tone.

"I'm good."

"Did you need something? I saw that you had called me twice. I was in prayer, and you know I don't answer my phones when I'm in prayer."

"Yeah, I figured you were."

"God is so good, Tamarra. He really is."

Maeyl was so perky that Tamarra almost wanted to change her mind about what she was about to do, what she was about to tell him. He hadn't been this happy since—since before finding out he had a daughter. Tamarra knew that Maeyl's total bliss had almost everything to do with the relationship he was forming with Sakaya. Tamarra knew she could never be as equally thrilled about the situation, which is why she had to break things off with Maeyl. The sooner the better. She knew she best do it now before she tried to kid herself and pretend she could go through with continuing a relationship with Maeyl.

"Well, you certainly sound blessed," Tamarra said. "Look, Maeyl, I was wondering if you could meet me at the park." For late November, the outdoors was beautiful and still had welcoming weather.

"Are you serious?" Maeyl questioned, still in a perky tone.

"Yes, is that a problem?"

"No, it was just that I promise on everything when I got out of prayer I was going to call you up and ask you if we could meet somewhere. The park will do just as fine. Why don't I call up Sasha and see if she'll let Sakaya—"

"Uh, Maeyl, I was kind of hoping it could just be me and you," Tamarra said as her skin crawled. She couldn't help it. Every time Maeyl reminded her that he had an extended family now, the green eyed monster showed itself. She was jealous. Jealous of the woman, jealous of the child, or both. She didn't know. She didn't care. She just knew right at that moment, with the way she was feeling, it only confirmed that she was about to do the right thing.

Maeyl paused. "Well, I kind of wanted to do it with Sakaya, but I suppose I could meet you alone. Can you give me about a half hour?"

"Sure," Tamarra said. "I'll see you then." Tamarra ended the phone call and sighed. This wasn't going to be easy. Breaking up with Maeyl, and then having to see him on a regular at church. Seeing him and Sasha and the child. Perhaps she'd just have to find some place to worship outside of New Day Temple of Faith. But for now, first things first. She went into the bathroom and sprinkled some water and setting lotion on her natural hair. She then went out to her car and headed toward the park, along the way practicing exactly what she was going to say to Maeyl.

"Yes!" Tamarra screamed. "Yes, Maeyl, I'll marry you." Those were far from the words she had practiced on the way to the park, but yet those were the words Tamarra had spoken. At the sight of the two carat diamond ring, Tamarra had forgotten all about the reason why she'd asked Maeyl to meet her at the park in the first place.

"She said yes!" Maeyl began to shout to total strangers that passed them by while they sat on the park bench. "She said yes." He then looked to Tamarra. "You have just made me the happiest man in the world. I knew you'd say yes. I just knew it. While I was praying earlier, when I missed your calls, I'd been praying about you, about us. I needed to make sure that what I was about to do—what my heart wanted so desperately to do —was the right thing. During prayer, I asked God to give me a sign. He didn't give me my answer right then and there, but I knew when I came out of my prayer room and saw that you had called, and then you asked to meet me at the park, I knew it was meant to be. It was at the park that I had envisioned proposing to you and you saying yes. Your calling me was my sign, Tamarra. This, us—" He held her hand he'd just placed the ring on. "We were meant to be."

A huge smile covered Tamarra's face as she watched tears form in the eyes of her husband to be.

"The only thing different than what I had envisioned," Maeyl continued, "was Sakaya being here."

Just at the sound of the child's name, Tamarra's smile faded. Maeyl was too busy telling the couple jogging by that Tamarra had said yes to his proposal to notice. Tamarra didn't know what it was that made her feel this way. The child had never done a thing to her, yet just the thought of her being the result of Maeyl's intimacy with another woman made her feel threatened. She never assumed Maeyl was a virgin. She was sure he'd slept with other women besides Sasha. But there was just something about a cute, little two and a half foot re-minder with French braids and beads on the end that she just couldn't stand. But then it dawned on her that she'd better get used to it because she had just agreed to marry the father of the cute, little two and a half foot reminder.

After spending another twenty minutes or so in the park, Maeyl and Tamarra each left toward their individual homes. The two agreed they'd take Sakaya out to dinner tomorrow and share the news with her together.

Tamarra returned home to find a car parked in front of her house with Maryland license plates on it. The only people she knew who would be visiting her from Maryland were her mother and father, but the sporty, little, red Honda wasn't the Chrysler 300 she knew her parents owned. Even if they had decided to get a new car and her mother not tell her, it sure wouldn't have been that hot rod.

The sun was almost all the way down, and with the tinted windows, Tamarra couldn't make out who the single occupant was that sat in the driver's seat. Instead of parking her jeep in her garage, Tamarra pulled up into the driveway and got out. The passenger of the Honda got out too.

"Aunt Tamarra?" the young, female driver called out.

Tamarra stood frozen in her tracks as the petite figure before her began walking in her direction. Tamarra hadn't seen the girl in ages, but she recognized her eyes, her skin complexion, and other tell tale signs. It was Raygene, Raymond's daughter. Tamarra's mother had given the girl her name, a name that Tamarra felt was too close to that of Raymond's, which is yet another reason why she never wanted to have a relationship with the child. Letting Raymond's daughter into her life would have meant having to acknowledge the fact that she even had a brother. She'd written them both off, but now here one of them was standing before her.

"Hi, Aunt Tamarra, it's me, Raygene. Sorry I didn't call first, but since you don't really know me from Adam anyway, I figured, what difference would it make?"

The beautiful, slender, bubbly girl stood before Tamarra looking every bit like her father. With such a warm spirit that shined even in that dark evening, the girl still resembled a dark past of Tamarra's life. One that prevented Tamarra from welcoming the girl with open arms.

"I used Mapquest to find you, and since it was on the way to where I'll be staying—"

"Staying?" Tamarra interrupted.

"Yes, I just transferred to a wonderful graduate program at Ohio State University. I'm going to be living in Columbus near the campus. Looks like we'll practically be neighbors now, living only an hour or so away from each other. Perhaps we can make up for lost time?" Raygene smiled. Tamarra didn't. "But then again, perhaps not. I mean, I'll be busy with my studies and all. And Granny says your catering business keeps you quite busy."

Tamarra remained silent.

Raygene could see that the wattage in her bright idea hadn't been powerful enough, as Tamarra wasn't the least bit enthused. "Well, it's late and my roommate is expecting me. I should probably get going. I just didn't want to pass family, you know, without at least stopping by to say hi."

Still, Tamarra said nothing.

"Well, it was good seeing you." Raygene dug into the purse that was on her arm. She pulled out a piece of paper and a pen, then began to write something down. "Here." She handed the paper to Tamarra. "This is where I'll be staying and my phone number. I'd love to hear from you if you ever get the time."

Tamarra looked down at the paper, but still said nothing.

"Anyway, like I said, I better get going. Hopefully you'll use the number." From the look on Tamarra's face and her complete silence, Raygene knew Tamarra would not be using her contact information. "Well, good-bye, Aunt Tamarra."

Tamarra watched the girl get back inside her car and drive away. She then got back inside her own car and hit the remote button to open the garage door. She pulled inside, all in somewhat of a daze. She got out of her car and headed inside, stopping at the trashcan on her way.

She looked down at the piece of paper in her hand. She then looked upward to God. She looked at the paper again before she threw it in the trash and went inside her house.

She knew forming a relationship with Raygene could possibly be a step toward complete healing and forgiveness, but it just wasn't something she was willing to do. Raygene was a part of Raymond, who was a part of her hurtful past. At that moment Tamarra decided for now she would leave her past behind her, all of it, and instead, move forward in her future with Maeyl. Whether she was making the right decision or not, only time would tell.

Chapter Thirty-six

It had been a few days since Lorain had been discharged from the hospital. Physically, she was well; mentally, she was well too, if the fact that she couldn't remember certain people and things didn't count.

The doctors concluded that Broady had saved Lorain's life by performing the Heimlich maneuver on her, but when he released her and she fell, the bumping of her head on the hard ground affected part of her brain. Although they couldn't diagnose just how long Lorain would suffer from this partial memory loss or if it was permanent, were certain that she was only remembering things and people that she wanted to. Her brain had suppressed things she most likely would want to forget.

It was Sunday, and Lorain had insisted on going to church. Eleanor thought that going to New Day would be too much for her since she would be trying to remember folks and things and all, so she talked her into going to visit Broady's church. Lorain was okay with that because what she did remember was that she loved the Lord and that He had been good to her. Surprisingly, she was okay with more than just going to church, but going to Broady's church. Considering she now only knew about Broady what her mother had told her, it probably shouldn't have been a surprise.

"What a lovely church," Lorain said as she entered into the sanctuary of the church with her mother. There was soft music playing and a few saints were at the altar praying. At

New Day, folks would have been chatting like they were in the halls of a high school catching up on all that had taken place over the weekend. At this church, they were setting the atmosphere, preparing the way for the Word of the Lord, Broady included.

As a leader, Broady was required to sit in the front couple of rows with all the leaders and ministers. They'd each arrived at church at least a half hour early for coffee and corporate prayer. From there they all headed straight for their posts. Their bishop's saying was that the devil ain't busy; the devil is simply doing what he's supposed to do, which is carry out his assignments. The devil ain't busy, he's just always at his post, in position to carry out such assignments. The saints should always do the same; be at their posts and in position to carry out their assignments.

"It is a lovely church indeed," Eleanor agreed. She especially loved the mauve, cream, and gold color scheme. And now there were Christmas poinsettias decorating the pulpit. The first time she visited the church she felt as though she were walking through heaven's gates. That's just how beautiful and powerful the anointing was in that place.

The usher at the door kept one gloved hand down to her side while extending the other arm out, giving the two women freedom to sit in any vacant chair. Eleanor chose two seats that were together in the fourth row. When the women sat down, they followed suit of the other saints and began to enter into prayer. When the musicians took their places behind their instruments and began to play live music, and when the exhorter began clapping her way to the microphone while speaking praises to God, all saints stood to their feet and joined in on the celebration of who God is.

From that point on, Lorain was in awe of how the service flowed. Everyone seemed to be in order and on one accord. From the outside looking in, Broady's church appeared to be the perfect church, but of course everyone knew there was no such a thing. Behind closed doors, every church had their isms and skisms. The praising and worshipping of the Lord seemed to go on for so long that Bishop really didn't need to give a message. God had spoken to each individual in that place. He had given them His Word personally, and on this given Sunday, God really didn't need to use earthly flesh to relay it.

The windows of heaven opened up, and glory just filled the sanctuary. It was a Holy Ghost experience indeed. When things seemed to settle down a bit, Bishop opened the altar to allow folks to step up and give testimonies. After a couple of people did, Bishop attempted to give a word, but a bolt of Holy Ghost power struck him, causing him to stomp the devil back and forth across the altar. At one point, he almost fell out, but fortunately, Broady was there to catch the bishop and help him keep his balance. Bishop's happiness in the Spirit seemed to be contagious as Broady began to dance in the Spirit upon touching his bishop.

Eleanor's eyes filled with tears as she shouted for Broady and the demons and devils he was stomping on. Lorain's face was covered with joy as she watched the man her mother was going to marry dance for the Lord. At first she was skeptical when she found out that her mother hadn't been dating him that long and was about to exchange nuptials with this man. But now, seeing the God in this man, Lorain could understand. Her mother needed someone like him in her life, a God fearing man to keep her on the straight and narrow. She knew her mother could be a firecracker at times.

As Lorain continued to watch Broady, the expression on her face turned from joy to horror. All of sudden things began flashing before her mental eye, things about Broady. There were newspaper articles that flashed before her eyes. The articles had pictures of him. She saw the words "Molestation," "School Girl," "Sexual Relations" and "Jail." She had a vision of court papers with Broady's name on it. Flashes of pictures of him on the computer screen came up. Lorain felt as though she were watching an eight millimeter movie. But she knew this wasn't a movie. She was confused at first, but then she realized that it might have been her mind reminding her of things, things that the doctor had told her she probably didn't want to remember, one of those *traumatic events*, she supposed.

Well, there was no doubt why she wouldn't have wanted to remember this if it were true. But it had to be true, right? Or how else would these visions have gotten into her head? It seemed so real, not like dejavu or anything. Not like her imagination was running wild. It seemed real.

The doctor had told Lorain that her complete memory may come back slowly, and that there was even a possibility that it could come back all at once. The doctor had also told her that some of the memories may be unpleasant. Well, these sudden memory flashes definitely fit the definition of unpleasant.

As Lorain looked over at her mother, she wondered that if these things were true about Broady, if her mother knew about them. "She couldn't possibly," Lorain mumbled to herself. There was no way her mother would know such things about Broady and yet was still going to marry him. There was no way Lorain would let her. "Mom? Mom?" Lorain said to her mother, who was too caught up in the Spirit to even acknowledge the voice of her daughter. "Ma?" This time Lorain nudged her mother.

"What, dear?" Eleanor almost had an attitude.

"My memory—I think—I think it might be coming back," Lorain told her. "But I'm not sure if what—"

"Oh hallelujah!" Eleanor started to shout after hearing only the first part of what Lorain had said, then cutting her off. "Praise God! Thank you, Jesus!" Eleanor began to dance and shout so hard, folks had to move out of her way so that she could get into the aisle. "Glory!" she shouted as tears poured from her eyes. "I'm a believer. God is everything everyone has claimed Him to be. He's a healer! He's a healer!" she shouted.

"Good Lord!" Bishop declared. "Sounds like we got another testimony that needs to be shared.

A couple of altar workers helped Eleanor up to the altar.

"Come on, sister, go ahead and speak on it," Bishop told her.

"Oh Lord! Oh Jesus!" Eleanor cried. She tried several times to speak about what Lorain had just told her, but every time she tried to say something regarding it, nothing but a praise came out. "Oh Lord, I can't do it. Let my daughter do it. It's her testimony anyhow," Eleanor said, out of breath.

If Lorain's face hadn't been horrified when those images had just popped in her head, it was certainly horrified now. *No she didn't*, is all her mind could say. "No, Mom, no," Lorain said, shaking her head. "I can't." She didn't want to. Even though she was ninety-nine percent sure those images held truth to them, there was still that one percent of confusion.

"Come on, sister. Don't be shy. Tell us what God did for you," the Bishop ordered.

Lorain still continued shaking her head, refusing.

"Tell 'em, daughter. Tell 'em how you lost your memory, and God just restored it, right here in this sanctuary." Upon Eleanor saying those words, the entire church, it seemed, began doing a praise shout and dance for what God had done for Lorain.

"Glory!" they shouted. "God is good. The God I serve is awesome. He's a healer!"

Once things calmed down a bit, Bishop said to one of the ushers as he handed him a microphone, "Go take this to the sister. She's too shy to come up front, so take the mic to where she is. God met her right there in her place of need, so surely you can too."

"Amen," the usher said as he made his way to Lorain and handed her the mic.

Lorain took the mic and just stood there without saying a word.

"Go on, baby, tell us what you remember," Eleanor insisted with a look that said, "Don't you make a liar out of me, child. Don't you embarrass me by acting like you really didn't get your memory back."

She stared at her mother. She then looked to Broady, and then back to her mother. She couldn't. She couldn't really tell them what she remembered. But it looked like she was going to have to. She knew God was present in that church today, and she wasn't about to stand before Him and lie.

"That man is not—he may not be—who you all think he is." Lorain couldn't believe she'd found the courage to let the words flow out of her mouth.

"Huh? What? Who? What man?" She could hear the confusion among the congregation.

Without looking directly at him, Lorain pointed to Broady. "Him, Broady. He's not the man you all think he is." Lorain looked to her mother. "Especially you, Mom. He may not be the kind of man you'd want to marry." There was still that one percent of doubt voicing itself.

Now Eleanor had a look of horror on her face. "Oh Lord, God done gave her her memory back, but now the devil done took her mind. Oh Jesus!" Eleanor said as someone had to hurry up and catch her in order to keep her from falling out.

"I'm sorry, Mom, but you forced me to have to do this," Lorain said. She stood there nervous as all get out, but convinced she was doing the right thing. "Broady is a child molester. I believe he's even been jailed for it, for having some type of sexual relations with a high school girl."

Lorain expected to hear the same confusing *Huh, what, and who's* she'd heard among the congregation just a moment ago, but they never came. She looked at her mother and expected to see her face covered with shock, but it wasn't. Lorain was the only one in the sanctuary with a confused look on her face.

The usher went to take the mic back from Lorain as he whispered, "Young lady, I think you should sit down now."

"No, let her finish," Broady insisted.

Lorain released the mic to the usher, a sign that she was finished. She'd said all that she had to say. She'd told all that she'd just remembered seeing.

The church was silent before Bishop finally spoke. "Sister?" he said to Lorain, "we know all these things about Brother Leary. He shared it with us when he joined our ministry five years ago after moving here from Phoenix. See, back in Phoenix—"

Broady put his hand up as if to stop the bishop from speaking. "Please, allow me, Bishop. It's my testimony; allow me to tell it; again." Broady stood down at the altar and faced the congregation. "Some of you already know my testimony, but for those of you who don't, I hope what I share may be able to help you or someone you know and love. The devil tormented me before about sharing this testimony with you all the first time, but now I'm especially glad that I listened to God and not Satan. Imagine how this moment might have turned out had I let the devil talk me out of it."

Broady looked to Eleanor. She shook her head and softly said to Broady, "Baby, you don't have to do this."

"Oh, but I do," Broady insisted as he continued. "See, I moved to Phoenix about twenty-something years ago or so just to start fresh. Wait, that's a lie. I moved to Phoenix because I was running, running from a situation that I thought if I ran far enough from, it would go away. I'd worked in the school system here in Ohio. In Phoenix I started off as a guidance counselor just like I had been here in Ohio. But just like here in Ohio, I found myself in another exact same situation with just a different girl. See, I had the urge for young women. Young girls. Under age girls. I was what most of you would call a pedophile—a pervert. In Phoenix I started having a relationship with a young girl. She told her parents about what I'd done to her, and the next thing I knew, her father was barging in my office, and I was looking straight down the barrel of a loaded shotgun.

"I swear—I mean, I promise, that my life flashed before my eyes. The father said a few choice and colorful words, calling me every low down dirty name in the book. Shortly thereafter his wife came in behind him. She was crying and asking him not to do it. But her husband was like a mad man. You should have seen the look in his eyes. That man wasn't going to leave until he blew my brains out. It was like slow motion, me watching his finger pull that trigger. All I remember is both me and his wife calling out at the same time, 'Jesus'!"

Broady's eyes filled with tears as he began to tremble. "I'd never been a praying man. I had never stepped a foot into church a day in my life except an occasional Easter Sunday here and there with my mom. But at that very moment I was made into a believer. I knew that simply by calling on the name of Jesus, my life had been spared. At the sound of the name of Jesus, the gun jammed. Through grace and mercy, knowing I was in the wrong, my life had still been spared. It was a second chance from God, an undeserving second chance. Without wasting tax payer's dollars on court cost, I pled guilty for what the father had accused me of doing to his daughter and went to jail willingly, without a trial, ready to serve my time."

Broady looked among the congregation. "But I was sick. I knew I was sick; that I had a problem. I knew it was something that nobody or nothing could fix. Not a judge and not time in prison. The same way the name of Jesus had delivered me from catching that bullet in the head, I knew only the name of Jesus could deliver me from that demon inside of me. The same way the power in just the name of Jesus had delivered me from the angel of death, I knew if I sought Him to deliver me from the pedophilic demon, He would do that too, and

He did. I came out of prison a changed man after serving a five year sentence."

There were hallelujahs and Amens among the congregation.

"Of course I was stripped of my license to work in the state of Arizona school system, so I came back here to Ohio, where to this day I still walk in my deliverance." Broady said this with such proudness. He was glowing in victory. It was apparent the devil had been defeated in his life.

"Once delivered," he continued, "like anybody who's ever gotten delivered from something, there is always a chance of backsliding if you choose not to walk in that deliverance. I needed to know that a watchful fleshly eye, not just the eyes of God, were watching me; holding me accountable for my actions. That's why I make it a point to share with those in my life that thing I've been delivered from. And it don't make me feel ashamed that the other youth ministry leaders won't leave me alone with the youth during any youth ministry events and functions. It don't make me ashamed that neighbors won't let their children come over my house and swim in my pool unless the parents come with them. It's just a constant reminder that God has His hand on me and my deliverance through His people. And I thank God for all of you." Broady's voice began to break as tears filled his eyes. "Especially for my wife-to-be, who didn't hold my past against me. Who still agreed to take my hand in marriage and marry the man who I am today, not the man I was yesterday. Glory be to God!" he shouted.

Eleanor walked over and embraced her husband-to-be as the congregation shouted out praises unto God for delivering their brother in Christ.

Lorain's eyes filled with tears as well. She felt so embarrassed, and it showed all over her face. She wondered if her mother would ever forgive her for humiliating her fiancé in such a way. But a half hour later, after offering and benediction and when stepfather-to-be was walking Lorain and Eleanor to their car, the same way God had restored and forgiven Broady, both Eleanor and Broady had done the same for Lorain.

"Again, Mr. Broady, I'm so sorry," Lorain apologized. "It's just that all these visions started popping up in my head, and I didn't know what was going on. Then Mother put me on the spot—"

"It's okay, sweetheart. Really it is," Broady said as he put his hand on Lorain's shoulder. Lorain turned to look at him. Something about her seemed so familiar to him. Truth be told, he thought she'd looked familiar the first time he'd seen her. "You know, you look like somebody I know. I just can't put my finger on it," Broady pondered.

"Uh, hello," Eleanor said, clearing her throat. "Could it be her mama? The woman you are about to marry?"

"Oh, yeah; I guess that's it," Broady concluded, although in the back of his mind it felt like he knew Lorain from somewhere else. Then again, perhaps Eleanor was right, so he just shook the thought away. "What do you two say we go eat somewhere? How does that sound? My treat."

"Sounds good to me," Eleanor declared. "Since you're buying, you lead the way to where you want to chow down, and we'll follow you."

Broady headed to his car as Lorain and Eleanor got inside of theirs.

"Viola Lorain," Eleanor said to her daughter, calling her by her real first name and middle name, "I thought I was gon' have to ring your neck back there in God's house." She laughed.

"Oh goodness, you're calling me by my first name; that means you would have really let me have it. Mama, you know I haven't gone by Viola since high school. I hate that name. I can't believe you named me that."

"Don't let your great-great grandmother Viola here you say that."

"She's been dead for years, so I'm sure she won't." Lorain chuckled as they waited for Broady to back out of his space and lead the way.

When he pulled out of his space, he drove past where Lorain and Eleanor were parked. Eleanor, who had driven her car, pulled out behind him. As the two women followed Broady's car, Lorain stared at his license plates. They read Leary 01. He'd had those personalized plates since the day he got his first car.

Staring at those plates, Lorain pictured them on the back of a teal green Buick, the car Broady drove back when he was Lorain's guidance counselor. The car where he'd had his way with her in the backseat. Just like in church, flashes and visions of her as a young girl and Broady began going through her head.

"Oh my God." Lorain said it softly under her breath, but she hadn't really meant to say it out loud at all. "I was the one, the situation he was running from here in Ohio."

"Excuse me? Did you say something, sweetie?"

Lorain looked over at her mother who was bubbling with joy as she followed behind her fiancé. So much was starting to come back to Lorain now. Things she wanted to tell her mother at this very moment, but she didn't want to make the same mistake she'd just made at church and embarrass herself. She believed in God and knew that she served a mighty powerful God. Yes, He was a God who could deliver a person from the pedophile spirit, even the homosexual spirit. And she was sure that God had, in fact, delivered Broady, and that God had forgiven him along with the rest of the church, including her mother. Her mother had to forgive him for his past in order to be even thinking about marrying that man. But Lorain couldn't help but ask herself if her mother would still be willing to marry him if she knew that her very own daughter was one of his victims.

Once again, looking over at her bliss-filled mother, Lorain decided that that would be something perhaps she'd never know.

Chapter Thirty-seven

"Can I get you anything?" Mother Doreen peeked into Bethany's bedroom and asked.

Bethany simply shook her head without saying a word. She hadn't said a word in a week, since being released from the hospital. The death of her husband and now her baby had taken its mental toll.

Mother Doreen looked over at the untouched dinner plate she'd delivered to her sister's room an hour ago. "I'm going to leave your plate, honey. You gotta eat something. Okay?"

This time Bethany didn't even nod. Mother Doreen shook her head in sadness, then pulled the door closed. She turned around to see Sadie and Hudson standing behind her.

"How's she doing?" Sadie asked.

"The same," Mother Doreen sighed.

"This is all my fault." Sadie began to weep.

"What did I tell you about that? Don't you say that, honey." Mother Doreen embraced her niece. "Like I told you before; God don't make mistakes."

"Auntie Doreen is right," Hudson told his sister, "it's not your fault."

"That's right," Mother Doreen agreed with her nephew.

"It's my fault." Hudson's comment caused both Mother Doreen and Sadie to direct their attention toward him. "If I didn't have a baby on the way, then you couldn't have told

Mama about it, and none of this would have happened. No one would have been arguing and Mama wouldn't have fallen and—" Hudson became too choked up to go on. He had to pause. "Anyway, Aunt Doreen, I hear what you're saying and all, but I think this time God did make a mistake. Maybe not with the baby, considering the circumstances. But I think God made a mistake when He took my father."

"Oh, Hudson, I understand." Mother Doreen opened one arm and invited Hudson in on the hug. Before anyone knew it, the three of them stood weeping in the hallway. They didn't even notice that Bethany had opened her bedroom door and was standing in the doorway.

"It's no one's fault," Bethany said, gaining everyone's attention. "Nobody but my own."

"Mommy, you didn't ask for this to happen," Sadie cried.

"I'm sorry to put you kids through all of this. And I couldn't lay in there and listen to you blame yourselves." She directed her comment toward her children. "It's my fault. I just didn't want to be alone. With your father on the road all the time—I just—" Bethany's words trailed off in tears. All anyone could make out of her next words were, "I just—didn't want to be alone—he was there for me—he's always been there for me—thought—he loved me—but—when I told him about the baby—everything changed—became a different man."

"All right, Bethany, that's enough," Mother Doreen said as she watched her sister begin to go into hysterics. She looked to Hudson and Sadie. "Children, go to your rooms for a minute."

The children didn't put up an argument as they made haste to their rooms.

"Bethany, honey, just sit down," Mother Doreen said as she led her sister back to her bed. "Now just calm down, and tell me what's really going on."

After several sniffles and heaves, Bethany was finally able to calm herself down long enough to say, "You were right. Sadie was right. The baby wasn't Uriah's. It was Pastor—"

"I know, I know, sweetie. You don't have to say it," Mother Doreen comforted her sister with a rocking hug.

But Bethany finished anyway. "Davidson's. The baby was Pastor Davidson's."

As Mother Doreen drove to Living Word, she was having the hardest time obeying the speed limit. She'd called up Pastor Frey and asked him to meet her there ASAP. Even with a mixture of snow and rain forming a slushy sleet on the ground, she was still too anxious for her meeting with Pastor Frey to obey the traffic laws.

After listening to her sister for over an hour talk about the affair she'd been having with Pastor Davidson for the past two years, Mother Doreen was beside herself. How could she have gotten it wrong? She had been so sure that it was Pastor Frey that Bethany had been having the affair with that she didn't look past that. That's when it dawned on her. She had been so sure. God hadn't told her a thing. Maybe He had, but her flesh had been so hell bent on keeping her eye on Pastor Frey and naming him as the accused, that she didn't even bother to hear from God any further on the matter. Now it seemed as though she owed Pastor Frey an apology, and that's just what she intended on doing, right before she got to the bottom of what was really going on. She had her suspicions, but as it was just proven so, her suspicions didn't mean a thing. Now she had to trust God to reveal the truth to her, the real truth. And some way, some how, Pastor Frey had something to do with it.

The more Bethany had talked, the more Mother Doreen was convinced that Pastor Davidson had been using his assistant pastor as nothing more than a decoy to cover his own tracks, a distraction. It had worked brilliantly up until now. What she thought was jealousy of Bethany not wanting Pastor Frey around Mother Doreen had really been fear. Bethany had been afraid that if the two got too close, Pastor Frey would tell her everything he knew about the affair.

"Davidson thought just the opposite," Bethany had told Mother Doreen. "He figured it better to use Pastor Frey as a means to keep you out of the way. From the first time he met you he realized that you had the gift of discernment, that you hear very clearly from God. He figured that if he planted the seed in your mind that Pastor Frey wasn't the man he claimed to be, that your flesh would get to out running your spirit man."

Mother Doreen could kick herself for falling for the trick of the enemy. She was now bound and determined to get back on track with God. This time she would cross her "T's" and dot her "I's." After leaving her sister sound asleep to rest after an emotional confession, Mother Doreen got on the phone and called the company Uriah had gotten his trucking assignments from. She had access to all of this information from when she had helped Bethany go through all of Uriah's paperwork for insurance and funeral planning purposes.

She just wanted a little bit of information concerning his runs and what not. Knowing the information might be private and that the company might not release it to her, she said a prayer that God would touch the hearts of those she spoke with, giving them compassion to want to help her get to the bottom of things. And that's just what He did.

The receptionist who had answered the phone was very helpful to Mother Doreen. She let her know that on the evening before Uriah drove home for Hudson's birthday celebration, someone had called on Uriah's behalf, stating that he was ill and would need to cancel his runs for the next three days. The receptionist confirmed that it was a male.

"I think the gentleman said he was Uriah's brother," the receptionist had told Mother Doreen. "Or perhaps he said, Brother Something—you know, how church people refer to themselves. We know Uriah was into church and all."

"How did you know that?" Mother Doreen inquired.

"Because his pastor was always checking in on him. Making sure God was showing Uriah favor by getting him plenty of runs so that he could provide for his family. His pastor called checking in on him and his runs more than his own wife had." The receptionist chuckled.

"You didn't find that strange?"

"Oh, no. I knew why that pastor was really calling, to make sure Uriah stayed on the road," the receptionist said in a knowing tone.

"Really?" Mother Doreen asked. Now she was really beside herself. How could the trucking company's receptionist know something that Mother Doreen didn't even know, and with it going on right under her nose?

"Yeah. He wanted to make sure Uriah was able to pay him back that thirty grand he loaned him to get in the trucking business in the first place."

"How do you know that?"

"Oh, Uriah mentioned it one time himself. He was frustrated when the price of diesel fuel started going up. Out of frustration, Uriah himself mentioned how between taking care of his family, and paying the pastor back who'd loaned him thirty grand toward his rig, would leave him with nothing to live off of while on the road."

Mother Doreen thought of how he must have struggled just to feed himself while traveling for days.

"But he never had a struggle out there on them roads," the receptionist said as if she had heard Mother Doreen's thoughts through the telephone. "That pastor of his always ended his calls by telling me that he'd keep praying for Uriah. And he must have been too, because everywhere Uriah went he had a story about how God had looked out for him. He'd deliver a load to Family Dollar store or something, and there would be a surplus of toiletries that the store manager would let him have. He'd show up at diners right before closing, and the waitress would give him, for free, the surplus food they'd prepared and would have to throw in the trash anyway. It was crazy." The receptionist paused for a minute. "I wonder where that pastor of his and his prayers were the evening Uriah's brakes went out and he got into that horrible, horrible accident."

"Yeah, I wonder too," Mother Doreen said suspiciously.

"Anyway, that's my other line. Can you hold?"

"Oh that's okay. You've told me everything I need to know and then some. You've been very, very helpful."

"Glad I could be of help. Uriah was a good, honest man. Tell the Mrs. how sorry we are, will you?"

"Certainly," Mother Doreen had said before ending the call, and in turn, making one to Pastor Frey, asking him to meet her at the church.

Mother Doreen had definitely gotten an earful. That sneaky rascal of a pastor had literally paid to have an affair with his church brother's wife. He knew keeping Uriah on the road would mean more time he could spend with Bethany. And he had probably used church funds to do it.

A red flag immediately flew up in Mother Doreen's head as she thought about what the receptionist had said about the phone call she'd received about canceling Uriah's runs. Uriah didn't have a brother, and the receptionist had talked to Pastor Davidson before. So if it had been him calling, he would have identified himself as such. And even so, she would have recognized his voice. It must have been a church brother, and she could put her finger on just which brother it might have been. That was why she was so anxious to speak with Pastor Frey.

After hanging up with Pastor Frey, it was put in Mother Doreen's spirit to call one more place. That was the salvage garage where Uriah's truck had been taken after the accident. Some young country bumpkin sounding fella answered the phone confirming to Mother Doreen what the police had shared with them. Brake failure had been the reason for Uriah's accident.

"It's possible the line just snapped, but according to the paperwork we found in his glove box, he'd just recently had break work done on his vehicle,"

"Is it possible that his brakes could have been tampered with?" Mother Doreen asked, and with good reason. Uriah always kept his truck parked in the lot not far from the house. Everybody knew that. Mother Doreen knew that only one somebody had motive to tamper with Uriah's breaks.

"Well, I guess anything's possible," the man said, and then Mother Doreen heard a buzzer sound in the background. "If you don't mind, ma'am, I have to tend to a customer."

"Thank you. You've been very helpful."

After Mother Doreen hung up the phone, she thought for a minute. The gentleman was right, anything was possible. That meant there was a slight possibility that Uriah's accident was actually no accident at all. "But when could he have—" Mother Doreen's words trailed off when she remembered Uriah telling them how Pastor Davidson had initially accepted his invitation for dinner, but then suddenly couldn't make it. Mother Doreen could picture him now cutting the brake line while he knew they were all at the house having dinner. "Son of a gun," Mother Doreen said with a snap of her finger.

The police had already closed the case, ruling it an accident, but Mother Doreen hoped that by presenting them with her new findings, they might re-open the investigation. Mother Doreen prayed for something even better, a confession. If she could get her most likely suspect to confess his faults, then an investigation wouldn't be necessary. The same way Pastor Davidson had needed Pastor Frey to help him with the entire scheme, she now needed him too. Would she be able to get him to switch playing sides?

"Mother Doreen, I got here as soon as I could."

Mother Doreen looked up to see Pastor Frey entering the church sanctuary. She was about to find out the answer to her question.

Chapter Thirty-eight

"Well, it's good to have you back," Deborah said to Lorain as both Eleanor and Lorain entered the doors of New Day. "I came back from my sabbatical last Sunday. When I asked about you, Pastor told me what had happened." Deborah paused for a minute and gave Lorain a puzzled look.

"Yes, Sister Deborah," Lorain smiled. "I know who you are."

Deborah laughed and hugged Lorain.

"I see Pastor didn't waste anytime putting you back to work," Lorain told her.

"Yeah, I'm the door greeter this week, and I'm putting up Christmas decorations next week," Deborah stated just as Unique entered the church behind Lorain. "God bless you, Sister Unique," Deborah greeted her with a hug. "Hey, little ones," she said to Unique's children.

Lorain turned and stared at Unique.

"Good morning," Unique said, slightly cutting her eyes at Lorain. She'd heard about Lorain's incident and the loss of some of her memory. Lorain may have forgotten about their last encounter, but Unique sure hadn't . And although she knew it wasn't pleasing to God, she was holding a grudge.

Lorain just stood there staring at Unique. Sister Deborah noticed the confused look on Lorain's face. "Oh, yes," Sister Deborah said to Lorain. "This is—"

"My daughter," Lorain interrupted and finished Deborah's sentence. "She's my daughter."

Eleanor, Deborah and Unique all shot looks at each other

while Lorain stared at Unique in silent awe. Then all of a sudden each of the women, with the exception of Lorain, burst out laughing.

"Girl, you being my mama would be like Jill on *The Young and The Restless* when she found out Mrs. Chancellor was her mother," Unique joked. "Obviously that little thing between you and me is something your mind chose to forget, so you know what, I'm going to forget it too. God bless you, Sister Lorain." Unique hugged Lorain, and then pulled away. "Or should I say Mother Lorain."

Once again, all the women laughed. Lorain feigned laughter as she headed into the sanctuary. *They can laugh all they want,* Lorain said to herself, *but that girl is my daughter. I just know it.*

Lorain took her seat in the sanctuary. Eleanor sat down next to her.

"You okay, daughter?" Eleanor asked Lorain. "Is this too much for you? You're not going to get up in here and pull one of them stunts you pulled at Broady's church, are you?"

"No, I'm fine, Mother," Lorain lied. Her mind was going ninety miles per hour with visions of Unique, documents, and newspaper articles. She kept seeing the words: "Baby girl found in trash can" and "Baby Doe up for adoption." Between the visions she had regarding Broady and the visions she had regarding Unique, she thought she was going to lose her mind.

As a strong headache came on, Lorain decided she would do exactly what Sister Deborah had done, go on a sabbatical. She needed to get her mind right. She would have sweet communion with the Lord and everything would come together. For now, though, she decided not to think anymore about Broady or Unique. She knew that one had something to do with the other, and if she just sat back and waited on God long enough, He would reveal it all anyway because that's the kind of God she served.

Chapter Thirty-nine

Pastor Frey entered the sanctuary to find Mother Doreen sitting on the front pew.

She'd been praying for the past eight minutes while she waited on him to arrive. She'd been praying that God would be in the midst of the situation at hand, not only to reveal some things, but bring closure and justice if need be.

Pastor Frey took notice of Mother Doreen's calm demeanor. "You sounded quite urgent on the phone." He now stood before Mother Doreen. He looked around the sanctuary as if there should have been some five alarm fire brewing somewhere.

"Thank you for coming, Pastor Frey." Mother Doreen said his name as if some boundary had been placed between them. It was as if some wall that he knew nothing about had been built between them.

"Of course I'd come running when you call," he assured her.

Mother Doreen stood. "You can cut out the shenanigans, pretending to be interested in me. I know what's going on. You're nothing more than Pastor Davidson's flunky. His side-kick. You should be ashamed of yourself."

Pastor Frey attempted to speak, but Mother Doreen cut him off before he could even get the words out of his open mouth.

"Don't even fix your mouth to say that you don't know what

I'm talking about. I'm talking about you playing the good and faithful servant by always being at my sister's bedside, just so no one would suspect that it was your leader who was the one actually in her bed. And then your so-called taking the time to have these working dinners with me to discuss the church's business just to keep me out of the way. And the phone call you made on Pastor Davidson's behalf to the place that gives Uriah his truck runs." Mother Doreen looked at him with such disgust. "And you call yourself a man of God. Humph."

Pastor Frey put his hands up in defense. "Look, Mother Doreen, if you'll just allow me to explain."

"Explain what? How you helped Pastor Davidson kill Uriah and made it look like an accident just so he could be with Bethany? Or maybe it was so that Uriah would never find out about the fact that the baby his wife was carrying wasn't his."

Pastor Frey's eyes went buck. "What? Murder? Baby?"

"Oh, please." Mother Doreen shooed her hand. "Like I said, you can stop pretending. I'm on to you. I'm on to your pastor too. Bethany told me everything."

"Uh, Mother Doreen, I uh—" Pastor Frey stammered.

"And now, on top of everything, you are trying to come up with a lie in God's house. Lord have mercy." Mother Doreen placed her hand over her heart, and then sat back down on the pew.

"Mother Doreen. Please." Pastor Frey asked for permission with his eyes if he could sit next to her. When Mother Doreen didn't respond one way or the other, he sat down anyway. "I'm not going to lie to you. Yes, I knew about Sister Bethany and Pastor. And yes, I am guilty of making a phone call on behalf of Pastor Davidson in order for Uriah to be able to come home for those few days."

"So that you two could get Uriah home so you could figure out a way to kill him. You kept him busy at dinner while Pastor Davidson cut his break lines."

Pastor Frey stood in anger. "Mother Doreen? Do you have any idea what type of accusation you are making? I would have never participated in something like helping someone commit murder."

"But you would participate in helping someone commit adultery? What's the difference? And by golly, you better give me Bible to back it up."

"Now listen here." Pastor Frey had his finger in Mother Doreen's face when a voice from the back of the sanctuary startled them both.

"He's telling the truth," Pastor Davidson said as he slowly walked to the front of the church with his head lowered. "Pastor Frey didn't know anything about the baby, not at first, and not that it was mine. He had no idea of the real reason why I had him place the call to Uriah's trucking assignment company."

"Pastor, don't," Pastor Frey said with an urgent look on his face.

"No, son, it's okay." Pastor Davidson rested his hand on Pastor Frey's shoulder. "I've asked you to do things that I know I shouldn't have. I know you only did them because I'm your pastor and you thought you were protecting me, but I can't allow you to do this anymore. I can't have your blood on my hands like this."

"But you can have my sister's husband's," Mother Doreen chimed in.

"Mother Doreen, when I had Wallace make that call to Brother Uriah's trucking place, it was so that he could come home and spend time with his family, mainly his wife. I knew about Bethany's pregnancy. She'd shared it with me. She also shared with me that she hadn't been with her husband in the time frame in which the child had been conceived. I only wanted Uriah back home so that he could, like I said, spend time with his wife, if you know what I mean. But he didn't."

"How do you know?" both Mother Doreen and Pastor Frey asked out of curiosity.

"Because in so many words, I asked Brother Uriah, and he answered me. I knew then that everything had been in vain. The day he left, he'd invited me and First Lady over to dinner, and I had every intention of coming. But I was being so convicted by God about taking my wife to go over there and break bread with the woman who was having my child, and I break bread with the man whose wife I'd impregnated." Pastor Davidson shook his head in shame. "I couldn't do it."

"So you decided to go to the lot where Uriah's truck was parked and cut his brake lines?" Mother Doreen surmised.

"No, God no," Pastor Davidson stated, appalled at Mother Doreen's accusations. "I decided that I'd take my wife out to dinner and tell her everything. The burden was becoming far too much to bear and a child would soon be here. I had to confess."

"What did your wife have to say about it?" Mother Doreen asked.

"Nothing," Pastor Davidson answered. "Before I got the chance to tell her, I received the phone call about Uriah's fatal accident. I had still planned on telling her once Bethany got through Uriah's death. I wanted the church to be there for Bethany, not shun her. I didn't want her to have to deal with an angry first lady on top of that. I was going to tell First Lady, but once the baby was gone, both Bethany and I decided to just let things be."

"But you never told your wife. Are you not still feeling convicted?" Mother Doreen inquired. Pastor Davidson had no words. "Does this mean that you and my sister are still—"

"No," Pastor Davidson was quick to say. "Bethany and I broke things off—for good. None of this was worth it. I've repented, and God has forgiven me. I pray that you can, Mother Doreen." He looked to Pastor Frey. "And you too, Pastor Frey."

There was silence. Both Mother Doreen and Pastor Frey knew that eventually they'd have to forgive him, they just didn't know if they were willing to do so at that very moment.

"Anyway," Pastor Davidson continued, "I'm going to be sitting down for a few months. Pastor Frey, I'd like you to run things during that time. I'll still be attending Living Word because I, more than anybody, really need to hear from God right now."

"I'll have to pray on it, Pastor," Pastor Frey replied. "I played a role in all of this too. I need to repent and hear from God as to whether He's going to sit me down or if He finds me worthy of delivering His Word to His people."

Pastor Davidson looked to Mother Doreen. "Mother Doreen, I promise you, I'd never do anything to take another human being's life. Uriah's crash has been ruled as an accident by the police. If it weren't an accident, I assure you I had nothing to do with it. I'm not the most trustworthy person right now, so I don't mind if you take the information you do know to the police. But I guarantee you that all it will do is open up a can of beans that I'll have to spill to my wife. You do what you have to do—or what God tells you to do." After a few seconds of silence, Pastor Davidson said, "Well, I'm going to go clean some things out of my office. Pastor Frey, I hope to hear from you over the next couple of days with your acceptance to pastor the church." He looked to Mother Doreen. "I do hope you'll find it in your heart to forgive me." Pastor Davidson exited the sanctuary, leaving Pastor Frey and Mother Doreen alone.

"Well, what are you thinking?" Pastor Frey asked Mother Doreen after the two had stood in silence for a minute.

"I really don't know what to think at this point," Mother Doreen stated.

Pastor Frey cleared his throat. "Well, Pastor Davidson is not the only one who needs to apologize here. I owe you an apology too. I should have never agreed to cover another man's sins. It's just that I—"

"You don't owe me an explanation," Mother Doreen told him. "That's between you and God."

"Well, do you believe Pastor about not having anything to do with Brother Uriah's accident?"

Mother Doreen hated to admit that she did believe the man. "Yeah, I actually do." Mother Doreen thought for a moment. "But I've been wrong before. But you know what? I'm going to simply trust God. This is in His hands. If vengeance is due, God will have it."

"Amen," Pastor Frey agreed. "Well, I better get going. Mother Headly got sent to the nursing home today. I need to go pray for her and her family."

"Oh, so that bit about being there for the sick and shut in really wasn't part of your act?"

"No, ma'am," Pastor Frey stated as he headed toward the sanctuary doors. "With all that has gone on, I'm sure you and Sister Bethany will be finding another place of fellowship. I mean, we'd love to have you here, but I understand if you all don't feel the same."

"Just like you, Pastor Frey, we'll have to pray on it." Mother Doreen let a faint smile cross her lips.

Pastor Frey responded with his own faint smile before heading out of the sanctuary doors. Before he had completely exited he turned back around and said, "By the way, I wasn't pretending; I really am interested in you."

Pastor Frey exited, leaving Mother Doreen in the sanctuary alone—with a big smile on her face. She had to admit, she had started to get a little sweet on Pastor Frey, so it was quite fancy to hear that he felt the same way. Although deep down inside she secretly imagined what it would be like if God sent her another husband, she never imagined that He would.

As she herself headed out of the sanctuary, she couldn't help but wonder if all this time, God had really sent her to Kentucky for another reason, to meet her next husband. Perhaps while she was praying on other things such as forgiving Pastor Davidson, taking the information she knew to the police, and whether she'd continue fellowshipping at Living Word, she'd have to pray on that too. But for now, she was simply going to be the best sister she could be to Bethany, the best aunt she could be to Hudson and Sadie, and the best great aunt to Hudson's little bundle of joy that was due in just four more months. She prayed that everything would get back on track without a hitch.

She let out a small chuckle before saying, "Who am I kidding? Been there, prayed that."

She put up her umbrella once outside the church in preparation to weather the storm.

Reader's Group Guide Questions

1)   Lorain judged Unique because of her appearance and her social status. Have you, or someone you know, ever prejudged a person by what was on the outside without taking the time to first learn about the type of person they were on the inside?

2)   Mother Doreen picked up and relocated to Kentucky. She felt she was on an assignment from God. Although when first arriving in Kentucky she wasn't one hundred percent sure about her being there, claiming to have had a mere gut feeling about why God had planted her feet in Kentucky. Still she was obedient and waited on God to reveal her purpose to her. Have you ever just done something because God had ordered you to without knowing exactly why? Did God eventually reveal the purpose?

3)   Tamarra seems to be tested in the area of forgiveness over and over again. Why do you think this is so?

4)   Do you feel that the pastor of New Day Temple of Faith is too passive? That perhaps Pastor should have done something more about Lorain and Unique getting in to it at church besides appointing them to work together? Do you feel that Lorain should have just immediately been removed from her leadership position? How would you have handled the situation had you been in Pastor's shoes?

5)   Mother Doreen is known for her sweet, gentle, and kind spirit. She seems to become an entirely different person around Pastor Frey though, becoming snippy and sharp. Is there a person in your life who always seems to draw you out of character? What are ways you have dealt with that situation or person?

6)   Do you agree with the fact that even though some of the New Day Temple of Faith members fall short of the glory, Pastor still puts them in leadership positions? Why or why not?

7)   Although Sadie and Hudson never seemed to be directly involved in all the drama that was taking place around them, they were well aware of it. Do adults sometimes take for granted, or perhaps maybe are oblivious to the fact, that every closed eye ain't asleep? Do they realize children are watching them and their own actions could affect those of their children?

8)   Do you agree with how Pastor handled the meetings with Unique and Lorain when they had complaints against one another? Instead of meeting with them one on one, Pastor had the three of them meet together? Why or why not?

9)   Lorain was shocked that Unique had much biblical knowledge, could pray, and could speak in tongues. Were you? Had you prejudged Unique as well? Is there anybody in real life you have done this to?

10)   What biblical story can you relate to Bethany and her husband's situation?

11)   Broady had been healed and delivered by God from the spirit of pedophilia. Do you have a hard time believing that God is powerful enough to do such a thing?

12)   Broady stated that by the church and the people in his life knowing of his past, they were able to "watch him" and

hold him accountable for his actions. Do you have anyone in your life besides God who is there to hold you accountable for your actions?

13) Do you think there are church leaders, such as Pastor Frey, who cover for the wrong doings of their pastors?

Urban Christian His Glory Book Club!

Established January 2007, **UC His Glory Book Club** is another way to introduce, **Urban Christian,** and its authors. We are an online book club supporting Urban Christian authors by purchasing, reading, and providing written reviews of the authors' books. *UC His Glory* welcomes both men and women of the literary world who have a passion for reading Christian-based fiction.

UC His Glory is the brainchild of Joylynn Jossel, author and Executive Editor of Urban Christian and Kendra Norman-Bellamy, author and copy editor for Urban Christian. The book club will provide support, positive feedback, encouragement, and a forum whereby members can openly discuss and review the literary works of Urban Christian authors. In the future, we anticipate broadening our spectrum of services to include online author chats, author spotlights, interviews with your favorite Urban Christian author(s), special online groups for *UC Book Club* members, ability to post reviews on the website and amazon.com, membership ID cards, *UC His Glory* Yahoo Group and much more.

Even though there will be no membership fees attached to becoming a member of *UC His Glory Book Club*, we do expect our members to be active, committed, and to follow the guidelines of the book club.

UC His Glory members pledge to:

- Follow the guidelines of *UC His Glory Book Club.*
- Provide input, opinions, and reviews that build up, rather than tear down.
- Commit to purchasing, reading and discussing featured book(s) of the month.
- Agree not to miss more than three consecutive online monthly meetings.
- Respect the Christian beliefs of *UC His Glory Book Club.*
- Believe that Jesus is the Christ, Son of the Living God

We look forward to the online fellowship.

Many Blessings to You!

Shelia E. Lipsey
President
UC His Glory Book Club

**Visit the official Urban Christian Book Club website at www.uchisglorybookclub.net

E.N. Joy currently resides in Reynoldsburg, Ohio where she is continuing work on the *New Day Divas* series, as well as working on the anthology series titled *Even Sinners Have Souls*.

You can visit the author at www.enjoywrites.com or email her at enjoywrites@aol.com to share with her any feedback from the story as well as any subject matters you might want to see addressed in future *New Day Divas* books.

About the Author

E.N. Joy is the author of *Me, Myself and Him*, which her debut work into the Christian Fiction genre. Forme secular author writing under the names Joylynn M. Jossel JOY, she decided to fully dedicate her life to Christ, whi meant she had to fully dedicate her work as well. She made conscious decision that whatever she penned from that poin on had to glorify God and His kingdom.

The *New Day Divas* series was incited by her publisher, Carl Weber, but birthed by the Holy Spirit. God used Mr. Weber to pitch the idea to E.N. Joy; sort of plant the seed in her spirit, of which she prayed on. Eventually the seed was watered and grew into a phenomenal five book series that she is sure will touch readers across the world.

"My goal and prayer with the *New Day Divas* series is to put an end to the Church Fiction versus Christian Fiction dilemma," E.N. Joy states, "and find a divine medium that pleases both God and the readers."

With book one, *She Who Finds A Husband*, launching the series, readers agreed that this project is one that definitely glorifies God in every aspect, but still manages to display in a godly manner that there are "Church Folks" (church fiction) and then there are "Christian Folk" (Christian fiction) and come Sunday morning, they all end up in the same place.

Be sure to pick up Book Three of the "New Day Divas Series" titled *Love, Honor or Stray*

Now that Deborah has finally let go of the past that has haunted her for so many years, is she ready to grab a hold of love? The handsome Lynox Chase certainly hopes so, as he tries everything to win Deborah's heart. But even with believing in her heart that Lynox is the husband God has for her, there still seems to be something separating the two—or someone.

The ringing of the wedding bells between Paige and Blake can still be heard echoing, but will the roar of temptation rear its ugly head when Paige begins to find comfort in the least expected old friend?

Just when it appears as though Tamarra has gotten the victory over one trial, here comes an even bigger tribulation on its tail. Will trying to plan a wedding with Maeyl, while continuing to throw dirt on her biggest family secret yet, take her to the breaking point?

Love, Honor or Stray is one of the most compelling books of the "New Day Divas" series yet.

WITHDRAWN

No longer the property of the
Boston Public Library.
Sale of th material benefits the Library